# QUARANTINE

## a love story

# QUARANTINE
## a love story

Katie Cicatelli-Kuc

Scholastic Press / New York

Library of Congress Cataloging-in-Publication Data available

ISBN 978-1-338-23291-2

10 9 8 7 6 5 4 3 2 1                    19 20 21 22 23

Printed in the U.S.A.    23
First edition, April 2019
Hazard symbol photo © MelnikPave/Shutterstock
Book design by Nina Goffi

To my mom, who first showed me what a magical place a library is, and to Mila, who continues to remind me

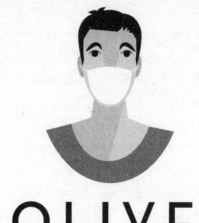

# 1. OLIVER

My eyes sting against the brightness in my room when I wake up. I didn't sleep well. I usually don't before I have to get on a plane. I try to concentrate on the sound of the waves crashing outside my room, but it just reminds me of how much open water my plane will be flying over. I haven't had a panic attack the entire trip, and I don't want one on my last morning in the Dominican Republic.

I get out of bed, grab some clothes, and head to the bathroom. I'm so tired as I brush my teeth that I drop my toothpaste cap down the drain. Which means I have to throw out the rest of my toothpaste. The travel-size tube is almost empty anyway, so it's dumb that losing the cap bugs me, but it does.

Annoyed, I quickly put on my clothes and head to the hotel lobby, which has been set up as a dining space for us volunteers. Everyone has their phones out and is swapping numbers and emails and stuff, including Emily, who is talking to Devon. She puts her hand on his arm, and I almost go back to my room, but she sees me and waves. I'm not sure if the wave means I should go over there or not, but I decide I should, even though Devon is less than thrilled as I approach their table.

Emily's eyes look even bluer with her new tan. Her smile turns to an expectant look. "Do you want to sit down?" she finally asks.

"Sure," I say, sitting. But I quickly spring back up. "I should get my breakfast first," I mumble.

"We'll save your seat," Emily calls as I get in line at the buffet table. I start to pile my plate with scrambled eggs, but in my hunger and tiredness I drop a bunch onto the platter of pancakes. I stand with the ladle in my hand, trying to decide if I should scoop the eggs off or just leave them, feeling my ears burn.

I decide to leave the eggs, but as I head back to the table, I hear someone behind me in line say, "Eww, someone dropped eggs in the pancakes. That's disgusting."

My ears feel like they're going to catch on fire as I sit down again.

Emily and Devon are both scrolling on their phones, so I'm not even sure if they've noticed I'm back, but Emily looks up just as I'm shoveling food in my mouth.

She asks, "Oliver, I heard you're not on our flight anymore?"

I've just taken a huge bite, so I nod. They both look at me, and I realize I'm supposed to say more. "Going back on the earlier flight," I finally manage to choke out.

Devon rolls his eyes. "What, big party in Brooklyn you need to get back to?"

My ears start to burn again. That's actually exactly why I'm going back early, but it's clear I can't tell Devon that.

"It's a sorta . . . family emergency," I lie.

Devon rolls his eyes again and grabs his breakfast tray. "Have a safe flight," he says, sarcasm dripping from his voice. Then he smiles at Emily. "See you at the beach in ten?"

Emily gives him a dirty look, but Devon leaves smiling. "He's such a jerk sometimes." She watches him walk away, then turns to me again. "So, really, why are you heading back by yourself? I think you're the only volunteer who actually *wants* to leave the Dominican Republic."

I fidget in my seat. "It's not that. Something came up last minute back home." Which is only 50 percent a lie. Kelsey mentioned the party on the first day of my trip, but she only actually invited me yesterday morning.

"Olive . . ." It's the nickname she thinks she invented for me. I haven't had the heart to tell her my aunt Jana has called me "Olive, because you're too little to be a whole Oliver" since I was three and it's never not annoyed me.

I avoid her eyes and pull my phone out of my pocket and start fiddling with it.

Emily quickly reaches across the table and grabs the phone from me. It's open to my pictures—specifically the one of Kelsey that I saved off Facebook. "Does *Kelsey* have anything to do with your early departure?"

Busted. Maybe I've talked about Kelsey too much with Emily. Maybe I've talked about Kelsey too much with everyone.

She raises an eyebrow at me, but I just sort of shrug, and she goes to my contacts to add her number.

"Trade you," she says, sliding her own phone my way. It's totally different from mine, so I fumble for a bit with her watching while I add my phone number. I include the *r* in *Oliver* without even really thinking about it, then worry she'll read into that, but I've already slid her phone back to her a little too hard. She barely catches it before it slides off the table.

I cringe, but Emily just laughs again. "Bye, Olive. Don't go breaking any hearts, okay?" She clears her breakfast dishes and heads out to the beach.

I watch her leave, and as I look at the back of her head, her hair reminds me of Kelsey's. I swear Kelsey used to wear her hair in a braid like that all the time. Maybe.

I sit at the table by myself and pick up my phone. I scroll through all my texts with Kelsey. I pulled her number off Facebook and saved her in my contacts months ago but never actually texted her. Then suddenly on the way to the airport she texted me 2 bad ur gone all spring break. I stared at the message for a while, telling myself she had probably meant to text someone else, even though I had just posted a picture of my suitcase. I composed and rewrote and deleted, and when my mom went over a bump, my finger tapped the guy-in-sunglasses emoji. I wanted to throw up at first. But then she sent the wink emoji back, and somehow we texted the whole spring break, even though we have hung out exactly once outside school, when a big group of us went ice-skating. That was four months ago, and since then I could count the number of conversations I've had with her on one hand.

I head back to my room to pack. I spent my junior-year spring break helping build houses in the Dominican Republic, so most of my clothes are dirty. I throw my crumpled and sweaty laundry into my suitcase. I look out my window one last time, at the beach and palm trees. I see Emily and Devon walking together, and I grab my suitcase and head to the lobby.

I'm the only volunteer on the little airport shuttle. We stop at a couple of resorts to pick up other travelers. One man has three huge suitcases, and the driver can't fit them in the undercarriage of the small bus. There is some rearranging, some yelling, and finally the man, who is now drenched in sweat, brings one of his suitcases on board. He doesn't make eye contact with any of us and fans himself with his boarding pass.

We're already running late, and some of the other passengers are grumbling, but it's fine with me, really. The less time I have to spend at the airport, waiting to get on a plane, the better. I wish there was a train that went from the Dominican Republic to Brooklyn. Or even a boat. Something lower to the ground that doesn't go tens of thousands of feet in the air. I take a deep breath, wipe my sweaty hands on my legs.

When we get to the airport, the sunburned resort-goers pile off the bus in front of me. Because I was the first one on the bus, my suitcase is the last one the driver pulls out. He wipes the sweat off his face with his shirt. I wasn't watching anyone else, so I'm not sure if a tip would be welcome or insulting. I opt for a handshake, which he looks confused about. I mumble *"Gracias!"* and walk into the airport. I should say more in Spanish—should *know* more Spanish, considering my dad was born in Mexico—but I don't.

The security line is long and moving slowly. My mom tries calling, but I feel weird talking on the phone with so many people around me. Then she texts—and she doesn't stop texting. Hope you're at airport. Did you get my last text? I can picture her pacing our pristine apartment, wiping down the counters for the third time this morning, the phone in her other hand.

I send her a quick message: Sorry, was packing and saying bye. I'll see you in a few hours.

She writes back so quickly I wonder if she already had the message composed: You're sure everything is okay? You're really just coming back early for a party??

I look up at the line, take a deep breath. Yes, Mom, just a party. At security.

A millisecond later: Okay. Let me know when you're on the plane.

I close out of the text with my mom and send a quick group text to Kelsey and Lucy asking for the address tonight, even though I was at

Lucy's house a few months ago when we had to do a history project together. I'm getting close to the front of the line, so I shove my phone into my bag. I look up, and a woman is trying to walk through the metal detector while on a phone call. She looks confused when the security workers make her hang up. No one else seems bothered . . . except for a girl at the front of the line, who I swear is wearing a flannel shirt that Kelsey has. She's looking around, and our eyes lock for a second. Without thinking about it, I roll my eyes and smile, and she smiles back at me.

She has a really great smile.

Airports suddenly seem a little less scary.

Flying in general seems less scary when I get to the gate and see that the girl is on my flight.

# 2. FLORA

I've been awake and packed and ready for this flight since dawn. I know how I must look: a surly teenager in jeans and boots and a flannel button-down, totally at odds with the vacation vibe. Even in the airport, I see people in flip-flops and swim trunks as if they've been dragged here straight from the beach.

Me? I can't wait to get out of here.

I grab a seat at the gate. I take out my phone and see that Goldy, my dad's new wife, has posted the selfie she took of us when they dropped me off. There's already a score of vapid comments:

OMG, u and ur stepdaughter could be sisters!

SO CUTE.

#hotmomma

The last comment is from my dad. I try not to gag as I untag myself from the photo. I fiddle with my settings so Goldy can't tag me in anything ever again.

It hasn't been much of a vacation, and not just because it rained almost all week. Since my dad remarried and moved to the Dominican Republic, he seems to think he's on some kind of permanent spring break. While they slept till noon, I spent my mornings cleaning up pizza boxes and salsa bowls and sticky blenders—only to have it all reappear the next day.

I'm used to cleaning up other people's messes. Which, you know, is fine. But it doesn't make for a great vacation.

I scroll through Instagram some more and look at the pictures Jenna put up last night of her and Becca hanging out in Becca's apartment. No wonder neither one of them responded to my texts. Clearly they were too busy posing with Becca's cat and burning brownies. I feel yet another jolt of anger at my dad for taking me away from my friends for an entire week. Jenna and Becca have never hung out without me before; they weren't even friends until I introduced them.

The gate agent starts boarding the plane, and since it's a smaller plane, the process is quick and I'm at my seat in no time. I sit next to the window, and the aisle seat next to me remains empty. I stretch out and open my book. I've already read *Gulliver's Travels* and started my notes for my paper, but I should probably do some more work. I'm tired, though. The bed at my dad's condo was way too soft, and the feathers in the pillows gave me a runny nose. They called it "my" bed in "my" room, but hadn't bothered to ask me about any of it. And the room really didn't suit me at all. There was animal print everywhere. Who knew it was even possible to buy a leopard-print tissue cover?

I look up and notice a guy about my age carrying a bag of McDonald's getting on the plane. He has dark hair, and even from where I'm sitting I notice his light eyes. He pulls one of his hands out of the bag and waves. I certainly don't know anyone in the DR besides my dad and Goldy, so

I figure he must be waving at someone behind me. I don't wave back, and he blushes.

I feel a little bad, so I try to smile just in case he *was* waving at me, but he's already looking away, his face bright red, and he climbs into the aisle seat in the row in front of me.

The flight attendant is about to close the plane door when one last passenger hurries onto the plane. He blows his nose as he climbs over McDonald's guy and sits down. I wrinkle my nose. A cold will be a great souvenir from my awesome junior-year spring break.

McDonald's guy is stuffing french fries in his mouth, but he looks over his shoulder as germ man blows his nose again. Their seats are close together, my seat is close to theirs, and I feel a little nauseous smelling the fries and thinking about the germs flying around. I sweat a little in my flannel, and I crank on the air-conditioning fan over my head.

"Good afternoon, ladies and gentlemen! I'm Maria, your flight attendant. Welcome aboard flight 4548, with nonstop service to Miami." I can barely hear the rest, because now germ man has a coughing fit.

The other guy pushes away his half-empty container of fries.

# 3. OLIVER

It figures that I change flights and end up sitting next to a guy with a cold. And I'm such a doofus to wave at the girl from the security line. Now I'm stuck in front of her for the next ninety minutes. My palms are wet again, but I'm not sure if it's from the anxiety that is slowly sliding into my brain or from the greasy fries I just inhaled to try to keep my nerves at bay. The man sneezes, and I move over in my seat.

I glance around the plane, wondering if maybe I should get off, if I should just go back on the later flight after all with the rest of the volunteers. But that's not for another six hours, and what would I say to everyone, that I had another change of plans? I can just imagine Devon's face . . . Plus my mom really would freak out. Which reminds me to text her: About to take off. Will text from Miami. See you soon.

I'll be tracking your flight. But let me know when you land just in case.

I stick my phone back in my pocket, but it buzzes again a second later. I wipe my hands on my jeans, dig out my phone again, and it's Lucy. She's sent her address and said c u 2nite? Which could mean she's just wondering if I'm going. Or it could also mean she's confused about why I'm going to the party at all. I wish Kelsey had been the one to text.

I take deep breaths, but then the man next to me starts coughing, and all I can think about is how I've just inhaled all those germs. I unbuckle my seat belt. I can't sit here anymore.

But the flight attendant is walking by, and places her hand on my shoulder sternly. "Sir, we are just about to take off. I need you to buckle your seat belt and put your phone on airplane mode." I slide low into my seat, wanting to disappear. I glance around again, look through the space between the seats, to the row behind me, where the girl from the security line is sitting. I feel my face turning red again thinking about that dumb wave, but luckily she has her head down, reading, and she doesn't see me get in trouble with the flight attendant. I look enviously at the empty seat next to her.

We push back from the gate, and we're taxiing. This isn't Newark with all its plane traffic. I look out the window, then quickly look away. I don't want to see all the water we're going to fly over.

The man next to me makes a little chorus of sneezes and coughs and sniffles. I adjust the air-conditioning knob above my seat and realize it's already on full blast. Aside from him, the flight seems eerily quiet, and the rest of the passengers' relaxation unsettles me. Doesn't everyone realize we're about to hurtle through the air in a tin can, thirty thousand feet above the ground, over a whole bunch of open water that is probably infested with sharks? I wipe my wet hands on my pants again. The woman ahead of me yawns loudly and stretches. With that, the plane races forward, and I sink back into my seat and dig my nails into the armrests as I feel the wheels lift from the ground.

I look next to me again—actually turn my head—and I'm startled by how awful the man looks. I thought flu season was almost over, but now I'm not so sure. His eyes are red, and his face is a weird grayish color.

Something dings, and I jump, but it's just the pilot telling us we've reached a safe cruising altitude and we can get up. I unbuckle my seat belt again, not sure where I'm going on the small plane except to get away from the guy next to me. There's nowhere to go but the bathrooms, so I step into one. I press down on the soap a bunch of times before turning the water on, then scrub my hands. I'm just about to leave the bathroom, but I decide to wash my arms too, just to be on the safe side.

I head back to my seat, and right as I'm about to sit down, I realize there's a dirty tissue on my seat belt. Before I even realize what I'm doing, I grab my backpack and head a row back.

The girl is scrolling through her phone, book in her lap, and she doesn't see me. Up close I notice that her hair looks reddish blond in the light coming through the small airplane window. I clear my throat, point at the empty seat next to her, and say, "Is this seat taken?"

She doesn't respond, and I realize she has earbuds in. I stand there for a second awkwardly, and then the drink cart comes from the back of the plane. The same flight attendant who scolded me earlier is pushing it, and I catch annoyance in her face as she sees me standing in the aisle. She stops before the row, waiting for me to move, so I slide into the empty seat next to the girl, feeling my face turn red.

As I sit, the girl finally notices me. She takes out her earbuds and gives me a confused look. "Isn't your seat up there?" She points to the row ahead, to my germ-infested seat.

I realize how poorly I've thought out this plan, and that I have no clue what to say. "It is. It was. I was hoping you wouldn't mind if I sit here."

"O . . . kay," she says, already turning back to her phone.

"I'm glad you were able to sneak that thing past security," I say, trying to make a joke about the woman who set off the metal detector. It's a lame joke even if it lands, and I can see by her confused expression that it doesn't land at all.

She furrows her brow at me. "I'm . . . just listening to music while I do homework, guy."

God, I'm an idiot.

She pops her earbuds back in, opens her book, and once again my hands are covered in sweat.

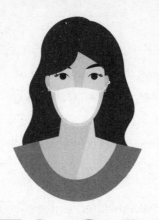

# 4. FLORA

I'm not sure who this guy is or why he waved at me or why he's sitting next to me or what he's talking about. I just file it away as guys being weird, and try to read.

Soon the flight attendants come to our row with the drink cart, so I take out my earbuds and order a ginger ale. The guy orders a seltzer, which explodes all over the flight attendant and all over her cart as she opens it. She slams the drink down on his tray table, then pushes the cart to the back of the plane to dry off.

I can't help laughing. "What'd you do to her?"

The guy blushes. "I think she's having a tough flight," he says. He looks at germ man, who is having another coughing fit. We both watch as he pulls himself up to stand. He's leaning heavily on the seat in front of him.

"Not as tough as him," I say.

The guy smiles, fidgets. "I have the worst luck when I travel."

He looks at me, and I notice the green flecks in his blue eyes. His face is still a little red.

"I hope your luck isn't contagious," I finally say.

He laughs nervously. "I don't know. It's only bad luck if you're alone with it, right?"

"Shared burdens are lighter, you mean?" I think about it for a moment. "I guess I disagree. I mean, say this plane went down right now. That's bad luck all around, isn't it?"

"Don't," he says. "Don't even joke."

I laugh a little, then my laughter stops in my throat. He's pale and gripping the armrest and looks genuinely freaked out. "Hey, sorry, it's all—"

But suddenly germ man loses his balance, and we watch as he falls into the aisle.

The guy next to me starts to move, like he wants to help or do something, but the flight attendant barks at him, "Please remain in your seat, sir!" before rushing over to help germ man. He's already sitting up, muttering that he's fine, and the attendant gets him back into his seat.

Germ man orders an orange juice, and I swear that when the flight attendant gives it to him, her hand is shaking.

The guy next to me looks horrified and embarrassed all over again. "It's probably just Ebola," I whisper.

I watch the flight attendant quickly walk up to the front of the plane and pick up the phone that connects with the cockpit. She has her back to the cabin, but she looks over her shoulder at the row in front of me. She nods a few times, hangs up, and disappears into the restroom.

The guy watches all this in stunned silence. He's breathing really fast. "Um, are you okay?" I ask, feeling a little guilty about the Ebola joke.

He smiles weakly at me. His face is sweaty now too, and my over-protective older cousin instincts kick in. When my cousin Randy gets trapped in his own head, it helps if I get him talking about something, anything.

I twist the knob above the guy's head to get some cool air blowing on him. "So, what were you doing in the DR, um . . . ?"

"Oliver," the guy next to me chokes out.

Well, at least he's talking.

"Oliver, do you live in Miami or are you going somewhere else?"

"Party tonight in Brooklyn." He's breathing even faster now.

Crap. I'm terrible at this today. "Hey, I live in Brooklyn too," I say, trying another approach.

Oliver nods quickly and looks at me.

"Um, my name is Flora?"

He keeps nodding.

"I was visiting my dad and his lame wife?"

"Your stepmom?" he says, his breathing slowing a little.

I fight the urge to scowl. "Yep," I say with gritted teeth.

He half smiles. "You don't like her?"

"HA!" I pull my phone out and find the Instagram picture Goldy posted. "Is there any reason to like her?" I say, waving my phone.

Oliver studies the picture for a second, and I feel stupid. He probably thinks she's hot, with her ridiculous Kardashian pose and glow-in-the-dark teeth. Straight guys are so predictable.

He looks away from the picture and up at me, takes a deep breath. "Ew," he exhales.

I feel triumphant.

Oliver smiles a real smile. His breathing is almost back to normal. He clenches and unclenches his hands. "Thank you," he says quietly.

"No worries," I say, like I never even realized anything was the matter.

Oliver goes back to fiddling with his phone, so I slowly put my earbuds in again, watching him out of the corner of my eye.

# 5. OLIVER

I stare at my phone, too mortified to move, too mortified to say or do anything. I can't believe I had a panic attack in front of a stranger. A cute stranger. I can't believe Flora didn't freak out when I freaked out. I can't believe I'm still sitting here. My anxiety had been bad lately, but never this bad. I should probably tell someone.

Flora is thumbing through her book again, like she sees people have panic attacks every day, so I try to act casual, and I start playing a game on my phone. The plane seems quiet again, and I realize the man in front of us has fallen asleep.

I think about the party tonight, about Kelsey, what Kelsey would do if I had a panic attack. The thought settles uncomfortably in my stomach, so I think about when we all went ice-skating in Prospect Park and how she smiled at me. I had just fallen and there was a tiny part of me that worried that she was laughing at me, but I had to remind myself my Kelsey was too kind for something like that.

There's another *ding*, and it's the pilot again, updating us about the weather. Flora is looking out the window. She takes out her earbuds, turns to me. "Hey," she says.

"Hey," I say.

She looks at me for a second and then goes back to the window. She starts playing with the shade, pulling it up and down. The movement wakes up the man in front of us, and immediately he starts coughing again.

Flora lets go of the shade and sits back. She sees me watching her. "You feeling okay?"

"Yeah," I say honestly. "Surprisingly." I laugh. Maybe she's forgotten about the panic attack.

"Good." But she still seems distracted.

"So are you on the flight to Newark?" I try.

"Hmm?"

"Your connection . . . you live in Brooklyn, so you're on the flight into Newark?"

She looks at me like I'm speaking a different language, then shakes her head. "Oh, no, sorry. LaGuardia, actually."

"Weird," I say, even though it isn't really.

"Yeah."

She looks out the window for a while, and I listen to some music. Then there are more *ding*s, and we're about to land. She peers out her window as we descend and touch down. Already there is a text from my mom. I see that you landed. Let me know when you're through customs. She probably knew my flight landed before the pilots did. I flip the airplane mode on and off a few times, seeing if that will make any other texts come through, but it doesn't.

We taxi for a little bit, then pull up to our gate. There's no *ding* from above telling us we can take off our seat belts, but people get up anyway, even as the flight attendants walk up and down the aisles and remind everyone to stay seated. A short doughy man starts to argue, tells the flight attendant he has a connecting flight, and another man joins in. The flight attendants look panicked. Suddenly, the pilot's voice comes over the loudspeaker. "Uh, folks, we're going to need to wait here for a few minutes."

There are groans, and the men try to argue with the flight attendants more. Flora is still looking out the window, but she turns to me suddenly, grabbing my hand. "Oliver!" she gasps.

I look down at her soft hand on mine, wondering how girls have such soft hands, wondering what Kelsey's hands feel like, but Flora is digging her nails into mine, which kind of hurts. Her head is blocking the window, so I have no clue what she sees at first, but then she sits back and I see the van.

We watch as a group of people get out and walk toward our plane.

They're dressed head to toe in hazmat suits.

# 6. FLORA

A woman a few rows behind us yells, "That's the CDC!" Suddenly the cabin of the plane is quiet. Everyone stops where they are and what they're doing. Some people are still sitting, some are standing in the aisles, and one man has his suitcase halfway out of the overhead bin. We all watch as four people in white hazmat suits approach the plane. I can't help it, but I feel an odd rush of excitement. It's the same guilty rush I feel whenever there's a chance of a snow day, or when a bad storm gets close to New York.

That excitement quickly fades when the hazmat-clad people get on our plane. The plane is filled with yelling all over again, and a few passengers run to the back of the plane. Which for some reason strikes me as funny. Really funny. I'm giggling so hard I can't unbuckle my seat belt. I turn to Oliver, but my laughter dies in my throat again when I see that his face has turned a horrible shade of greenish white.

One of the people in the suits grabs the PA microphone, but it's impossible to hear what he's saying over all the yelling and movement on the plane. He looks at the flight attendants, clearly frustrated, but they look back at him helplessly and shrug. Finally, a second suited agent grabs the microphone, and the force of her words cuts through the noise. "I NEED YOU ALL TO REMAIN CALM."

We all quiet down and look at her like scolded children.

"Thank you." And she smiles. Which is weird. "I know we're a scary sight, and I know this is not how you envisioned your vacations going, but we've been alerted to a possible situation on this flight."

And then, duh, I look down at the row ahead of me, where the man is slumped over in his seat, his eyes half-open.

"I'm sure most of you have heard of mononucleosis—"

The word *mononucleosis* sets off a rush of conversation among passengers across the plane.

"Wait, wait, this is a joke, right? Are you telling me you're here because of some dumb teenage kissing disease?" It's one of the men who was arguing with the flight attendants a few minutes ago. His face is pale and blobby like uncooked dough.

The woman in the hazmat suit continues, "Which, while uncomfortable, is not usually a serious illness. However, in recent days, our organization has been made aware of a mutation of this disease that has proven fatal in the elderly and the very young."

"Which none of us are!" dough man yells.

The woman doesn't look at him but says, "And I'd imagine none of you would want to pass this on to any of your elderly family or friends, or the children in your lives."

Oliver is breathing hard, so I absentmindedly grab his hand again.

"We are calling this new disease tropical mono, due to where we believe its origins are. Since your flight has just arrived from the Dominican Republic, and since there is a suspected incidence on this flight, we need to take all of you to quarantine to monitor you for symptoms and keep a close eye on your temperatures before we can let you continue to your final destinations."

The words *quarantine* and *suspected incidence* are muttered back and forth between passengers, and everyone looks around, until Pillsbury points to the row ahead of me. "It's him, isn't it?" I'm slightly alarmed by the sudden rage behind his eyes, the redness of his face.

Slightly alarmed and suddenly really annoyed. He's my dad's age, and just like my dad, he looks like he's trying too hard. I look at the stupid beads he has strung through his thinning hair, the overpriced watch on his wrist. Of course all he cares about is himself. He probably abandoned his wife and daughter too.

Before I can stop myself, I blurt out, "Hey! It's not all about you. He's sick. Probably thought he had a little cold. But you know what? He made a mistake. He's not out to get you or ruin your day. Not everything is about you!" Hot tears suddenly sting my eyes, and I sit down.

Pillsbury opens and closes his mouth a few times, narrows his eyes at me.

I feel Oliver looking at me as I dab at my eyes and angrily dig through my bag, even though I'm not looking for anything.

"If everyone could *please* remain calm," the CDC worker says. "These suits are only a precaution. Everything we've learned about this strain indicates that it's just like the mono you probably already know about. It's usually found in saliva and passed through close contact, like kissing, or being in close proximity of someone coughing or sneezing. Luckily, you can't catch it as easily as a cold. You all have to be monitored and have your vitals checked every two hours, just to be one hundred percent safe."

A quick flurry of whispers and groans erupts among the passengers.

Most of the passengers are concerned, but some sound more inconvenienced than anything else.

The CDC worker raises a hand to quiet down the passengers once more. "The first sign is a fever, which typically appears within twenty-four hours after the illness has been contracted. Other symptoms take a few days to manifest themselves. So if any vitals checks reveal a temperature of one hundred or above, you'll be going to an extended quarantine for thirty days."

There are gasps around the plane, and the CDC worker says, "However, we think the chances of that happening are highly unlikely, and as long as your vitals checks remain normal for the next twenty-four hours, we'll be able to release you by tomorrow afternoon."

Though I know I should be grateful, I feel a vague sense of disappointment that I'll be back on my way to Brooklyn so soon. On my way back to my mom, who will grill me about everything Goldy said and did, about my dad's weird new clothes and his blond-tipped hair. On my way back to school, back to Becca and Jenna and their new amazing friendship. Back to the annoying everydayness of it all.

"We're going to deplane you all from this flight and onto our vans, which will then travel to a sterile quarantine site where we will monitor your symptoms and check your vitals."

Pillsbury says, "Well, I'm no doctor, but I can tell you that guy has a fever." He points an accusatory finger into the row ahead of mine.

My fist clenches around a pencil in my bag as I stare at the doughy man. As his eyes meet mine, the pencil snaps between my fingers. He looks away from me quickly.

"Please try to maintain an orderly fashion as you exit the plane, and remember that there is no reason to panic." And with that, the CDC worker hangs up the PA microphone and smiles again at the flight attendants, who seem to automatically smile back at her.

The passengers who have run to the back of the plane return to their seats sheepishly and gather their things. One woman wraps a scarf around her face, and another has a bottle of Purell open and is rubbing it onto her arms and legs like she's at the beach applying sunscreen.

One of the CDC workers walks to the row ahead of Oliver and me and begins talking to the man. I try to listen, but everyone is deplaning and the worker looks at me and waves his arm forward, gesturing that I need to move.

"You all right?" I ask Oliver. I try to say it brightly, but my patience has shredded.

He smiles uneasily, looks guilty. "I need to get back to Brooklyn. I should probably text my mom, but she's going to freak out. I'm freaking out a bit." He laughs nervously, and we get off the plane and onto the van. My head begins to throb a little, and I realize how long the next twenty-four hours in quarantine are going to be.

# 7. OLIVER

As I climb onto the van, I tell myself I can't have another panic attack in front of Flora. I'm not sure why she got so mad at the guy on the plane, and I'm not sure I want to find out. I'm covered in a cold sweat, and I clench and unclench my fists, trying to make the tingling in my fingers go away. I try to calm my breathing, try to follow the advice that I looked up online, but suddenly I can't remember any of it. I need to get home. This trip was a mistake, and home is safe and I need to be there. I can't believe I thought I could handle a plane trip. I can't believe the CDC is here. I can't believe we're going to quarantine. They're saying it's mono, but I bet it's Ebola. I bet Flora was right. The words the CDC worker said don't compute with the level of anxiety I'm feeling, with my numb hands, with the sweat covering my body.

I sit down, and Flora is still next to me, looking a little worried and maybe a little annoyed. Her mouth is moving, but I can't hear any words coming out.

I look at my phone, which I didn't even realize I was holding, and I start a text to Kelsey, but I have no clue what to say, and my hands are shaking and I still can't feel my fingers, and then I feel guilty for even thinking about her and start a text to my mom, but I'm stumped about what to say to her.

The ride feels short, and we pull into a huge industrial yard and stop outside a warehouse that gives me the creeps. Flora grabs her things and looks at me. "You all right there?"

I take a shuddery breath. "I've been better." It's my attempt at humor, and Flora half smiles at me.

We're ushered off the van to the outside of the warehouse, where CDC workers holding clipboards are taking names of all the passengers from the flight. Flora tugs me along to one of the workers, though I don't even know if she realizes she's holding my hand. The way she grabs it seems so automatic. The worker sizes us up. "You two together?"

Flora looks at me, looks at our clasped hands. "Yeah."

"Names?"

*Together.* The word echoes in my head. It's not a word I've ever been able to use to describe myself with anyone. Flora is holding my hand to make me feel better, to prevent any other panic attacks, and that's why she said we're together, but there is something weird in my stomach and I realize it's guilt. I wonder what Kelsey would think if she saw me holding hands with Flora, my fingers wrapped in Flora's soft fingers. I should probably just take my hand back, but suddenly it's free, and Flora is once again looking at me expectantly, and I realize she's been talking to me.

"Dude. What's your last name?"

"Huh?"

"You're Oliver . . . ?"

Flora and the worker are peering at me.

"Oh, right. Russell."

"Okay, Oliver Russell and Flora Thornton. You're both minors, correct?"

I stare at the worker blankly. "Like, coal?"

"Um, no, like you're both under eighteen," the worker says slowly.

"Yes, we're minors," Flora says impatiently.

"Okay. Well, once you're all settled inside, just be sure to tell one of the interns or nurses that you're minors and you can call your parents together. We'll need their consent." She's writing something on her clipboard.

"Yep, sure thing," Flora says.

She and the worker both look at me again, and I say, "Right."

"You're all set. Hey, no kissing in there." The worker laughs like she's said something hilarious.

I feel that weird guilty feeling in my stomach again at the mention of kissing.

The inside of the warehouse is cozier than I was expecting. There are tidy rows of cots, and oddly enough a couple of TVs on the walls that are turned to one of the food channels. I don't know what else to do, so I follow Flora as someone on TV cracks an egg into a mixing bowl. Flora plops her stuff down on a cot and takes out her phone again. She could be riding the subway for how at ease she looks. It baffles me.

There are CDC workers milling around, talking to passengers, and people are filling out papers, having their temperatures taken.

My pocket vibrates, and I jump. It takes me a few seconds to retrieve my phone, which I must have put back in my pocket at some point. It's my mom calling. I look at the phone in my hand, watch it ring, ignore it. She calls back again, and again, and then finally leaves a voice mail. "Oliver! I hope to god that isn't your flight on the news. Please call me immediately."

She calls again while I'm still holding the phone. I answer, "Hi, M—"

"Why didn't you answer my phone calls? Are you okay? Oh, Oliver, I've been worried sick."

"Mom, it just happened. You can't have been worrying that long." I don't know why I'm attempting humor.

She doesn't even seem to hear me, though. "Oliver, I want you to come home right now. You don't need to be in quarantine, you're not sick. And I know you wouldn't sit close to another sick passenger, right? I know you wouldn't do that, right?" There is desperation in her voice.

"No, Mom, of course not," I lie.

"Is there anyone I can talk to there? Someone who can speed this along?"

"Mom, it's okay, I'll be home tomorrow. It's less than twenty-four hours of quarantine."

My mom's voice gets that fluttery edge to it like when she's crying. I've heard that flutter a lot over these last few years, ever since my dad died. "I wish I could be there. Does it seem safe? How many adults are there?"

I look around the warehouse, at the other passengers, at the CDC workers. "I don't know, a lot." A man in a hazmat suit is talking to Flora and taking her vitals, including taking her temperature, and then another one walks over to me. He gestures at my phone.

"Mom, I'm sorry, I have to go."

"What? Why?"

But the worker is shaking his head at me and gesturing at my phone again.

"Um, maybe I don't need to go?"

"What is going on?" my mom asks.

The worker snatches the phone out of my hand. "Hi, Ms. Russell, I understand your son is a minor."

I can't hear what my mom says to him but I know it's probably not very nice. He listens for a bit, then abruptly says, "For the safety of your son and anyone else who may come in contact with him, yourself included, do you give consent for him to spend the night in Miami?"

He listens more, then says, "Thank you, ma'am." He hands the phone back to me.

"She agreed?" I say, shocked.

The CDC worker says, "Uh-huh."

I want to ask him more, or maybe apologize if she was rude to him, but he's wheeling a little cart over to me. He wraps a cuff around my arm to check my blood pressure, sticks a thing on my finger to check my pulse, and jams a thermometer in my mouth. My arm tightens in the cuff, and a second later the thermometer beeps. I think he says, "Good, normal," and walks away.

The CDC worker with Flora is using her phone now, and I catch myself eavesdropping as he talks to someone who I assume must be Flora's mom.

"Yes, ma'am, she's safe and healthy and we'll keep it that way."

He's quiet for a second, then chuckles. I wonder if Flora's mom is funny. I wonder why my mom isn't.

My phone buzzes yet again, and there's a text from Kelsey: OMG, r u ok? Is that ur flight on the news???

*Is she worried about me?* The possibility makes my face feel warm, and I'm glad my temperature check is already over.

But seeing her name on my phone reminds me I need to be on my way home to the party. I need to be on my way home now.

Flora is fiddling with her phone. She says without looking up, "Everything is fine."

It's a statement, not a question, but I find myself starting to say, "No." Flora just looks at me with her eyebrows raised.

"Are you always this high-strung?"

I'm taken aback, but I sputter, "Um, are you always this calm when we could possibly have Ebola?"

Flora throws her head back and laughs, and her laughter just makes me mad. "Oliver, it's mono. We're lucky we don't have to worry about Ebola as much as people in other parts of the world do. Do you know how many people Ebola kills every year? Do you know how lucky we are?"

She looks at me seriously, waits for it to sink in, then says more lightly, "You're not one of the high-risk people, anyway. Even if you have been making out with lots of ladies on your spring break, the worst it'll do is make you a little sleepy and give you a bad cold like the guy on the plane. Would time away from school, away from . . . reality . . . be so bad?" She almost sounds wistful.

I don't know what to say, so I blurt out, "How do you know I was on spring break?"

She rolls her eyes. Then she flops back on the cot and watches the cooking show. I pace around my cot, and when I look over at Flora again, she has her eyes closed. Something has shifted. Her patience for me seems to have ended as quickly as it started, and I wonder why I care, and I hate that I ever felt guilty about anything.

I watch her sleep for a while, envious at her ability to relax, to not freak out. My mom calls again, and she seems a bit calmer. She's still got that fluttery edge to her voice, but it's slowed down from hummingbird to pelican. She's had her nightly glass of wine. I promise fifteen times I'll be safe, that I'll wash my hands every twenty minutes, that I'll be home tomorrow.

When I hang up, I look through my texts, look back at the one from Kelsey. I realize that when she watched the news, she thought about my flight, which meant she had to have been thinking about me, right? It gives me a squishy feeling in my stomach. I settle into my cot and text back, Yeah! Kinda scary! In quarantine now.

She keeps texting me, and she sends me a picture of herself holding a sign saying GET WELL SOON! Which I'm touched by, but it also worries me a little.

"Get well soon" is what you say to people who are sick. And I'm not sick. There's no way I can be sick.

I hope.

# 8. FLORA

Someone is shaking my shoulder, and when I open my eyes it's a man in a weird suit and I jump. And then I quickly remember where I am, why I'm here.

He laughs. "Sorry about that, Flora. You looked so peaceful, but we're supposed to check vitals every two hours."

Now that I'm waking up, I realize he's younger than I thought. A college student, maybe? And he's pretty cute too.

I smile at him. "It's okay"—I look at his suit, like I'll find a name tag—"you're just doing your job."

"Well, my internship, anyway," he says, grinning. "And it's Joey."

I look into his eyes as he puts the thermometer in my mouth, and I think there are certainly worse places to be than here with him. The thermometer beeps, and I jump again, and he laughs again as he looks at it. "Still normal." He makes a note on a clipboard, and he's off. It's silly, but I almost feel jealous that he so quickly moves on to the next passenger.

Oliver is sitting on his cot, staring at the TV. I feel a little bad for giving him such a hard time before, but I had a lot on my mind, and his anxiety was stressing me out. My mom always says I have a good bedside manner, that I could be a doctor or nurse, but there are limits to how much I can handle. "Hey," I say softly.

"Oh, hey," he says, playing with his phone.

I grab my phone and see it's only 5:00 p.m. I would have been landing at LaGuardia right about now, greeted by my mom, who would be irate at the traffic, but really I'd know it was anger she had for my father. My cousin would be in the back seat asking me a bunch of super-specific questions about the planes I took, questions that I wouldn't be able to answer, which would frustrate all of us.

Being here reminds me of the long flights I used to take visiting my dad before he married Goldy and moved to the DR, that powerful feeling of being nowhere, having to do nothing, be nobody. The three years of flights I took over summers and school breaks from New York to San Francisco were some of my most relaxing experiences. I was flying away from at least one parent, away from at least one set of emotions I didn't want to get involved in or deal with, and I love Randy, but sometimes I just wanted a break from being the overprotective older cousin.

I decide to watch TV to take my mind off everything, and it works, because seeing people make cupcakes on TV is mesmerizing. My phone vibrates against my leg sometime during the next show, which is about some kind of bread-making competition, and it's my mom calling. Finally! I texted her hours ago on the van from the plane to the warehouse, telling her about the quarantine and flight delay and telling her not to worry. I know I'm not really sick, but I'm still happy that the woman who gave birth to me wants to check on me.

"Hi, Mom."

"I *knew* I shouldn't have let you visit your father and that . . . that woman! I had a bad feeling about this trip all along. Maybe if your father could think about someone besides himself, he'd realize how selfish he is, how you have enough going on at home with your cousin—that you don't need international travel thrown in. God, I can't stand him. And her! Has she had more work done since you saw her last? I saw that Instagram picture she put up and she looks even more like a Barbie Doll than before . . ."

I begin to tune out, and those hot tears that started on the plane have returned. My mom prattles on and on. "I know he has all the time in the world, but my life is planned down to the second, and today is my day with Randy while Uncle Craig is at work and—"

"It's just one day, Mom," I interrupt, wiping at my eyes. "Don't worry. I'll be home tomorrow."

My mom sighs. "Tomorrow is no help for me today."

"Well, I'm sorry. And quarantine is awesome, thanks for asking."

I hang up and turn my phone off, tossing it back on my cot. Oliver must have heard everything. He catches me looking at him and blushes a little.

"You feeling better?" I ask, trying to distract us both, and before he can ask me about the conversation I just had.

He studies my face for a second before speaking. "Yeah. I guess. So far everyone here seems to be okay. That dude from our flight is in thirty-day quarantine somewhere different, but he's the only person sick so far. His fever wasn't even that high after all. Can you believe that?"

I don't say anything. I look around the room, at people lounging on their cots, some reading, some watching TV. Everyone seems pretty relaxed now, and even Pillsbury is snoring on his cot. The late-afternoon light streams through the warehouse windows and casts a pretty glow across the room. I push the conversation with my mom even farther back in my brain and wiggle against my pillow. "Does this remind you of camping at all? Or do you feel like we're on a big boat out in the middle of the ocean?" I ask.

Oliver looks confused. "No?"

I feel silly for saying it, so I change the subject. "Where in Brooklyn do you live, anyway?"

"Park Slope. You?"

"Wow, fancy-stroller capital of the world. Nice. I'm in Bay Ridge."

Oliver looks mad for a second, then smiles. "Yeah, yeah, yeah. And my mom is a member of the co-op too."

I like his smile.

"We'll be back at the airport before you know it," I say, to fill the space. For some reason I don't totally believe myself.

He looks at me for a long time, and his smile leaves his face. "I hope you're right," he finally says.

Later, we get pizza for dinner. Who knew quarantine could be so tasty? One of the CDC workers checks my vitals again after I eat, and I wonder if the hot pizza will affect my temperature. I'm oddly disappointed when she says "Normal" and moves on to Oliver.

Oliver barely looks up from his phone as the cuff is placed on his arm and the thermometer is placed in his mouth. He's been messing around with the thing all night.

The worker says "Normal," but Oliver is so focused on his phone that he doesn't hear her. She says "Normal" again, but he still doesn't hear her. The worker is clearly annoyed and in a hurry, so she yanks the cuff off and pulls the thermometer out of his mouth.

Oliver looks up, startled, but the worker has already walked away. He rubs his bottom teeth. "Ouch," he says quietly. He starts to pick up his phone again, but sees me watching him. "The service here is awful!

I'm hardly getting any texts, even with Wi-Fi. Somehow my mom's messages keep coming through." He laughs nervously.

I want to tell him that the service isn't the problem, but I don't have the heart. Or the strength to help him through another panic attack. I turned my phone back on, but I'm not getting messages from anyone besides stupid Goldy, whose most recent message is a cartoon koala bear with a big bandage over its fuzzy ear. Great. Goldy is more concerned about me being in quarantine than my own mother is.

I watch TV the rest of the night, until they get turned off at ten. I doze a bit, but we all get woken up every two hours for vitals checks. Oliver is pretty groggy through the checks, but finally during one of them he rolls over to face me, and I wave at him.

He looks a little startled, but says, "Aren't you tired?"

I ball the blanket up in my hand. "The sooner I go to sleep, the sooner I have to wake up and go home," I say.

"Don't you mean *get* to wake up and *get* to go home?"

I realize how bitter that sounded. "Yeah, something like that."

He looks at me for a second, then yawns.

I can't help asking, "What's your hurry to get home, anyway?"

Oliver fidgets. "Oh, there was this party last night. It's over with now, but I'm still hoping to see someone when I get back. I hope, maybe." He looks at me sheepishly.

"Of course there's a dumb girl," I say to myself, but Oliver's cot isn't that far away from me, so he hears me.

"Good night, Flora." He looks hurt, which just annoys me even more, and makes me feel even more terrible about everything.

Around 10:00 a.m., the workers bring us bagels. I think I hear Oliver humming as he eats his, which fills me with a rage I don't understand.

Shortly after, people are actually cleared to go back to the airport, and the passengers are joking and laughing, and I'm starting to feel a little panicked at how quickly the night went. Dread sits in my stomach like a lead weight.

Then it's just Oliver and me. A worker stops by for our last vitals checks, but clearly the novelty of it all has worn off for her. She's looking at the TVs, which have been switched back on and are now showing a soccer game somewhere in Europe. Before I really think about what I'm doing, I take the thermometer out of my mouth, rub it between my hands a few times, and pop it back in my mouth again.

# 9. OLIVER

I watch Flora, baffled. When the thermometer beeps, the CDC worker looks startled at the result. She looks at Flora and sighs wearily.

I start to open my mouth, to tell the worker what I just saw, but Flora catches my eye and shakes her head furiously.

"But you—" I say.

I don't know if I really intend to tell on her. I never finish the sentence. Because suddenly Flora grabs me by the shirt, pulls me forward, and gives me a kiss.

On the lips.

There are gasps all around us, and the CDC worker sighs again.

"Thirty-day quarantine for you two officially starts now."

# 10. FLORA

Oliver pulls away from my kiss quickly. Up close I see the green flecks in his blue eyes again. His eyes remind me of looking out an open window on a spring day, feeling a cool breeze on my face.

He pulls away farther from me, keeps backing up until he's in the corner of his cot. His mouth is opening and closing, but he isn't making any actual sounds, any actual words.

I sort of expect there to be huge blaring sirens, air-raid horns, something loud and noisy happening. Or at least more running, more panic, more yelling. But the only thing I hear is my heartbeat drumming in my ears. The workers calmly shuffle around with clipboards, making hushed, quick phone calls. It's weird that no one is talking to us. I feel like someone should be talking to us, telling us something, and I feel a bit like a mouse in a laboratory. I wonder if there's a pamphlet—*So You're Going to Be in Quarantine for Thirty Days*—or something.

Oliver keeps staring at me from the corner of his cot. I hear his phone vibrate in his pocket, but he either doesn't feel it or doesn't care, because he just keeps staring at me.

He finally shapes his mouth into a word, but speaks so quietly I wouldn't hear him if he was farther away from me. "Why?" he says hoarsely.

I don't say anything. I wish I knew what to tell him. I wish I had an answer for him.

# 11. OLIVER

I want to push her off my cot. I want to kiss her again. I want to rinse out my mouth with acid. I want to call Kelsey. I want to know what's going through Flora's head. And Kelsey's head. I want a do-over on my first kiss.

The air feels very thick in the room, and I want to get off my cot but I can't because Flora is there and I want to touch her and never touch her again. And my first kiss was supposed to be with Kelsey, and I was supposed to have gone to a party with Kelsey last night, and now I can't see her for thirty days, and it may as well be thirty years.

Thirty days. A month. I quickly add thirty to the current date, and it's the middle of April, and two days before spring formal, and it's not fair, and why did Flora do it, and why were her lips so soft? And why haven't I told on her yet? Why am I letting her get away with this? I could stop this all now, tell the workers what I saw. But would they believe me? And then what—they take our temperatures again, Flora fakes the fever again?

And I don't know who I'm supposed to talk to anyway. I watch the workers milling around, and I have the sensation of being stuck at a restaurant while trying to get a check and not knowing who to ask. I never know who to ask about anything.

And why is Flora sitting so calmly on my cot, and why won't anyone tell us anything, and why does my leg feel so weird? I put my hand in my pocket, realize my phone is buzzing. I take it out, look at it, put it back in my pocket, realize I didn't actually read what was on the screen, and take it out again. Eleven missed calls from my mom. And a text from Kelsey: OMG. 30 days of QUARANTINE?! Can I be your nurse? ;)

And the idea of her taking care of me is sweet and amazing and makes my chest feel warm, until I remember she's in New York and I'm in Florida. And that Flora just kissed me. And I'm going to be in quarantine for thirty days. But Kelsey is flirting with me. I think. Maybe quarantine won't be all bad. And how long can thirty days really be?

# 12. FLORA

Oliver keeps taking his phone out of his pocket and looking at it like he's never seen the thing before, like he doesn't understand what it is or how it got there.

Watching him reminds me I should probably call my mom and tell her that I won't be coming home today after all. I think about her getting Randy ready to go to the airport, which I know is no small process, especially if he doesn't think he's ready to leave yet. I think about them sitting in traffic, Randy asking my mom a million questions, him getting frustrated when she can't answer because she's concentrating on the traffic. A tiny little flame of guilt starts to burn in my stomach. I remind myself how awful my mom was on the phone, how selfish, and it's not like thirty days is *that* long.

I dig my phone out of my backpack, and I'm a bit startled when I see all the notifications and texts. I scroll through, see that there are five missed calls from my mom and two voice mails. And somehow a few missed calls from my dad and Goldy and one voice mail from Goldy.

I listen to the first one from my mom. "Flora, I'm sorry about last night. And I'm sorry you were in quarantine and were stuck in Miami overnight. I know that must have been scary." She pauses. "You're a good cousin to Randy and you make your uncle Craig's life easier." She pauses again. "I don't know why I'm talking like I won't see you in a couple hours! Anyway, I just wanted to apologize and get that all out of the way. Have a good flight home, and I'll see you soon."

Oh god. She called this morning. The time stamp is 11:13, just a few minutes before I messed with the thermometer.

The flame of guilt is getting hotter.

I listen to the next voice mail from my mom, which came in just a few minutes ago, at 11:26.

"Flora! I'm watching the news right now . . . please tell me that there is another flight with two teenage passengers who are going to *thirty-day* quarantine. Call me back!"

I start to feel warm. Maybe I really do have a fever? I'm just about to listen to the voice mail from Goldy when someone in a hazmat suit approaches our cots. I realize it's Joey, the guy who woke me up from my nap yesterday to take my temperature.

He smiles. I guess I was too tired yesterday to see his dimples. I start to feel even warmer. "You ready?"

Oliver has been sitting on his cot tapping furiously at his phone and talking to someone who I assume is his mom. I've been too distracted to really hear much of what he's been saying, but I'm still surprised he snaps out of his daze to say, "Ready for what?"

Joey looks confused. "For your transfer to quarantine?"

Oliver looks around, waves his arms. "Isn't that where we are? Quarantine?"

Joey throws back his head and laughs. Oliver nervously chuckles, and it's clear he's just as confused as I am.

"Flora has a communicable disease whose mutation we don't fully understand yet. And, Flora, you might have spread that communicable disease to your boyfriend"—he flips through the pages on his clipboard—"Oliver. This could be the very beginning of an epidemic!" I'm both comforted and disturbed by his excitement. "You guys are going to the hospital. Same hospital as the man from your flight. I'd say you guys could all hang out, but that whole quarantine thing."

"He's not my boyfriend!" I say quickly. "And hospitals are for sick people," I add without thinking.

Joey looks at me sympathetically.

Oliver seems too embarrassed to look in my direction. I think of how fast he pulled away from my kiss, like my lips were full of poison.

I don't like when people feel sorry for me. And I don't like feeling poisonous. And I don't like that Joey thinks Oliver is my boyfriend.

I wish I were back in Brooklyn and I could go for a walk like I do after a crummy day. Most times I start out in different directions, but I always end up at the little community garden two blocks from my apartment. It's usually locked by the time I get to it, but I love looking at the statues. My favorite is one of a little girl with her head thrown back in glee, birds resting on her upturned arms.

I suddenly really need fresh air.

Joey is still watching me. He takes a pen from his clipboard, jots something down.

"Okay, let's get ready to go!" he says brightly, like we're about to head out for ice-cream sundaes. "Before we can transport you both, we'll need to talk to your parents again. Since you're both minors, your parents will need to give consent to any medical supervision and procedures. The head doctor of the communicable diseases unit is going to meet us by the ambulances."

"What if they say no?" I say quickly.

"If who says no?" Joey asks, furrowing his eyebrows at me.

"Our parents. What if they refuse to give consent?" I ask, feeling suddenly hopeful that maybe there is a way out of this mess.

"Oh, well, then we'd have to get a court order to put you in quarantine," Joey says without skipping a beat.

"Court?" I've never even been in detention before.

Joey is grinning. "Any other questions?" he says.

I have a ton, but it feels pointless to ask any of them. "Nope," I say, with tight lips.

"All right, let's go," Joey says, slapping his knee.

We walk through the warehouse, wheeling our suitcases behind us, and I'm in a daze. I need to figure out how to explain to Joey, to Oliver, to everyone, that I don't want Oliver to be my boyfriend. I didn't kiss him because I liked him. I kissed him because . . . I'm still trying to figure it out when we walk outside. There are two ambulances with their doors open and two stretchers with huge plastic covers waiting for us.

# 13. OLIVER

I wonder why there are ambulances outside, then realize they are for us. We can't exactly walk to the hospital, but the stretchers with the plastic covers look . . . claustrophobic. As I'm looking at them, a woman in a hazmat suit walks between the two ambulances. She nods at Joey, who retreats into the warehouse. Through the woman's hazmat suit I can see that her dark hair is pulled into a tidy ponytail.

She shakes my hand, then Flora's. "I'm Dr. Demarko. I'm sorry we have to meet under these circumstances, but I promise we're going to take excellent care of you both. You'll be in a shared room, but one of your walls is entirely made up of glass, and medical personnel will constantly be in and out of your room. If necessary, we will add a video camera to your room." She looks at us both, waits for that point to sink in. I feel my cheeks turn red as I realize she's referencing the kiss. *The kiss.* Flora kissed me.

"Wait, so we'll be . . . roommates?" Flora says. "I'll be spending thirty days in the same room as him?"

She gives me a look of shock and something else I can't figure out.

Disgust? Dread? Clearly she's not thinking about the kiss. Or maybe she is.

"Yes. It's easier for hospital staff to monitor you if you're in the same room. We won't have to dispose of as many hazmat suits either."

"So this is a matter of saving a few pennies?" Flora says sarcastically.

"It's more than a few pennies," Dr. Demarko says, unfazed. "Anyway, as I said, you'll be in a shared room, but if either of you starts to display symptoms beyond a fever or develops a fever of 101.5 or above, then you will be moved to isolation."

"What if the fever doesn't come back? What if it was a . . . mistake? What if, say, the thermometer was tampered with?" Flora says.

Dr. Demarko says, "Unfortunately, the fever has been recorded. Even if it was only a onetime thing. Even if it was a mistake. We have protocols we have to follow."

"Right," Flora says softly. She thinks for a second. "But isn't a fever a sign of being sick?"

"It is. But fevers in and of themselves aren't contagious. The symptoms of the fevers are what we're worried about. If either of you starts coughing, sneezing, vomiting, or experiencing diarrhea, or, as I said, develops a fever above 101.5, you'll be moved to isolation."

I feel myself blushing again. I don't like hearing about poop with anyone, much less the first girl who kissed me.

Flora seems unbothered, though. "What is isolation like?"

"It's not much different than the room you're going to, actually. But don't worry about that. Just know that your room has a thick curtain dividing it in half, for privacy. And remember that you will be monitored *very* closely."

Flora asks, "Can we see our parents? Our moms, at least?"

"We are currently doing more research to decide if and when you can have visitors. I'm going to recommend that your parents head to Miami anyway, so if and when they have received clearance to visit, they can get to the hospital right away."

Flora asks, "How long will that research take?"

"Hopefully just a few days," Dr. Demarko informs us. "Oliver, do you have any questions for me?"

"Sorry," Flora says. "I always do that."

Dr. Demarko looks at me, waiting for an answer. "I don't think so." The only question I want to ask her is why Flora kissed me, but I don't think the doctor has the answer to that. I wonder if Flora does.

"Now, let's call your parents before they have to find out anything else from the news about their children."

I'm looking at the stretchers again, and when I pull my eyes away, I realize Dr. Demarko and Flora are both staring at me. Flora has her phone in her hand. I think I'm supposed to do the same thing, so I pull my phone out of my pocket.

"Flora has offered to let me talk to your parents first," Dr. Demarko says.

"Oh, it's just my mom," I say. But I'm wondering why Flora wants me to make the phone call first. I'm sure she's overheard me talking to my high-maintenance mother, so is she doing it as a favor, or to be mean?

"I understand," Dr. Demarko says. "Why don't you talk to your mom first, and then I can jump in after a few minutes?"

"Are you sure you don't just want to make the phone call yourself?" I say, trying to make a joke.

Dr. Demarko looks at me sternly.

"Right, okay," I say, and call my mom.

It rings a half ring. "OLIVER. Why haven't you answered any of my calls?" She's beyond fluttery now, and I think about how a group of crows is called a murder of crows.

"Sorry, Mom. Um, there's been a change of plans."

"A change of plans? Thirty-day quarantine is a change of plans? Oliver, what is happening? The news is exaggerating, right? Everything is always exaggerated, right?" There's that desperation in her voice again that scares me.

"We're going to the hospital—"

At the word *hospital*, she starts crying.

Dr. Demarko and Flora are both watching me, and I hand the phone off like it's a hot potato.

Dr. Demarko calmly introduces herself, and even though she's a few feet away from me, I can hear my mom wailing over the phone.

Flora touches my hand lightly. She's got her phone facing me, and on her screen is a video of a seal waddling out of the water at the beach and onto a patch of sand. The seal is on an inlet, and as it puts its head down, a huge wave splashes it in the face. The seal sneezes out the water and waddles to a new patch of beach on the sand, looking annoyed.

Flora watches my face. I have no idea why she's showing this video to me. But I don't object when she plays it again and again. It gets funnier each time.

So funny I don't hear what Dr. Demarko says to my mom, but suddenly she's handing the phone back to me.

"I'm getting on a plane tomorrow morning, Oliver! I'm looking at hotels now, and I found one right by the hospital, so even if I can't see you, I'll be close to you." Flutter, flutter.

"Isn't that great news?" my mom says. She sounds so different than before. Almost excited?

"Yeah, Mom, great," I say. But she doesn't notice my lack of enthusiasm. My brain is going a million directions at once.

"And just you wait. The doctor said a girl kissed you! But she's not your girlfriend? When I get clearance to visit you, I'm going to give her a piece of my mind. Why would she kiss you when she knows she's sick? Who does that?"

I look at Flora, who is still showing me the seal video. She sees me looking at her, gives a half wave.

Maybe my mom has a point. Who does that?

# 14. FLORA

I hit STOP on my seal video. Becca showed it to me the day I found out about Goldy and I watch it whenever I need to laugh. I know it's a lame attempt to help Oliver feel better, but I'm relieved he at least smiled.

Dr. Demarko nods at me.

My mom's phone rings four times before she answers, sounding breathless. "Flora! I've been so worried. So, so worried. Is it true what they said on the news? Are you really going to quarantine for thirty days?" All the anger from her voice the last time I talked to her is gone, and I miss her so much it takes my breath away for a second.

"I'm sorry," I say, just as she says, "This is all my fault."

"What? No, Mom, this isn't anyone's fault," I say.

"No, it is. I just . . . How are you feeling?"

"I feel okay," I say honestly.

I look at Dr. Demarko, say, "The head doctor is actually with me. She can talk to you, explain more."

I hand the phone to Dr. Demarko, watch her talk to my mom, explain what quarantine will entail, that she's not allowed to visit yet, but she should still think about coming to Miami soon. Oliver is scrolling through his phone. He looks up at me. "I'm trying to find a video to make you feel better. But maybe you don't need to feel better? I don't hear your mom freaking out like mine did."

"Oh, she's freaking out in her own way," I say, then feel guilty. "Anyway, what kind of video did you find?"

Oliver shakes his head. "Oh, nothing that great. Just a cat sneezing and, uh, passing gas at the same time."

"Not great? That's a scientific miracle!"

"Isn't that an oxymoron?" Oliver says.

"Farting and sneezing at the same time?"

Oliver blushes and says, "No! Why are we talking about farting? Can a miracle be scientific? I think it's an oxymoron."

"I think you just want to show off a word you learned in your English class."

"Well, we'll have thirty days to find out," Oliver says.

"Why you used the word *oxymoron*?"

Oliver exhales loudly. But he smiles at me.

His eyes crinkle up when he smiles. It's nice.

Dr. Demarko snaps me out of my trance, though, and hands me my phone.

"Flora, I'm coming to Miami!" my mom says.

"You are?" I say, surprised. "What about Randy?"

"Your uncle and I will make arrangements. You don't need to worry about that."

"Yeah I do, he's my cousin."

"And he's my nephew," my mom says, speaking a bit more sternly. "Please don't worry about anyone but yourself now."

Dr. Demarko is waving to someone, and I turn and see that Joey is coming back. "I think I have to go now," I say.

"Let's talk when you get to your hospital room." Her voice sounds a little quivery, but she clears her throat.

"Yep," I say, afraid of the quivers in my own voice if I attempt to say anything else.

"I love you, Flora."

"Yep," I say again.

I hang up, and seeing Joey again helps a little.

He gestures to the stretchers. "Your chariots await. Hop in!"

"I'll see you at the hospital," Dr. Demarko says. "Have a good ride."

I look at Oliver, and his eyes are bugging out of his head, and it suddenly dawns on me that he didn't tell Joey or any of the CDC workers or Dr. Demarko about my fake fever.

And I have no idea why.

# 15. OLIVER

I look at the stretchers in front of me. I watch Joey help Flora get into one. He zips her in, and she looks like a scared animal in a cage. It's her fault, I know, and she got herself into this mess, but I should put a stop to it. I could put a stop to this. I just need to open my mouth and tell Joey what I saw Flora do. But I keep thinking about Kelsey's texts—thinking how I'm the only guy in school who is in quarantine. I feel like there is an edge to my otherwise boring life for the first time ever.

As I climb into my stretcher, I snap a quick picture. The light filters through the plastic in a cool way and there is a little rainbow in one of the corners. I think about putting it on Instagram, but how would I even caption it? *No pot of gold at the end of this rainbow? Quarantine over the rainbow?*

Joey zips me in, and I look at Flora in her stretcher. I think about her kiss. How Joey called me her boyfriend. Then a little thought starts somewhere in the back of my brain and gets bigger and bigger, like a speeding train coming down a tunnel. What if she really *was* sick and just got me sick? What if I have tropical mono? The CDC worker on the plane said it could be fatal in the elderly and very young. I'm not elderly, but am I very young? How young *is* very young?

Since the disease is passed through saliva, maybe I can just spit out the germs. But I'm sure I've swallowed since Flora has kissed me. Though I guess it's never too late to try. Flora is being wheeled into an ambulance by Joey and two EMTs in hazmat gear, so I turn my head to the side and spit a little bit. But my mouth and throat are dry so nothing comes out. I take a few big deep swishes, and finally spit out a little trickle. But it sticks to my lips. I wipe it away just as Joey hops back out of the ambulance.

"You okay, dude? You didn't puke, did you?" He has the clipboard again, and he looks alarmed.

My mouth and throat are so dry I can't speak. I clear my throat, try again. "No, I'm fine," I finally croak.

"You sure?"

I swallow desperately, nod again.

I can tell he doesn't believe me. He scribbles something furiously on his clipboard.

Two EMTs pop out of the second ambulance. Joey whispers something to them, and they all look at me. It's weird, but I suddenly feel like I miss Flora.

The workers and Joey all load me into the ambulance, none of them saying anything to me. I don't dare try to get any more of the spit out of my mouth.

Joey hops out of the ambulance again. "I'll go with Flora. Since she's the only sick one . . . for now." He gives me a pointed look, and I try to smile, but it feels more like a grimace.

I've never been in an ambulance before. And I've certainly never been in an ambulance in a stretcher covered in plastic on my way to quarantine with EMTs in hazmat suits. I want to take another picture, but it's hard with the EMTs staring at me. Instead I send the one I took when I first got in the stretcher to Kelsey.

She sends back It's like a movie! with the gasping emoji. I wonder if that means she thinks I'm a movie star?

Then I wonder what Kelsey has heard, if she knows I'm going to quarantine because Flora kissed me, and that makes my stomach churn in so many directions at once that I really do feel like I need to throw up.

My mom calls again, but I don't know what else to tell her, so I ignore her call.

I find a news site on my phone, and at the bottom is a tiny story: *First suspected case of tropical mono reported in an American airline passenger. A teenage girl is being transported to a Miami hospital to be quarantined, along with her seatmate, another teenager. Both are high school students from Brooklyn. It's unclear whether the second teen has exhibited symptoms or is being transported out of an abundance of caution.*

My mom keeps calling and I keep not answering.

There are palm trees outside, and I see trickles of sweat on the EMTs' faces as they pull me out of the ambulance. Flora is getting pulled out of her ambulance at the same time. I'm relieved to see her, but I don't know why. Then I see the way she and Joey are looking at each other and I feel like an idiot for protecting her secret. I just need to tell someone what I saw Flora do—even if they don't believe me, even if it doesn't change anything. But first I can't wait to rinse my mouth out.

# 16. FLORA

I'm still in a daze as I'm wheeled through the hospital. I don't much like hospitals. But then again, who does?

The ambulance ride was sort of exciting, especially with Joey sitting next to me. He told me the hospital we were going to was one of the best in the country. I wanted to scream at the top of my lungs, "I'm not sick!" But I didn't. He didn't bring up Oliver's name once, and neither did I.

As we are brought in, we are greeted by at least a dozen members of the medical staff, all in full-blown hazmat suits. Just like the workers in the warehouse, the medical staff are surprisingly calm, and I'm kind of disappointed things aren't more chaotic, more exciting.

We finally stop in a hallway. There is a room on the right side and a room on the left side. I can see into both rooms because the walls are made of clear glass. The rooms look like a movie set.

My stretcher is turned toward the room on the right side of the hallway, and then I'm wheeled through a plastic antechamber, then we're in the room. The curtain between the beds is open. I hear the workers pushing another stretcher into the room. I'm wheeled over to a bed, then turned, and I see Oliver in his stretcher, getting wheeled over to his bed, looking just as bug-eyed as before. There's a lot of to-do getting us off the stretchers, and it's clear one of the workers in particular wants nothing to do with us, keeps hanging back but getting beckoned forward by the other doctors. I see his nose wrinkled behind his hazmat suit. I don't like the way he looks at me.

The staff are all speaking in medical jargon, and it sounds like a different language to me. I watch them all like I really am watching a movie. Oliver is watching them too, and somehow I notice his side of the room has a window, and off in the distance I see an airplane. I wonder where it's going, wonder if the passengers have heard about tropical mono, wonder if they're worried yet. I think how anxious Oliver was, how hard that panic attack was on him. I think about Randy, how hard it is when he gets worried, anxious. It hits me like a slap in the face how little I've thought about this plan, how many people I might affect. Somehow, though, all I want to do is laugh, and I feel like I did on the plane, almost hysterical, and I bite my lip to keep from laughing out loud.

The workers lift me onto a bed with a thin mattress, then start to shuffle away. None of them have said anything to me, even Joey. "Wait!" I yelp.

One of them turns to look at me, like she's surprised that I know how to speak.

"What do we do now?" I ask.

She looks at the other doctors and nurses, and a few of them shrug. "Um, you're looking at it?" she says, gesturing around the room.

One of the nurses chuckles, and I force a smile onto my face and say, "Super, thanks," as sweetly as I can. Joey gives me another sympathetic look, and I feel like a patient at a hospital, remind myself that I *am* a patient at a hospital.

They exit through the plastic antechamber, where I watch them take off their hazmat suits. They throw the suits in something that looks like a big trash can, just in regular scrubs now. I watch them through the window as they walk down the hall, and for some reason I feel disappointed again. I still feel like things should be more exciting somehow. Like some kind of fast-paced punk song should be playing somewhere. But everything seems so quiet.

I fluff my pillows a bit harder than I need to. When I'm done, I get up, get out of bed. Oliver is staring blankly at the TV on his side of the room. It's bolted into the ceiling, just like mine, and I wonder if TV theft from hospitals is really a thing. It occurs to me it's our first time alone. Though it's hard to really be "alone" when one of our walls is made up entirely of glass and doctors and nurses and other medical personnel are constantly walking by.

As I look at him, our kiss flashes into my mind again. I couldn't help but notice that his lips were softer than I was expecting. He seemed so anxious, so prickly, so full of edges, and I was surprised at the softness of his lips. Then I think about how he immediately pulled away like I was poisonous. Soon he'll tell someone what happened, that I faked the fever. I fluff my pillows again.

Oliver rips his eyes away from the TV, which I realize isn't even turned on. "Do you have to do that?"

"Sorry, I've seen kitchen sponges thicker than these pillows."

"Well, we are in a hospital. In *quarantine* in a hospital, in case you for—"

"Oliver, I'm sorry." I say it almost automatically. I've spent my life being an apologizer, saying "I'm sorry" for things. But I don't even know what I'm apologizing for this time, where to begin. So he missed some party back in Brooklyn and didn't see some girl. Big deal. The world will keep spinning. There is a part of me that wonders if this girl even knows that Oliver exists. A mean part. I wonder who the girl is. Someone from school? His rich neighborhood? The daughter of family friends?

Then I wonder why I care.

He shakes his head, breathing hard, and I fear he'll have another panic attack. I want to help calm him down, like I did on the plane, think about holding his hand again, but he looks at me with such disgust, such anger.

"Look," he spits out acidly, "I'm sorry your life is so hard, that your dad married some bimbo. But you know what? I like my life okay, and you just ruined it."

I feel my blood boil. He doesn't know anything about me. Goldy is the least of my problems. "How *dare* you," I say coldly.

He looks taken aback for a second, and I see concern flash across his face, but it quickly disappears again.

I want to punch a wall; I want to slam a door. I want to do something that makes a lot of noise. I want to blast the punk song that I think should be playing. I look around the room desperately. The only door is the door to the bathroom, and it's closer to Oliver's side of the room, and I don't want to get any closer to him. I snap the plastic curtain between our beds shut. It barely makes a sound. I feel even angrier.

# 17. OLIVER

I sit on my side of the room, hear gulping sounds from Flora's side, and then of course my mom calls again.

I take a huge breath. "Yes, Mom," I say sharply.

"Oliver, I hate that I can't see you. I'm so worried you're sick. You're not sick. Are you? Please tell me you're not sick. Your dad never seemed sick, he wasn't sick, and he went to work and died at his desk and I never got to say good-bye to him." She sniffles.

I want to remind my mom that she and my dad were divorced when he died, and neither one of us had spoken to him in years. But I don't. And I want to remind Flora that she's the reason we're in the hospital, stuck in quarantine. But I don't. Instead I wait for my mom to stop crying, like she always does, like I always do.

"I told the doctor to take the best care of you. I know how fragile you are."

"Fragile? Thanks a lot, Mom."

"Oh, honey, it's okay to be fragile after everything we've gone through."

What we've gone through is dealing with the death of someone we barely knew anymore. But I don't feel like pointing that out to her. I don't feel like pointing anything out to her. I just want to be done with the phone call.

"Hey, Mom, it's probably good for me to get lots of rest, not exert myself on things like phone calls. You know, to stay healthy." I'm proud of myself for how quickly I've found an excuse to get off the phone.

"Okay," she says, unsure. "Call me as often as you can?"

"Yeah, okay," I say.

"I love you, Oliver," she says, and I hear her crying again. "I'll be in Miami tomorrow!"

"I love you too, Mom," I say.

I hang up and see I've gotten a text from Kelsey. Seeing her name on my phone makes me feel guilty. I wish the doctors hadn't told my mom about Flora kissing me. Now that she knows, she'll never unknow it, and I won't be able to wish it away as much as I want to. At least . . . I think I want to. Of course I want to. I shake my head, read the text from Kelsey. Did u see what I put on Facebook?

I open Facebook for the first time since last night. The notifications start popping up, and I see that Kelsey has tagged me in a post. Prayers for Oliver in quarantine!!

At first I'm excited. I want to frame the moment somehow, put it in a scrapbook to look at later. I do the closest thing, actually, and take a screenshot. But then I look at all the comments, most from people I don't know, some from people I sort of know.

I hope you feel better, from a girl in my English class.

How scary. Hope you're okay! from a guy in my chemistry class.

Didn't he switch schools last year? from Clayton Crowl, whose locker is two down from mine and who I see almost every day.

I scroll through, see some more *get wells*.

Then, **Isn't mono a kissing disease? Who'd kiss him?** from Blaine Robert. We were friends in elementary school, used to play *Star Wars* together. We stopped being friends when he started being popular.

I open my texts, write to Kelsey, Thank you! Though I don't know why I'm thanking her for making me feel like crud.

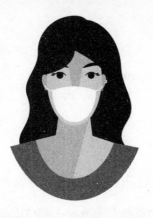

# 18. FLORA

My phone makes a noise, and I realize it's my dad trying to video chat me. I figure it's a mistake, that he probably sat on his phone or something, so I ignore it. The phone makes the noise again, so I tap the ACCEPT button skeptically. Immediately an image of my dad pops up. He's wearing the same tattered bathrobe he's had since I was little. It reminds me of pancakes and Saturday mornings.

"Flora!" he says. There's some expression on his face I don't recognize. "Are you okay?" His voice sounds funny too, and I realize the expression on his face is fear.

I don't know why, but I feel tears well up in my eyes. I just saw him yesterday, but suddenly I desperately miss him. I want to breathe in the smell of maple syrup and him again. The smell of his aftershave, of him reading the funnies with me, the smell of him carrying me to bed after I fell asleep on the couch—like he used to before he and my mom got divorced.

Then Goldy pops in the frame and the spell is broken. "Flora!" she says. "We've been worried sick about you. Did you get my texts? Did you see my posts?"

The *we* makes me shudder. "Yep, sure did." As usual when I talk to Goldy, I don't try to hide my annoyance, and as usual she doesn't seem to notice it anyway.

"I'm so sorry we invited you to visit us right where this disease started. We had no idea," my dad says.

*We, us, we.* I shudder again.

"Do you have the chills? Are you okay?" My dad suddenly leans forward toward the camera, and his voice echoes around the hospital room. I'm aware of how quiet it is on Oliver's side of the room, wonder what he's doing over there, remind myself I don't care. Remind myself what he said about me ruining his life.

"Your mother called me to tell me what happened. She said that you had a fever but otherwise your vitals were okay and you weren't showing any other symptoms yet."

"I'm okay, Dad." His concern just makes me mad all over again. Especially when I see Goldy's hand on his shoulder.

"I should probably go, though. Get some rest. Save my energy." I just heard Oliver say something similar to his mom and I hope he doesn't think I'm ruining his life by borrowing his excuse.

"Of course. We understand," my dad says.

*We.* I resist the urge to shudder.

"We love you."

I wait a second, both of them looking at me, then quickly say, "Love you too," and hang up the video call before they can say anything else.

It's still quiet on Oliver's side of the room, and I look around again, wanting to slam a door and throw something and yell and stomp my feet. But I don't do any of those things. I can't do any of those things.

I look out the window, to the empty room across the hallway.

I wonder if anyone will be in that room. I wonder if anyone else will get sick. Sick. Everyone thinks I'm sick.

Someone is outside our door, slipping into a hazmat suit. I can't tell if it's a man or a woman, not that it matters. The person steps through the antechamber, and I realize it's Joey, and he's holding two trays. "Lunch!" he says. "Sorry it's so late. It's almost time for dinner! I don't usually handle food deliveries, but the food staff was freaked about giving you food. Not that they think you're gross or anything, just that you might be crawling with germs, so I volunteered." He grins at me.

Does this mean he wants to spend time with me? I feel that giddy feeling again but resist the urge to giggle. I am *not* a giggler. I have no control over the grin on my face, though. He pats my head, a gesture I find both comforting and disorienting since his hand is in a huge rubber glove in a hazmat suit. He puts the tray on my bedside table and goes to Oliver's side of the room.

As I'm picking at my food, my mom calls. It's hard to concentrate on what she's saying.

"Good news, I'm on a flight to Miami in two days. I wish I could get there tomorrow! But your uncle and I are trying to find care for Randy, and he hasn't had that many sleepovers, and the soonest he can stay with someone is tomorrow and—"

"Mom, please, you don't need to explain yourself," I say gently. "I'm just really . . . happy you'll be able to come down. Thank you for going to all that trouble." I feel so guilty for what I've done that I'm dizzy.

"It's no trouble, Flora," my mom says.

We're quiet for a second, and my mom says, "Dr. Demarko said you're in quarantine with another teenager. A boy?" She stops, waits for me to say something. It's just like when I was a kid and she tried to lead me to admit that I cut my Barbie's hair.

"Yeah," I say carefully.

"She also said the reason the boy is in quarantine is because you kissed him?" It's the way we used to talk before my dad left us. Back when we were happy, when we could talk about other things besides Goldy being dumb and being mad at my dad. "Flora, was that your first kiss?" She says it softly, calmly.

I don't say anything. I'm suddenly very aware of Oliver's silence on the other side of the curtain.

My mom is quiet too, waiting for me to continue. But then I hear Randy's voice in the background, asking my mom where the stapler is. "Right side of the desk in Flora's room," she says. Then she asks me, "Do you want to talk to your cousin?"

"Nooooo!" I hear from my mom's end of the phone. She sighs. "Sorry, Flora, he can't find what he's looking for. You know how it goes. I know that I put—"

"Wait, Mom, before you go," I interrupt.

She's quiet, and I hear Randy really lose it.

"I just want to say I'm sorry. Again."

"Flora, honey, for what? Why do you keep saying that? You can't help that you got sick. It's not like you did it on purpose."

I laugh uneasily. "Right, of course not."

"I need to help Randy. You just worry about getting better, making that fever go away, okay?"

"Okay," I say in a small voice.

Just as I hang up, a woman in a hazmat suit walks through the antechamber and into the room. "Vitals check." She seems so bored, like she wears a hazmat suit every day. She probably does, come to think of it.

Vitals! Right! They'll figure out I don't actually have a fever, that I'm not actually sick, that Oliver won't get sick. Which means maybe we can both go home, and it can be just some big misunderstanding that Oliver and I will laugh about someday. Not that I'll ever have a someday with him.

The woman looks at the clock on the wall and mutters something.

"What did you say?" I don't know why I'm trying to make conversation with her.

She looks at me, eyes narrowed, like she smells something rotten. "I said that I'm late. This isn't my usual floor. I'm not really familiar with where I'm going."

"It's okay, I'm not *really* sick," I say without thinking.

She looks at me through the clear ⎓⎓⎓⎓ ⎓⎓ her face. "Never heard that one ⎓⎓ ⎓ ⎓," she ⎓⎓⎓, then rolls her eyes.

"No, really. I'm not really sick. It's all a misunderstanding."

I hear Oliver rustle around on the other side of the curtain, hope he's listening.

"Oh yeah? What kind of misunderstanding would that be?" The nurse looks at me sympathetically, pouting her lips, like I'm five years old.

"I didn't really have a fever. I faked it! Can we go home now?"

The nurse rolls her eyes again and jabs the thermometer in my mouth.

When the thermometer beeps, she pulls it out and looks at the number, looks at me. "Absence of fever," she mutters, squinting. She holds the thermometer between two fingers like it's venomous. I feel suddenly defensive of my saliva. I'm not poisonous. I'm reminded of how Oliver recoiled from me and suddenly I want to grab the thermometer from her fingers and poke her in the eyeball with it.

# 19. OLIVER

I hear the grumpy nurse finish up Flora's vitals checks. I feel a creeping sense of dread. It's like a bad dream. We're not sick, and we're stuck in a hospital room and no one believes us. Isn't this what used to happen in old insane asylums? Or maybe it was in a movie I watched. Or a book I read. Or a book based on a movie based on an actual event in history.

Suddenly the curtain rips open, and I see Flora for a split second. The nurse closes the curtain again, looks me up and down. "Vitals check," she says, sounding even more bored than when she took Flora's.

She waits for the thermometer to beep and for my blood pressure and pulse to be read. "Normal," she drones. Then she's gone.

It's quiet on Flora's side of the room. The curtain separating our beds is dark, so I can't see her outline.

Kelsey keeps texting me, and I want to tell her it's all a big misunderstanding, that Flora faked her fever and kissed me, but at the thought of Kelsey knowing Flora kissed me, I want to throw up again. I realize how completely and utterly trapped I am.

*There's no way out*, I keep thinking.

Kelsey is telling me about a movie she's watching with Lucy. The plot sounds complicated. Or maybe I'm just not paying close enough attention.

I turn on the TV, catch the news, and there's a quick story about two teenagers in quarantine in Miami, and I realize the story is about Flora and me. They can't show our pictures or release our names due to patient confidentiality and all that. But it's weird to know a news story is about me. It's like when I hear a recording of my own voice: It's something that's familiar but feels so distant and foreign.

*There's no way out.* I click off the TV, check Facebook, the post that Kelsey put up, but I can only read *who's Oliver?* twenty times before I want to close the app again. But there at the bottom is a comment from someone named Jenna: Eww. I think he's sharing a room with Flora.

*Eww.* It sears into my brain. But wait, who is Jenna and how does she know I'm sharing a room with Flora?

A second later my phone buzzes. It's a new text from Kelsey. Oliver! You didn't tell me u had a roommate! Should I be jealous? But she adds one of the emojis that is crying and laughing. Because of course she knows she has nothing to be jealous of, since no one would ever get jealous over me. Because I'm Oliver. I suddenly have the urge to tell her I'm in quarantine because Flora kissed me, but the thought feels mean. And I still don't know how I feel about the kiss. And I still don't know why she did it.

I touch my lips for a second. The kiss was quick, but I still noticed how soft Flora's skin was. Even her hands grabbing my face were soft. I think about how she held my hand on the plane, how she wasn't freaked out about my panic attack. I think about that seal in the video she showed me when Dr. Demarko was talking to my mom. I feel like a scumbag for what I said about her dad marrying her stepmom.

I wonder if Flora has kissed lots of people. It's weird being so close to her and not talking to her. It's weird that we are completely and utterly stuck in this room.

Joey brings in dinner trays a little bit later, and I don't mean to eavesdrop on him talking to Flora, but I also have no choice when her bed is only a few feet away from mine. I know he's studying to be a doctor or whatever, but he doesn't strike me as particularly intelligent.

He says something to Flora about visiting Times Square when he was a kid and she actually says, "I love hanging out there." Which has to be a lie. No New Yorkers actually like going there.

There is something in her voice that isn't there when she talks to me. It reminds me a little of the flutters in my mom's voice.

Now they're talking about basketball and Joey is saying something about the Brooklyn Nets. Flora says she loves basketball, but for some reason I don't think she means it. I haven't heard her mention sports teams once. Not that it's been that long since I've known her. And not that I'll ever know her anymore since we're not talking to each other.

They keep talking and I keep wondering why he's not leaving yet. I feel territorial of my room, my space. And, I realize, of Flora. I'm the one she's supposed to be talking to, not Joey.

After what seems like hours, he finally says something about giving dinner to "your boyfriend," and I hate how grossed out Flora sounds when she says, "He's not my boyfriend!"

Then Mr. *Grey's Anatomy* says, "So why did you kiss him?" But he says it in a joking way, one that shows he doesn't actually want an answer. I wonder yet again why she did it.

Joey pulls open the curtain, and I see Flora. She has a different kind of smile on her face, one I haven't seen yet. It lights up her entire face, and it's so infectious I can't help smiling back at her. But the smile quickly changes into a scowl when she sees me looking at her, and she closes the curtain again.

"Dinner, dude!" Joey says. I wonder if he's ever in a bad mood.

"Thanks," I say.

He watches me open the tray, and I wonder again why he's still in my room—*our* room.

I pick at the iceberg lettuce in my salad, and Joey writes something down on his clipboard again. Finally he says, "You'll see me or one of my fine colleagues tonight for vitals checks. And tomorrow we'll do it over again." He salutes me, and I don't even know what the proper gesture in response would be, but luckily he doesn't wait around.

It seems even quieter in our room now with Joey gone. It's 7:30 p.m., and it feels weird not to be doing homework, getting ready for a new week of school.

I text with Kelsey a little bit more, but she's talking about some other movie now that sounds even more complicated. My mom of course calls, and she sounds calmer. She's all packed and ready for her flight. I also know she's had her nightly glass of wine.

Then it's 10:30 and I hear Flora go into the bathroom. She comes out a little bit later, smelling like coconuts and mint. I hear her settle into bed, and I realize I should probably do the same. I dig around in my bag. I wish I had actually done laundry before I left my hotel because now all I have is a pile of sweaty, gross clothes. There is a stack of hospital gowns on the chair in my corner. I grab one that's blue and head to the bathroom. I brush my teeth, change into the gown, and am a little shocked by how much I look like a patient in a hospital.

I climb into the bed, fiddle with the different positions so I'm not sitting so upright, flip on the TV again. Same news story about us as before. Or about "two teenagers."

I try to sleep. I hear Flora breathing deeply, wonder if she's asleep. It suddenly dawns on me that I'm spending a night alone with a girl. I spent last night sleeping next to Flora, but we were in an open roomful of people. Now we're alone in this room together. Well, as alone as we can be when one of the walls of our room is made entirely of glass, and doctors and nurses are coming in and out for vitals checks. But still more alone with a girl than I ever have been before.

# 20. FLORA

It's 3:23 a.m. Oliver is snoring. It woke me up, but it's oddly comforting. Much more comforting than getting a thermometer jabbed in my mouth and a cuff wrapped around my arm every five minutes. I hop on Twitter for no reason in particular, but everything just annoys me. Becca and Jenna tried to start a Kickstarter thing to "find a cure for tropical mono," but so far they have only raised ten dollars. Of course they had to hang out to make the page, and take a million pictures and post them saying how worried "we" are. The "we" reminds me of my dad and Goldy.

I look at the ceiling, look at my phone again to check the time. It's 3:42, and Oliver's still snoring. I can't sleep, but somehow I don't care.

# 21. OLIVER

It's nice to wake up on my own, not to be woken up by a thermometer being jammed down my throat or a cuff tightening around my arm. It's light in the room. My phone tells me it's 9:37. I hear Joey come in, and he's talking to Flora about basketball again. Well, more like talking *at* Flora. He's telling her about some game he went to and some amazing free throw. I almost feel bad that Flora has to listen to him. Almost.

I look at my texts, trying to tune out Joey's voice. Kelsey sent a message a little while ago, still talking about one of the two movies she watched, and then, Hope u feel ok!

I feel better than okay reading it. Just great, I reply.

I open my email but don't find anything interesting. I don't feel like looking at my Facebook to see anyone else I know say they don't know me, so I look at Kelsey's Facebook, then her Instagram. Just some selfies of her and Lucy watching their movies.

My mom calls to tell me she's on her flight. There are all kinds of announcements in the background, and she's talking really loud. I pull the phone away from my face a bit, tell her I'm fine, no fever yet, yes, I'm eating well, and then Joey opens the curtain. For once, I'm actually happy to see him. "Mom, I need to go. One of the doctors is here."

"Okay. But really quick—I wanted to let you know I've spoken with the doctors about visitors. I'll have a definite answer one way or another by tomorrow. They seem confident it'll be okay, and I'll be able to see you soon! And I'll be in Miami in a few hours!"

"Mom, I really gotta go. Have a good flight." Joey is watching me on the phone, scrawling away at his clipboard like usual.

I hang up and he says, "You heard the rumor about visitors? No girl-friends, though, Romeo. We can't have you kissing anyone."

I hear Flora snort on the other side of the curtain. Joey hears it too, then tries and fails to hide a grin behind his hand.

"Breakfast," he says, sliding me the tray. He checks my vitals, writes some more on the clipboard, then exits through the antechamber. *Funny how quick his "checks" are with me versus Flora*, I think, annoyed. And why did she snort like that?

It's only 10:16 a.m. This is going to be a long day.

# 22. FLORA

I look out the window of my room at the hospital hallway. Joey left an hour ago, but he walks by again and waves. It's funny that now he looks normal to me in his hazmat gear, and when I see him in only his scrubs walking by, he seems out of place to me. It's like seeing a teacher outside of school, out in the real world. Except that I can't help but notice he fills out his scrubs nicely.

I feel like I should chase that thought out of my head, but I don't know why.

I look at the curtain between my bed and Oliver's. I'm still angry at him for what he said about Goldy, but I also want to talk to him again. He needed my help on the plane, then he got annoying, and then it got weird. I can't figure him out. He's an anxious guy for sure, but something tells me it's not his fault.

But it's *my* fault he's in this mess.

My mom has been texting me, telling me that she heard from my doctors and that she can probably visit soon. I feel itchy and restless, get up and pace around my room. I look at the curtain between my side of the room and Oliver's again. His TV is on, and I hear the canned laughter of some old sitcom. There is a little patch of sunlight coming from under his curtain. Is he looking out the window? I wonder what he sees out there.

I close my eyes for a second, take a deep breath, and pretend I'm back home in Brooklyn. Last I checked it was almost noon, so I'd be having lunch in the school cafeteria. I pretend I'm sitting with Becca and Jenna, and we're talking about our spring breaks. They're telling me they missed me, that it wasn't the same without me. Then someone else, a girl I don't know, sits down and says, "If they miss you so much, why aren't they texting you?"

My eyes snap open, and I grab my phone. I feel itchy and mad again when I see I don't have any texts from them. I look at the fund-raising page, but the donation amount still sits at ten dollars.

I hear more laughter from Oliver's TV.

Joey brings lunch in, but he doesn't stay long, and for some reason this annoys me. I remind myself he has other patients. I pick at the soggy bread on the ham and cheese sandwich, then nibble the cheddar.

I pace some more, make my bed again, reorganize my suitcase, refold the clothes. I miss the warehouse. I miss the open space. I miss talking to Oliver.

I miss Oliver.

I pretend I'm in the cafeteria again. But Becca and Jenna are already gone, and I'm alone.

My eyes snap open as a thermometer is being shoved in my mouth and the blood pressure cuff is being wrapped around my arm. I must have fallen asleep. I look up. It's not Joey in the hazmat suit this time, but the same grumpy nurse from last night.

She takes the thermometer out, looks at it, takes the cuff off, looks at the screen on her little cart. "Still normal," she says. She studies me, hand on her hip. "Your temperature should have gone back up by now," she mutters.

I spend the rest of the afternoon listening to the canned sitcom laughter on Oliver's side of the room, envious of the characters, of their problems being wrapped up in thirty minutes. Thirty days is so much longer than thirty minutes.

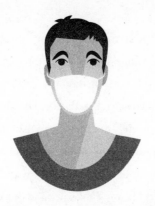

# 23. OLIVER

The third morning in the hospital starts the same as the day before: me not knowing where I am when I first wake up, then quickly remembering, then doing the breathing exercises I found online. And then, of course, checking my phone. First I check my texts, then my email, then Kelsey's Facebook, then Instagram. It makes a nice little circle in my head, and the routine comforts me.

My first check reveals a new text from Kelsey, just an emoji of a stack of pancakes. We've been texting about what we like to eat when we're sick, and I told her waffles, especially Eggos. I don't understand the emoji, but then think she must know the difference between waffles and pancakes and is trying to joke with me. Or maybe she was trying to tell me she thought pancakes were better and was just teasing me? Or maybe there isn't an emoji for waffles, but there is one for pancakes? Sometimes I hate emojis. I wish girls had instruction manuals.

My email, Kelsey's Facebook, and Kelsey's Instagram don't reveal anything very exciting or new, so with my morning lap done, I put my phone down. The curtain between my bed and Flora's is closed. Which is fine; I still don't want to talk to her, and I know I can hold out.

My parents once went thirty-three days without speaking to each other. I was eight, and I marked each day on a calendar. I'd drawn cake and balloons next to the twelfth day, my birthday. The only present I wanted that year was for them to talk to each other. But when that wish finally came true, I regretted my birthday wish. Thirty-three days of no talking erupted into one of their worst arguments and ended with my mom ripping pages out of her wedding album and trying to put them in the paper shredder. I hid in my closet until it was over.

I stretch in bed, look over at the closed curtain again, wonder what Flora's doing on the other side, wonder if she's still asleep. Not because I care about her. I just wonder if I should be getting all the sleep I can, just in case. Just in case . . . what, I'm not sure, because she's not really sick, and I'm not really sick, and this whole quarantine thing is her fault, and I know that she knows I know that she's not really sick. But I can't bring myself to tell on her. Especially when Kelsey keeps texting me.

I grab my phone again and text Kelsey. Good morning. I add an emoji of a sun too.

She writes back, I'm just about to have some waffles. And she adds the picture of the pancakes again.

Ha-ha, I write back.

Waffles r funny?

Now I really can't tell if she's messing with me about messing with me, and my head hurts.

I think I hear Flora moving around on the other side of the curtain. I remind myself I don't care and go back to my text with Kelsey. I send an emoji of a doughnut, and I guess I pass whatever test I somehow have accidentally agreed to take, because she writes back with lol.

I exhale, just as I hear someone walk in our room.

# 24. FLORA

It's hard to really know what counts as my day starting since I'm woken up every few hours for vitals checks, and every time I'm just about to fall asleep it's time for a check again. I haven't seen sunlight in a while either. It seemed like it was only fair that Oliver got the window after I dragged him into this mess. Though it's not a mess, it's more of an adventure, I remind myself for the millionth time. An adventure with Jell-O pudding cups and fruit cocktails and mashed potatoes that are a weird gray color. Our new living quarters are a far cry from the HDTVs and bagels and pizza from the warehouse. The hospital is fine, but it is just very much . . . a hospital.

I look up to see who has walked into our room. I expect it to be Joey—hope it'll be Joey. But it's not. It's someone I haven't seen before, and he's carrying a basket almost as big as him. It's stuffed full of all kinds of food.

"Um, excuse me, I have a package for you." His eyes are big in his hazmat suit as he nervously looks around the room, taking it all in.

He puts the basket down in the doorway, gives me a quick look, and

I see a brief wrinkle in his nose that I've come to recognize as disgust. He scoots out the door quickly.

I look at the curtain between Oliver's bed and mine. He's quiet over there, though I heard him moving around a little while ago, so I think he's awake.

I climb out of bed, scoop up the basket, and grab the card that's sitting at the top. It's addressed to me, and I'm surprised at how excited I am. The excitement immediately turns to disappointment when I see that it's from Goldy.

*Hope this helps make you feel better soon!* I'm surprised she managed to spell everything correctly, but I figure whoever put the basket together probably fixed all the misspellings and typos.

I grab the food out of the basket. It doesn't look great, but it has to be better than the room-temperature pudding I've been eating. I open a bag of cookies and take a nibble. It's not bad, but it tastes like it's missing something. I look at the bag more closely and see the words *gluten free*. I pull out the bag of chips, same thing. I dig around some more, and everything seems to be gluten free, even down to the box of raisins. "Because raisins are usually loaded with gluten," I mutter. I doubt she even knows what gluten is.

"What did you say?" Oliver's voice on the other side of the curtain makes me drop the box of raisins.

I don't know what to say. I look around in the basket some more. At the very bottom is a box of gluten-free pancake mix. "Good thing I have my hot griddle with me here," I say. I don't know why, maybe it's the lack of direct sunlight, maybe it's the lack of fresh air, maybe I just don't know what else to do, so I slide the box of pancake mix under the curtain in our room. For some reason I think Oliver might get a kick out of it.

He yelps, then rips open the curtain. He looks like he's seen a ghost. "How did you know?"

"Oh god, you're gluten free too?" I ask. "I mean, I know it's a really serious allergy, but I also know a lot of people like dieting trends, including Goldy." I hate that the first conversation I have with Oliver in two days is about her.

"What?" He looks confused. "No, no. Gluten is good. I guess. I don't know. I've never really given it much thought." He shakes the pancake mix. "But waffles are not the same as pancakes!"

I have no clue what he's talking about, but he looks so ridiculous in his hospital gown holding a box of pancake mix that I start laughing.

"Waffles are funny?" He starts laughing too. I don't know what he's laughing at, but I'm so relieved to see him happy again, and I'm so happy to be having a conversation with him, even if I have no clue what he's talking about.

# 25. OLIVER

My face hurts from laughing. It feels good to stretch out the muscles in my face. But as my laughter dies down in my chest, I snap out of my hysteria and quickly remember where I am, why I'm here. Flora is just laughing so easily. Seeing her so happy makes me mad all over again.

I think Flora notices my anger, because she suddenly stops laughing and we both look at each other for a moment in silence.

"I messed up," she says plainly, unemotionally. "I know you wanted to get home, I know there's a girl, and I'm sorry."

Her frankness—her genuineness—isn't something I'm used to, and it's throwing me off. I'm waiting for the catch, waiting for her to pull something on me, but her expression is so totally open. There wouldn't be any of this weird waffle/pancake confusion with her.

"I need to know . . . I need to know why . . ." I trail off.

"Why I did it? Faked the fever?" She says it so I don't have to.

"Yes. Please tell me you have some amazing reason."

She shrugs. "It was so cozy before. I know I said my stepmom is terrible, but my real mom isn't always easy, and taking care of my cousin is never easy. I guess I wasn't ready to go home yet. And maybe I don't always feel very interesting. I don't know."

"I think you're interesting," I say before I can stop myself.

I want to ask her about the kiss, but I'm embarrassed and I can't make my mouth form the words.

Flora is still looking me in the eye, and I'm reminded of her calmness on the flight, the way she helped me, a stranger, get through a panic attack. I think of the way she defended the sick passenger, the way she stood up to the other guy on our flight. Of the goofy seal video she showed me.

"Well, that's nice of you to say." She waves her hand. "But, I was thinking, we still have twenty-eight days here. I still feel like I owe you."

"Owe me?" *Say something about the kiss, Oliver.*

"Yeah. For all of this." She waves her hand again, this time gesturing at the hospital room.

*My first kiss.*

I shake my head, trying to focus on something that isn't her lips on mine. I look around us. Now that the curtain is open, I can see her side of the room. Her bed is neatly made, her clothes are folded on a chair, and even her tray of food looks tidy. I look around at my messy side of the room, my tray of picked-at food, my rumpled sheets, the socks that seem to have multiplied and are peeking at me from every corner of the room. I kick at one with my foot, shove it under a chair, but Flora isn't paying attention to what I'm doing.

She's got her phone out; she's mumbling to herself. "Quarantime? Quarantining?" Then, after a moment, "Oh, quaranteen! That's it!" She looks up at me, beaming.

"What are you doing?" I ask slowly.

"Making our hashtag."

"Our what?"

"Hashtag!"

"Right, sorry, I know what a hashtag is, but what is *our* hashtag? *Why* is our hashtag, err . . ." I trail off.

"Have you ever seen pictures from inside a quarantine?"

"I mean, everyone has seen pictures of some kind of quarantine, right? They're pretty depressing. And awful."

Flora doesn't seem to hear me. "I bring you the world's first hashtag for quarantined teenagers. Or should I say . . . quaranteens!"

I'm still confused. "Why are we doing this? Or why are *you* doing this?"

"What's her name?"

"Kelsey," I say without thinking. How did I know who Flora was even asking about?

"*Kelsey* will think it's pretty cool to see her name in the first hashtag-quaranteens picture, won't she?"

"Flora, what are you talking about?"

She finally looks up from her phone. "Making the girl fall for you, of course. And becoming your own personal girl assistant/girl handbook author."

She's so riled up, so excited, and we're talking after not talking at all for two days, and I'm still confused about the kiss, so I don't know what to say. I suppose "thank you" is a place to start.

"You can say thank you," Flora says.

"Wait, did you just read—"

"Yeah, I'm a hashtag creator and mind reader." She shrugs. "Consider it part of my double X chromosome."

She's pointing her phone at me. She puts it down and comes over to my side of the room. She ruffles my hair, and I resist the odd temptation to grab her hand. She backs away and looks at me, proud of her work. "Perfect bedhead," she says, pleased.

She points her phone at me again and shows me the picture. My hair is sticking up, my mouth is hanging open. It's a terrible picture.

"What's your number? I'll text it to you and you can say something about Kelsey and use our hashtag. She's going to fall for you so hard."

I don't say anything, so she looks up at me again, expectantly. "Your number?"

"Oh, right." I give her my number.

A second later my phone dings, and the terrible picture of me shows up on my screen.

"Okay, get to work."

"What exactly am I supposed to do again?"

"Make Kelsey fall for you," she says, like it's as easy as ordering a pizza.

"And *how* am I supposed to do that, again?"

"By charming her. And by being the perfect boyfriend in quarantine."

"Wait, boyfriend?"

"Remember that thing I said about being the author of the girl handbook?"

"Yeah?"

"I'm the author of the sequel too."

I wonder if Flora really does have a fever that is causing some kind of dementia. Then I fiddle with the picture on my phone, waiting for further instruction from Flora. But she just keeps watching me.

"I just don't get how a picture is going to make Kelsey fall for me," I finally say.

Flora rolls her eyes. "Give me that." She snatches the phone from my hand, taps a few things on the screen, and hands it back to me.

Whatever filter she used has washed me out, so my doofusy face isn't so brightly lit, and she's added the hashtag she was talking about: #quaranteen. She's also added #hikelsey. "Hike l-l-l." I stop, unable to parse out what the second word is.

Flora rolls her eyes again. "Hi Kelsey?"

"Right," I say softly. "Why am I doing this again? To show Kelsey that I can still be a dweeb even when I'm in quarantine?"

Flora jabs my arm lightly with her shoulder. "You're not a dweeb. Just please trust me? She'll totally dig this. Girls love when guys think about them from far away. Especially to call attention to it on social media, when so many people have already heard about the quarantined teenagers on the news. You'll have a date for spring formal by the time we're out of here."

"How did you know I wanted to ask—"

"Kelsey to spring formal?" Flora taps her head again and winks.

"You're a little creepy," I say before I can stop myself.

Flora grins evilly. "You'll thank me later."

I swallow hesitantly and hit SHARE for all Instagram to see.

# 26. FLORA

For the past twenty minutes Oliver has been even more glued to his phone than he was before, and I wonder for a second why I've created the hashtag. It was nice talking to him, but now he's silent on his side of the room, scrolling down and refreshing the Twitter post.

I can't help it, but I'm on Twitter now too, looking at my hashtag. *Our* hashtag. *This is for Oliver*, I remind myself.

I see Kelsey's reaction before he does. OMG. Can I be ur nurse??

I wince. How creative. But I also know Oliver is going to love it. I look at him out of the corner of my eye, notice a blush spreading across his face, a little smile following. Though it isn't the full-blown ecstatic reaction I was expecting. Have I misjudged the power of my hashtag? It seemed so perfect. Girls love getting called out on social media like that. Not that I would know . . . but so I've heard.

Oliver is still silent. I keep refreshing the post, waiting to see what he will say back to Kelsey, but he doesn't post anything. I look at him out of the corner of my eye again and his eyebrows are furrowed.

"Is everything okay? I think Kelsey said something back to you." I try to play dumb.

"You're checking the post?" He seems surprised.

"Well, the hashtag was my idea, wasn't it?" I mean to say it teasingly but even I hear the defensive tone to my voice.

Oliver studies my face for a second before looking down at his phone again. I wait for him to speak but he keeps his head down.

"You should say something back!" I say encouragingly.

"Hmm?" He's distracted. "Oh, right, yeah, I should."

I try: "I think she said something about being a nurse? That's pretty . . ." I trail off, searching for the right word.

"Repetitive," he offers, his head still down.

I'm confused. Did she post something twice? "I'm not following."

"Nothing. It's fine!" Oliver smiles, but it looks forced.

And then we're back to not talking to each other again, and I wonder how this is any better. Great.

I keep refreshing the post, but Oliver doesn't say anything back. I go on Instagram and look at pictures of Jenna and Becca. They've been texting me a little here and there. I start a text to them about kissing Oliver, but I don't actually send the message. Because then they'll know why he's in quarantine, and then maybe they'll wonder why I'm in quarantine, and they'll figure it out about the faked fever. Maybe. I don't know. Maybe I'm just making excuses.

Goldy has posted a bunch of dumb "inspirational" quotes on Facebook about smiling when things are hard and all her dumb friends are asking if she's okay. I'm fine. Just worried about someone close to me.

I hope she isn't talking about me and I hope she doesn't think she's close to me.

Oliver yelps and jumps out of his bed. His hair is still sticking up in the bedhead I styled for him, and I resist the urge to run my fingers through his hair again.

He wiggles the phone in front of me, trying to show me the screen, but in his excitement he accidentally turns the phone off. He's flustered, and I try not to laugh. We both stare at the logo of the home screen as it turns on again.

He finally pulls up Twitter, refreshes the post one more time, and triumphantly flips the phone to face me. "We're trending!"

I look at his screen but my eyes glaze at all the #quaranteens.

"What are people saying?" I try to act nonchalant, try to hide my surprise.

"This is crazy!" Oliver says. "I don't even know who these people are." He's still got his phone in front of me, and I force my eyes to focus.

I touch his hand to make him stop scrolling. "Wait, let me read some of this stuff."

He looks at my hand on his, and I quickly pull away.

He clears his throat. "Um, okay, so some people are saying we must be the same teenagers from the news. Some people are freaking out and are worried they're going to get sick. But, ha, look, this girl is telling her girlfriend she wants to go to quarantine with her."

I lean closer to him again to look at his phone. "Ha, that girl says she wants to go to quarantine with you! Oh, look, another one says the same thing!"

Oliver's blush is spreading to his neck. "Why would anyone want to go to quarantine with me?" he says.

I look at his cool-breeze eyes, think about running my hands through his hair, think about his soft lips when I kissed him.

I can think of a few reasons why.

He keeps reading me more but my brain can't keep up. I knew my hashtag was a good idea, but I didn't think it was *that* good of an idea. I must be on a roll: two impulsive, split-second decisions in one week.

# 27. OLIVER

I keep refreshing the post, and every time the number of likes and comments multiplies. Gone are the **Who's Olivers** and now come the **I've known him since kindergarten** and **We hang out all the time.** Even Emily chimes in, **My bestie from spring break.** And then there are all the people I really don't know, the complete and utter strangers. People asking their friends who they'd want to go into #quaranteen with. Who they'd hate to go to #quaranteen with. What illness they wish their ex could be sent to #quaranteen with.

Some other people say they want to go into #quaranteen with me, which I think must be a joke.

I keep scrolling, and I almost scroll right past the tweet, **Looking at airfare to Miami now! My uncle already said I can stay with him!**

My thumb hovers over the words, frozen. It's from Kelsey.

Flora looks up at me a couple of minutes later, grinning, but something about her smile also looks a little forced. "Now Kelsey is joking about visiting you!"

"Oh, you saw? Right, she's just joking!" I clear my throat. "I mean, Joey did say we could probably have visitors . . ."

"Does *she* know Joey said we could probably have visitors? I mean, nothing is official."

"Not yet."

Her smile looks further strained.

"I mean, should I tell her? You're the expert—the author of the girl handbook!"

"Ha, right, that's me," she says, but it feels half-hearted. Her enthusiasm from before seems to have dissipated.

Over her shoulder I see a nurse in scrubs approaching our doorway. He slips into a hazmat suit and enters our room, pushing the vitals cart. He takes Flora's temperature, blood pressure, and pulse, then writes down the results, sanitizes his hands, gets a new thermometer, and takes my vitals. The whole thing takes less than two minutes, but the entire time I'm wondering what I'm supposed to do next—tell Kelsey next. Wondering why Flora seemed so excited before and now she doesn't. I keep getting notifications about the hashtag, and my phone keeps buzzing and lighting up and making all kinds of sounds I didn't know it could make.

I look up from the beeping and dinging and vibrating to see Dr. Demarko come in. "Well, it's nice to see my celebrity patients," she says. "That sure happened fast."

Flora squirms on her bed. "Yeah, about that—"

"It's okay. I know you need to pass the time somehow. You're teenagers, after all, and there's nothing wrong with some harmless social media stuff, right? I think Joey might have hinted at it, but it's official: You will be allowed to have visitors, starting tomorrow. With a few caveats, of course."

My eyebrows shoot up in attention, and I think Flora notices.

"Your visitors will have to remain in hazmat suits the entire time, and their visits are limited to only one hour at a time, three times a day. No more than two visitors at a time for each of you. Even if you're not exhibiting symptoms, Flora, you did have a fever, and you did pass those potential contagions on to Oliver orally. You both need lots of rest to prevent any further illness in yourselves or others. And it should go without saying, especially since your visitors will be in protective clothing the entire time, but absolutely no oral contact of any kind."

She says it medically, not using the word *kiss* once.

# 28. FLORA

I should be excited that I can have visitors. Ecstatic, even. But everything just feels weird. Things were so nice and cozy at the warehouse, and then it got weird with Oliver, and then we came to the hospital and it was weird again and then it was nice for a few minutes, and now there's a hashtag and we're trending.

I knew Kelsey would like the hashtag, but I didn't think anyone else would really find it all that interesting. Except for maybe Kelsey's friends.

But now random strangers are talking about #quaranteens. Girls *and* boys are saying they want to be in #quaranteen with Oliver.

No one is talking about me, though, because I guess everyone forgot that there are *two* #quaranteens.

Except, oh god. I look at Facebook. Goldy has tagged me in a post. **Thinking about my beautiful #quaranteen.**

Her friends chime in to tell her how hard this must be on her. Right. Of course. On her.

I look at the post again, notice she has tagged my dad in it too. I don't know why, since he hasn't bothered to text me to see how I'm doing.

Jenna and Becca text me within thirty seconds of each other, and I know they must be hanging out after school. They both say that they saw my hashtag, that they hope I'm feeling okay. I wonder if I should invite them down to visit me. But then I think about them putting on hazmat suits together, talking about quarantine, about my hospital room, and the idea of them sharing the experience together, when it's *my* experience, *my* quarantine.

And Oliver's too. I just know Kelsey will want to visit when Oliver tells her we're allowed to have visitors. *Maybe he won't tell her*, I think hopefully. Or, more likely, her parents won't agree to it. What kind of parent would knowingly let their kid visit someone with a possibly mutating, possibly highly contagious and dangerous disease? But I don't know why those thoughts make me feel optimistic. I agreed to help him win over the girl, after all.

"Tell Kelsey to come!" I try to sound enthusiastic. "She can be your nurse!"

"How did you know I was going to ask you if I should invite her?"

I want to tell him it's not rocket science, that I know he's obsessed with this girl, that the chance he's thinking about her at any given second is about 90 percent. But I like that he thinks I'm some genius about girls, so I say, "I could feel it in the air."

Oliver seems to buy it. "What do I tell her? I've never invited anyone to visit me in quarantine before."

I think of what I'd want to hear, if anyone ever wanted me to visit them, like my dad did. It was kind of cute, actually. He sent me an online invitation saying I'd be a guest of honor at his house. I was almost able not to be mad at him for a little bit when I saw it. Almost.

"Do something to make her feel special, like she'd be a VIP."

"She *is* my VIP, isn't she?" He looks wistful. Then he looks at me.

"But how do I tell her that? I can't exactly send her a wristband in the mail inviting her to Club Quarantine."

"No, but what about an invitation?"

"An invitation? I can't send one of those in the mail either."

"Oliver, what century do you think this is? An online invitation."

"An online invitation? But she's the only person I'm inviting. Well, besides my mom, but it's not exactly like I invited her, she's just coming. Like always." He mutters that last part.

"You're missing the point. It's to make her feel special. Anyone can send a text. That takes like three seconds. But making an online invitation just for her? It's creative. Romantic, even."

"Are you sure it's not overkill?"

"I wouldn't use *kill* in a hospital setting."

He snorts. "I see your point."

He's back on his phone, fiddling with an online invitation. His brow is furrowed, and it's kinda adorable how seriously he's taking this. I see a baseball and the words *Can't wait to catch up with you.*

He sees me watching him, stands up and comes to my side of the room. "It's great, right?" He shows me his phone, so proud of himself.

I choke back a laugh. "Yeah, if you were inviting your eight-year-old cousin to visit you. Think more romantic."

"Catch up with you? Come on! That's genius!"

I give him a look that I hope is stern, but he starts laughing.

"What's so funny?" I ask, trying to look sterner, which makes him laugh even harder.

"Nothing, I'm sorry." But he's laughing again.

I'm trying to glare at him now, but he's clutching his stomach and laughing.

"Fine, fine," he says between fits of laughter. "When you try to look mad, your nose gets these wrinkles. It's really . . ." He stops, suddenly serious. "It's really—"

But Joey steps into our room. Somehow, I didn't see him in the hallway slipping into his hazmat gear. "Hey, gang!" he says. "Or should I say, *quaranteens*."

"Hey," I say, but I'm still looking at Oliver, and he's still looking at me. I think I might know the word he was going to say, and I think maybe he might not need as many lessons as he thinks he does from the girl handbook.

"You heard the good news? It's official! Party time in room 702." He doesn't seem to notice that Oliver and I are looking at each other. "The girls will be fighting over you, Romeo," he says, nudging Oliver. But something about the way he says it is mean.

Oliver breaks his eye contact with me and glares at Joey. "Actually, I *am* inviting a girl." He stands up straighter. "Flora was just helping me with an invitation."

"An invitation! Planning your wedding already?" Joey hoots. He looks at me, but I don't join in on the laughter.

On Oliver's face I see all the times he's been in this situation before, being picked on by someone bigger and older, and I can picture him as a nine-year-old, getting pushed off a swing by a middle schooler.

"She'll like it. Girls like that kind of thing," I say hotly, glaring at Joey. "Girls don't like when guys make fun of other guys."

Oliver looks at me, and I guess I'm doing the nose-wrinkle thing, because he starts laughing, and Joey only looks confused. "See, look, he's laughing. Who's making fun? Just some teasing. We're buddies, right, Oliver?" He nudges Oliver harder than he needs to.

I don't say anything, and Joey checks our vitals quickly. He doesn't stick around to chat, and for the first time, I'm relieved.

# 29. OLIVER

Flora is sitting next to me on my bed, and I'm trying not to freak out that there's a girl on my bed. I can't believe I almost said her nose wrinkles were cute. Are cute. They're adorable. I've never been able to compliment a girl on anything, and the first thing I go for is nose wrinkles. I can't believe how easy it was to say it. To almost say it. She looks up from her phone, flips it to show me the screen, and I jump.

"How about this?" She shows me the invitation, and it's just a simple *You're invited . . .* written on little flags. She clicks to the next page, and it says, *. . . to visit me in quarantine! Hazmat suits will be provided. :)*

I tap the screen, looking for more. "That's it?"

"What do you mean that's it? It's perfect!"

"I dunno. Don't you think it needs more?"

"More what?"

"I don't know! More . . . pizzazz! More—"

"More baseball jokes?" She lightly jabs me in the side with her elbow.

I jump again. This time she notices. "Sir Jumps A Lot," she says, jabbing me again. "Don't be nervous. Just trust me—we should keep the invitation simple."

"Yeah, that's what I'm nervous about, the invitation." I mean to say it quietly, but Flora hears it. She doesn't say anything for a second, and I worry that she'll hear my heart thumping in my chest.

"I think you're overthinking it, Oliver," she says finally.

"Overthinking what?" How does she know I'm thinking about her? Trying *not* to think about her.

"The invitation? What we were just talking about? And what we're working on?"

I laugh, trying to clear the air. "Right."

"Anyway, I think this is the one. Keep it simple. Don't overthink it."

"But you're making me overthink it!"

"No, I'm not. I'm telling you to make it look simple. Keep it simple."

"Right. Simple." Then why does everything feel so complicated?

"So you'll send it?"

"Send what?"

"Oliver! Focus!" She taps me on the head, and I jump again. "Just type in her email address and we'll send it and be done with it."

And with Flora watching me I tap in Kelsey's email address, inviting her to visit me, though I'm not sure anymore that I actually want her to visit me.

"There." Flora stands up, and I realize the left side of my body is warm from how close she was sitting to me.

My phone makes a noise, which it's been doing a lot since Flora created the hashtag, and I see a text from Kelsey: OMG, looking at tickets now 4 real! I check Twitter and see Kelsey has tweeted a picture of Flora's invitation with #quaranteen and #VIP and #2days.

Flora's hair tickles my neck as she leans over to look at my screen, and I smell coconuts and mint. "Well, that was fast!" she says. "Her parents are okay with it? I mean, isn't it expensive?"

"No, her aunt is a flight attendant, so she gets really cheap airfare."

"But aren't they worried about her getting sick?"

"She told me her dad thinks the media is overhyping it, that we're a country of germaphobes."

"You didn't mention that before." Her smile looks strained again.

"I didn't think it mattered?"

"Right, of course not," Flora says. She seems a little frustrated, almost like I've offended her.

But before I can question it, my phone pings with a text message from my mom. Can't wait to see you tomorrow!!

Then, another text, this one from Kelsey. Just got ticket! See you in 2 days!

I can't figure out why I'm not more excited. And I can't figure out why I don't immediately tell Flora.

She doesn't bring up Kelsey's name the rest of the day, and neither do I.

# 30. FLORA

Every time I'm woken up for vitals checks, I look at Twitter to see if the hashtag is still trending. And every time I'm greeted with more people talking about how #quaranteen sounds like a vacation, more teenagers who want to go to #quaranteen with Oliver. And, weirdly, some people wonder who the second #quaranteen is.

**Wait, hold up, aren't there two #quaranteens?**

**Are the #quaranteens related?**

**Is the other #quaranteen as cute as Oliver?**

I read the posts like I'm reading about someone else's life. How *did* this become my life?

I look to see if Kelsey tweets that she's not coming after all, that her parents changed their minds. She doesn't.

After the 7:00 a.m. check, I stay awake, listening to Oliver's snoring. Then I hear him wake up, yawn, and unlock his phone. I'm sure he's checking in on Kelsey World.

Now he's on the phone talking to his mom, saying he'll see her soon.

I'm suddenly nervous about meeting her. I know I'm probably not her favorite person, seeing as how it's my fault her son is in quarantine.

I can't wait to see my own mom, who should be in Miami tomorrow night. I know she got down here as soon as she could, but I still wish it could have been sooner.

I should feel nervous about meeting Kelsey too, but I don't. I mostly just feel . . . dread. Maybe I *should* invite Becca and Jenna. I text them: Good news! We can have visitors.

Becca writes back: My mom would never let me!

Jenna: We have school, quaranteen! Sorry. Hopefully we'll raise more money for you soon!

Nurses come and go, and Joey stops by too. It's nice to see him, and I feel a little bad for what I said yesterday about him picking on Oliver. I don't know why dudes think it's funny to pick on other dudes. He's talking about basketball again and, even though I don't really care that much about sports, I try to listen to him. It's a nice distraction from having to think about Oliver. And Kelsey. I really don't want to think about Kelsey.

Joey suddenly switches topics from free throws. "So who's the lucky someone that's going to visit you?"

"Ha-ha," I say, though it makes me happy he thinks I *have* a lucky someone.

"Come on. Oliver is inviting a girl. Surely there must be someone you want to invite." He kind of smirks when he says Oliver's name, which bugs me. But he's also thinking about the people in my life.

"It's only twenty-six more days," I say. "I think everyone can wait to see me."

"Well, if I went to high school with you, I'd already be on a plane on my way down here."

I giggle nervously. He made me giggle.

"Okay, duty calls!" Joey announces. He grins at me, salutes, and marches to Oliver's side of the room.

I'm still thinking about what he said as he pulls the curtain open, and just as I'm wondering if Oliver heard it too, I see Oliver on his bed, giving Joey a dirty look. Oliver sees me looking at him, and he rearranges his face into a smile, but it looks more like a snarl.

"Hey, buddy!" Joey says.

I haven't known Oliver long, but I know he's not a "buddy" kind of guy. I almost tell Joey that, but he pulls the curtain closed and I'm alone again, listening to two guys who clearly don't like each other talk. Could I be the reason they don't like each other? No, that seems like a silly thought . . . right?

I hop on Twitter again. Still no canceled flights from Kelsey. And more people who want to know about the second #quaranteen. Who want to know about me.

Joey finishes up with Oliver and walks out, removes his suit, and walks off in one direction. From the other direction, a woman approaches with Dr. Demarko. The doctor helps the woman climb into a hazmat suit, and I notice she has Oliver's blue-green eyes. I can't hear what they're saying, but I don't need to be a professional lip reader to see that she's saying, "My baby!"

Oliver's mom practically runs through the antechamber, and then she looks around the room, eyes wild. "You!" She's looking at me, her voice shaking with rage. I sink back into my bed as she approaches.

I'm just about to push the CALL button on my bed when Oliver rips open the curtain. "MOM!" he yells.

She tears her eyes away from me and scoops up Oliver in a tight hug. "My baby!"

Oliver hugs her, then pats her back like she's the child and he's the parent. I can see where he inherited his anxiety from. But I'm surprised at how calm he is with her, how quickly he calms her down. He pulls away from the hug but still holds on to her arms. "Mom, stress is not good for prevention in spreading diseases."

*Nice one, Oliver*, I think.

"I'm sorry, Oliver. You have no idea how hard this has been on me. You wouldn't even be here if it weren't for *her*!" She spins on her heel to face me. I'm flat as a pancake on my bed.

"Why did you do it?" she asks, her voice shaking. "Why would you do something so reckless? Why would you endanger my baby like that?"

She glares at me, and I see that Oliver is peering over her shoulder, waiting for an answer too.

"I'm sorry," I say in a small voice. "I wasn't thinking."

"Well, that much is clear!" his mom huffs. "That still doesn't explain *why* you did it. I know you're not Oliver's girlfriend." She sneers when she says it, and I feel disgusting and contagious and diseased. Like a nobody, a nothing, like pond scum. Like gum stuck on the bottom of a shoe.

"Why don't you think she's my girlfriend?" Oliver crosses his arms over his chest.

"Why *would* she be your girlfriend?" Oliver's mom looks me up and down. I can tell she doesn't like what she sees.

"I wish she *were* my girlfriend, Mom. She's amazing. And strong, and smart, and brave. And she stands up for what's right."

None of us says anything for a moment, their blue-green eyes staring at me.

"Mom, meet Flora. Flora, meet my mom, Patty."

Patty's face softens a bit, and she says quietly, "I'm sorry. I'm still not sure what is going on, but I hope you feel better soon. I need to catch up with my son now." She pulls the curtain shut, and I'm alone again, replaying everything in my head that Oliver just said.

# 31. OLIVER

My mom is prattling on and on about all the research she's done on tropical mono, and how nice everyone in our apartment building has been and how Mrs. Thompson even made her a green bean casserole, but I only hear every other sentence. I'm thinking about what I just said. I want to pull the curtain open and find out what Flora thinks about everything I said. If she's even thinking about it, or if she's back to thinking about Joey. Or maybe she's thinking about who she's going to invite to visit her. She told Joey there wasn't anyone, and she hasn't mentioned anyone to me. But everything I said about her is true, so surely there must be someone in Brooklyn who thinks the same thing and wants to see her.

My phone is on the tray next to my bed, and I see that I get a text message from Kelsey, but . . . I don't bother picking up the phone.

But my mom sees my phone light up. "Kelsey? I didn't know you were texting with her."

"Mom!" I snap. I don't feel like talking about Kelsey right now, when Flora is only a few inches away.

"She's friends with Lucy, the girl you study with? She's one of your Snapchat friends too, right?" My mom has my Snapchat friends list memorized.

"Yeah, something like that." I try to change the subject quickly. "So, did Mrs. Thompson say how her dog is feeling? She took him to the vet last week, didn't she?"

"Well, why is she texting you?"

"Mrs. Thompson?"

"No! Why is Kelsey texting you?"

"I don't know. She's probably just seeing if I'm feeling okay. Our hashtag is trending," I say weakly.

"I don't know what that sentence means."

My phone lights up again, and my mom cranes her neck to read the message. "The letter *c*, the letter *u*, the number *2*, and *morrow*. See you tomorrow? What's going on?"

"It's no big deal, Mom. What *is* a big deal is Bugle! Is he feeling better?" I say, desperate to change the subject.

"Oliver," she says in a warning voice.

I sigh. "She's coming to visit, yes."

My mom gasps. "You didn't ask me first? I'm your mother!"

"I asked the hospital," I say in a small voice.

"Well, *I* don't think it's a good idea for her to come."

For once, I actually agree with my mom.

"Even if she's in a hazmat suit, what if this thing is more contagious than originally thought? Could you live with yourself if someone else got sick? And I don't like the idea of sharing my visiting time with someone else!" Then she whispers, "And what about Flora?" But my mom has never been a quiet whisperer, and our hospital room isn't very big.

"She's allowed to have visitors too," I say, playing dumb.

"That's not what I meant. Do you think it's a good idea to have a girl visit you?"

I wish I knew what Flora was doing over there. For once I wish Joey would come back.

# 32. FLORA

I don't think I've breathed properly since Patty showed up. First, I feared for my life, then Oliver's. I thought for sure his mom would give him a harder time about the kiss. Not like she could punish him in quarantine, but I expected more of a scolding or something. Instead she seemed to make Oliver's quarantine about her. Talking about her special treatment in her apartment building, all the research she had done. She reminds me of my dad in a way. My dad, whose dumb new wife seems more concerned about me than he does. Goldy—not my dad—texted me earlier and told me they're looking at airfare to come visit. But I told them it would be better for my recovery to keep my visits to a limit. Another line inspired by Oliver.

I can't believe Oliver just said all that stuff. I'm sure he was saying it to get his mom off his back. But something feels different in the air, and I'm suddenly aware of how close he is to me.

Patty is still prattling on about how hard all this is on her when Joey suits up and comes in. I'm happy to see him, but I'm not sure if it's because I actually want to see him or because he's about to tell Patty that visiting hours are over.

Patty objects at first, saying the first visit in quarantine should be longer than just one hour, can't he make an exception, Oliver is incredibly anxious and fragile. I hate that she says that about Oliver. He might be a little anxious, but he's not fragile. If his mom actually listened to him, she'd realize that. Oliver remains quiet through the conversation, and I will him into saying something, but he doesn't say a word.

"I'm sorry, Ms. Russell," Joey says diplomatically, "but this is a medical establishment, and rules are rules. I know you want your son to feel better as soon as possible, don't you? Following hospital rules and procedures ensures that."

"Fine," Patty huffs. "But I'm not happy!"

"I'll take it up with my manager," Joey says facetiously.

"I should hope you would."

"I don't actually have a manager? It was a joke?"

But Patty either doesn't hear or doesn't care, because she's closing Oliver's curtain and briskly walking out of the room. Well, as briskly as one can in a hazmat suit. I watch her gingerly remove it and place it in the bin. She retrieves a compact from her purse, reapplies lipstick, smooths her hair, and is off.

Joey is still in the room, finishing Oliver's vitals check, and then he's on my side of the room. He rolls his eyes and mouths the word *crazy*. I don't know if he means Oliver or his mom, but I don't care to find out.

I don't say anything, and Joey does it again, smiling even bigger. I keep my face empty of emotion, and he nudges me. "Lighten up, Francis," he says. I think he's making a reference to something, but I don't know what it is.

I hate that he has dimples. I hate that when he touches me, usually I feel a jolt of electricity, even through the hazmat suit. And I hate that he keeps making fun of Oliver.

"The Nets are playing today," he says. "Maybe we can watch part of the game together?"

"Yeah, maybe," I say, hoping he'll leave.

He must pick up on my mental wish, because he gives me a salute and says, "Catch you later." And then he's gone, and it's just Oliver and me again.

But this time I'm more aware than ever that we're alone.

# 33. OLIVER

The curtain between my side of the room and Flora's is closed. I want to open it. I need to open it. And then what? Where would I even begin? Ask her why she kissed me? Tell her that everything I told my mom is true? Tell her that I don't want Kelsey to visit—I don't think?—even though I've had a crush on Kelsey for years and she's coming all the way down to see me? The pre–spring break Oliver would think he's died and gone to heaven.

But I'm not that Oliver anymore, and I don't want to be that Oliver—the pre-Flora Oliver.

I have no clue what she thinks about me either. I do have a clue what she thinks about Joey, though. And I have more than a clue what he thinks about her. Not that I can blame him. But I can blame her. He's a dolt, even if he's supposedly in medical school.

I hop on Twitter again. People want to know about the other #quaranteen. I wonder if Flora wants people to know about her. She made the hashtag for me and now Kelsey is coming to visit me and I should repay her. If she wants. I should ask her.

Flora is rustling around on her side of the room. She's video chatting with people, I think two girls, and I can tell they're all close. They're saying how much they miss her, how she'd better hurry home. They say they wish they could visit. I can tell Flora is disappointed, but I don't think her friends realize it. They talk for a while longer, and there's lots of giggling, though more of it seems to be coming from the other end of the call. Then I hear Flora walk around, showing them the bathroom, how her bed goes up and down, and then she comes to the curtain and says, "Knock, knock."

"Um, come in?"

Flora opens my curtain. She's standing in front of me, her cheeks red, holding the phone out in front of her. "Uh, this is Oliver," she says to her phone, looking down.

She whips the phone around to face me, and I see she is indeed talking to two girls. They wave at me, and I say, "Hi."

They look at me and there's an awkward silence, then everyone starts talking at once.

"We should probably go," from them.

"He's a great roommate," from Flora.

"Flora is the best," from me.

Flora looks at me over the phone. Her friends are saying something to her, but she isn't paying attention to them.

"FLORA!" they both finally yell in unison.

She jumps, looks down. "Right, sorry, what were you guys saying?"

"We were saying we have to go."

"Of course. You guys are busy." I hear the sarcasm in her voice, but they don't.

"Let's talk soon!"

"Yeah, sure, my schedule is pretty free."

Flora ends the call, but she's still standing on my side of the room.

We just look at each other. "You're the other quaranteen!" I blurt out. Flora looks at me, confused.

"The hashtag," I say. "People want to know about you. People deserve to know about you!"

"Deserve?"

"Yeah, I mean, after all, you did think of it, and now Kelsey is coming, and people should know . . . should know you exist," I finish lamely.

"Okay," Flora says, smiling a little. "And how will that happen?"

"Um, let me take your picture, like you did for me." I pull out my phone, and she smiles again. It's a really sunny afternoon, and the light makes Flora's red hair glow. Her entire body seems to glow.

I snap a few pictures. "So should I send them to you and you post them? Or, wait, is that dumb? Should I post them?"

"Oliver, I'm not the quaranteen manager."

"You're not?"

"No. I don't think hashtags work that way."

"Right." I look at the pictures of her on my phone. I look up, at the real Flora with the glowing hair.

Flora kind of shakes her head. "So, anyway, Kelsey gets here tomorrow! Need any other tips from my girl handbook?"

"Sure, I guess. What do you have?"

"I mean, it's a simple one. But figure out what she likes, if you haven't already, and learn about it."

"Learn about it?"

"Yeah. Like, if you find out she likes Indian food, you don't have to enroll in culinary school, but learn the difference between tikka masala and palak paneer."

Her eyes glaze over for a second and she licks her lips. I can almost smell the samosas at the Indian place down the street from my apartment.

"I miss takeout food so much," she says.

"Me too." I inhale sharply, but all I can smell now is the hospital room antiseptic smell.

"Oh, and another thing. Look into her eyes. Girls really like that. Trust me."

I stare back into her eyes. "Like this?"

Flora laughs, and for the first time since I've met her, she seems nervous. "You've got this, Oliver," she says softly.

And then our door opens, and Joey is there with our dinner trays, and I've never wanted Indian food so much in my life.

# 34. FLORA

I sleep terribly. Every time I manage to fall asleep for a few minutes, I'm woken up to get my vitals taken. My mind is racing with everything Oliver and I have said and not said to each other. He's not snoring tonight, and I hear him tossing and turning too.

No boy has ever called me strong or brave before. I mean, I'm pretty sure I am, but in the same way that I'm pretty sure my hair is strawberry blond. It's just something that is, something I don't have time to think about.

No boy has ever called me amazing before either. That one I'm not so sure about.

I keep thinking about my video chat with Becca and Jenna, them giggling together. If I'd hung up, they wouldn't even have noticed I was gone.

My phone pings and I see that I've been tagged in something. It's a picture of me—one that Oliver took yesterday. I'm smiling in it, and I look so . . . relaxed. He's tagged it #quaranteen and #roommates. Roommates. It sounds comfortable and cozy.

I bet Oliver is comfortable to cuddle with.

But he's my roommate in quarantine because of what I did. And then I remember that my mom is coming tomorrow and I can't stop thinking about how guilty I feel. I've made her already-difficult life so much harder. How will I ever be able to tell her that I faked my fever *and* that I intentionally dragged Oliver into this? She's going to be so disappointed in me. *I'm* so disappointed in me.

Oliver should be disappointed in me too, and knowing that I could disappoint him feels awful.

I toss and turn some more. What have I done?

# 35. OLIVER

Kelsey has been texting me all morning. Everything feels so confusing, but I'm still a little excited to see her name pop up on my phone. She's complaining that she couldn't sleep, that there was a bird outside her window that kept her awake. I miss birds. I wish a bird would wake me up instead of someone in a hazmat suit sticking a thermometer in my mouth or a blood pressure cuff on my arm.

Then she complains that the diner she goes to for breakfast is crowded and she has to wait for a table. The pepper pieces in her omelet are too big. I realize I miss crowds, diners, ordering food off a menu.

I tell her I'm sorry about her morning, and she tells me it's okay, she's just stressed. Her flight was an hour late leaving and it really threw things off for her.

She doesn't say if she's seen my #quaranteen post. Not that it matters if she sees it. It's no secret that Flora and I are roommates. Kelsey herself even made the joke about being jealous. But I still feel a niggling sense of guilt. Maybe because when I took the picture, Kelsey was the furthest thing from my mind.

I scroll through people's comments. The mysterious #quaranteen appears.

The second #quaranteen is pretty, pretty, pretty.

The #quaranteens have to be the two teenagers from the news.

Yep, I'd go to #quaranteen with her.

The two #quaranteens sure would make a cute couple.

*Couple.* Oh god. I should probably make sure Kelsey has seen my post.

I wonder if Flora has seen it, and all the comments.

She's watching her TV and flipping through a magazine. She's been quiet this morning. "Excited to see Kelsey today?" She smiles, but she looks tired.

"Yeah. I feel kinda guilty, though. I think the trip has been hard on her."

"On *her*?" Flora scoffs. "Um, she knows you're in quarantine, right?"

"She's probably nervous or something."

"Or something," Flora mutters.

I laugh uneasily.

"Anyway, I hope you've told her you're excited to see her."

"I don't think dudes say 'excited.'"

"Fine. Looking forward to seeing her?"

"Am I meeting her for a job interview?"

"I don't know. You're the dude. You put it in dudespeak for me."

"I thought you were the author of the girl handbook?"

"I don't know. Maybe I need a ghostwriter today." She's rubbing the sides of her head.

I look at her more closely, see how tired she really is. "You okay?"

"Yeah, I'm just feeling really tired today. I couldn't sleep. I'll be fine." She waves her hand.

My phone dings. I look away from Flora and read my latest text from Kelsey: OMG, it's so hot here!

I think I even miss sweating.

I write back: Will be *cool* to see you today!

She doesn't respond.

# 36. FLORA

Patty is back with Oliver when I hear people come in. I assume it's another vitals check, or another meal or a snack. Considering how little Oliver and I can actually move, the hospital staff sure do like to keep us fed.

But then I hear my mom's voice, and my eyes shoot open. She's in a hazmat suit, looking at me with tears in her eyes, and the guilt feels like a shotgun bullet.

Dr. Demarko is with her, and she says, "Please be in touch with any questions, Mrs. Thornton. Your daughter is in excellent hands. I have kids. I know this is scary."

"Thank you."

Dr. Demarko walks out, and before she's even out the door I'm up out of bed.

"Mama!" I say. I haven't called her that since I was super small, but it just slips out.

"Flora!" she says, arms already out. She wraps me up in a big hug, and it's so nice to be touched by someone familiar—by my mom. "I got on an earlier flight. I wanted to surprise you. Oh, it's so good to hug you."

"You too, Mom." I realize I'm shaking, and I don't know why.

"Oh, Flora, I'm so sorry." The tears in her eyes are welling over and rolling down her face.

I want to tell her everything. The faked fever, my desire to escape life back in Brooklyn, how much my dad has changed and how much I ache for the dad I used to know—the dad that I'll never know again. But seeing her so worried about me, when it's actually my fault, makes hot guilt sizzle in my stomach.

"I'm sorry too, Mom."

"No, honey, you don't know how sorry I really am. I wish I hadn't insisted that your dad invite you to visit him."

"I know, Mom."

She bites her lip the same way I do when I want to stop crying. It never works for either one of us. "I just . . ." she starts. She tries to rub her eyes, wipe her nose, but the hazmat suit is in the way, and then the tears really flow.

I've seen my mom cry before, but her tears have never made me doubt her strength.

She takes a deep breath. "I just wanted you to like her. It kills me, but that's all I wanted."

"I know, Mom," I say again.

"There's one thing I didn't tell you, though." My mom is talking fast now. "When I told your dad to invite you, he said Goldy had been saying the same thing. She'd actually been looking at airfares for you. Ordering stuff online to decorate your room. She even made one of those Pinterest boards and called it 'My Daughter's Room.'" She laughs bitterly again, the way she always does when she talks about Goldy. But something is different behind her eyes.

"What are you talking about, Mom? You hate her."

"No, Flora. I hate the idea of her. I hate that, to me, she represents my marriage falling apart, my life falling apart. But it was already falling apart before she came along."

I'm supposed to hate Goldy. I rub my forehead.

"And, Flora . . . we all agreed that you need a break—deserve a break."

"A break from what?"

"From taking care of Randy."

"What, so now I can't even take good care of my cousin? Thanks a lot, Mom."

"No, honey, not at all. It's the opposite. You take such good care of him. But you need to take care of yourself too."

"And sending me to spend time with someone I hate—*you* hate—is me taking care of myself? Especially when it wasn't even my own father's idea?"

"I know, it doesn't make much sense. But please understand that it was a decision made out of love. Love from *all* of us." She studies my face, lets everything sink in.

"So after four years of hearing nothing but horrid things about her from you, just like that, poof, I'm supposed to like her? And what about Dad? He's so different than when you guys were married. Sometimes it seems like he doesn't care about his life before Goldy at all."

"Honey, I'm so sorry. I hate that I've made you so angry. I hate that you've ever doubted your dad's love. I pushed him away from us so hard."

My head is swimming. Through the whole conversation I'm vaguely aware of Oliver's presence on the other side of the curtain. But I'm not ashamed or embarrassed about anything he might hear. It's weird, but I want him to hear it all—I want him to know all these things about me, about my family. I want him to know me.

My mom and I talk more, but it's idle chitchat compared to everything we've just talked about. I tell her how the hospital food isn't that bad. She reminds me of when I got my tonsils out when I was eight. She tells me how much Randy misses me. I almost confess everything to her when she says she saw him crying in his room the other night looking at a picture of me. But I keep my secret. My secret and Oliver's secret.

When the hour is up, Dr. Demarko comes back to get my mom. My mom gives me another huge hug, tells me she'll see me in a few hours. She pulls away and says quietly, "I want to meet Oliver next time."

I make shooing motions, and she smiles as she walks out with Dr. Demarko.

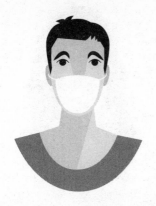

# 37. OLIVER

I didn't mean to listen to Flora's conversation with her mom, but there really is no such thing as privacy in a shared hospital room. I tried to listen to my mom and tune it out, but it was impossible.

I feel bad for Flora. I feel bad for her mom. I feel bad for Flora's cousin, who she hasn't talked much about yet. I even feel bad for Goldy, who seems to have good intentions.

Who would my dad have married next?

After Flora's mom and my mom finally leave, I hear Flora breathing deeply. I want to comfort her, I want to tell her everything is okay, that her family is amazing, that she's amazing. I stand up to go over to her side of the room to do just that. But I sit back down again. I stand up again, but Flora turns on her TV, and I listen to her watching TV.

# 38. FLORA

I'm looking out my window into the hallway, still processing everything my mom and I talked about. I'm watching everyone walk up and down the hall. Joey waves every time he passes. I hate how such a small gesture makes me feel so giddy.

By now I recognize everyone who walks by. The woman in scrubs with a completely bald head. Like, not even cut short, but just bald. She's beautiful. The man whose lab coat has an ink stain on the pocket. I wonder if he's washed the coat and the stain won't come out, or if he hasn't washed it yet, or maybe he just keeps getting the same ink stain on every single lab coat he owns. The woman with the bright dragon tattoo on her forearm. I've named the dragon Spike.

The room across the hall is still empty, and I hope it stays that way.

But now I see someone I don't recognize at first. It's a teenage girl, and she's got her phone out, clearly taking selfies. She's trying to subtly practice looking nervous or scared, her hand to her mouth, her eyes open wide. She taps her screen, doesn't like what she sees, and tries another pose, this time with her hand on the side of her face. She seems to like this one better, so she keeps walking. Until she stops right outside our room. She looks up, checking the number on the door, then sees me and jumps.

That's when I recognize her.

Kelsey is here.

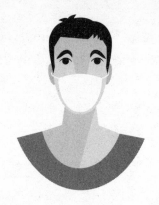

# 39. OLIVER

Kelsey is here. Outside my hospital room. With a doctor, showing her how to put on a hazmat suit. She told me she was leaving her hotel, then getting in a cab, then walking into the hospital, so I don't know why it's so surprising to see her. But it is. I wonder if she's seen my post about Flora yet.

I didn't think it was possible to look adorable in a hazmat suit, but she does. She tries to take a quick selfie, then follows the doctor into the antechamber, and now she's in my room. Kelsey's eyes are wide in the mask as she looks around.

Flora is watching her. "Hi, I'm Flora," she says in a voice I haven't heard her use before.

"You're the roommate! I hope you've been taking good care of my Oliver. I can be his nurse now."

"Yep! Though he's not actually sick!" Flora says, still in the weird voice.

"And he won't *get* sick, especially if I'm taking care of him," Kelsey says.

The girls are looking at each other, and I wish I could have some privacy with one of them, but I'm not entirely sure which one I'd want to be alone with.

I clear my throat, and both of them whip their heads toward me. Flora has a weird smile on her face to match the weird voice she's using, but Kelsey is just beaming at me. "Oliver!" she squeals. She runs the short distance to my side of the room and throws her arms around my neck. I've never even touched her before, and now suddenly she's hugging me. I notice how small she is in my arms. I smell vanilla; I think I can smell her hair through the hazmat suit? She pulls back, and my brain feels like it might explode from trying to process all her features so close up.

"You don't look sick at all!" She grabs my face, turns it from side to side in her hand, looking me up and down.

"Oh. Ha-ha. I'm not actually sick."

"Right. I keep forgetting that part. Quarantine is confusing. She's sick, though, right? She looks awful!" Kelsey doesn't even bother lowering her voice as she jabs her finger in Flora's direction.

"She had a fever. She's not sick. And she doesn't look awful." I feel so nervous all of a sudden that I realize I can't feel my fingers. *I cannot have a panic attack, I cannot have a panic attack.*

"Wait, so she had a fever, but she's not sick . . . why are you here, then?"

I hear Flora softly snort.

"Um, it's like the articles and the news have been saying. I'm here out of 'an abundance of caution.'" I don't know why I can't just tell her that Flora kissed me. I could tell her that I like Flora, and maybe Flora likes me, and we really just need some time alone, but we're never alone with all the vitals checks and doctors and now all the visitors.

"How was your flight?" I blurt out.

"Um? It was annoying? Like I said, we were an hour late taking off!"

I try to muster up some outrage at her ordeal, but all I come up with is, "I'm sorry."

"S'okay. It's not your fault. Actually, it is, because I'm here visiting you. I mean, taking care of you! Speaking of, I need to take care of you!" She looks around the room again. "Um, do you want some water? I know it's good to stay hydrated if you're sick."

"I'm not—"

"Right, sorry. I mean, to keep from getting sick." She grabs the plastic pitcher off my tray. "Oh, there's no water in here. How do I get you more water?"

"Uh, I don't actually know. Joey brings it in for us."

"Oh. Who's Joey?"

"He's in charge of taking care of us, sorta."

"So he's a doctor?"

"Yeah, something like that."

"And you call him Joey."

"I guess he's an intern or resident or something." I hate that we're talking about Joey.

"Shouldn't you have someone, like, higher up taking care of you?"

"There are other doctors too. Lots of them. And nurses. They're all pretty nice."

"Well, that's . . . nice."

"Yeah, it's nice." I cringe, unsure why my vocabulary skills aren't working.

"So! What should we do?" Kelsey says.

"Do?"

"Yeah, I mean, what do you usually do all day?"

"Uh, text with you?"

Kelsey looks pleased, but then says, "Okay, and what else?"

"I talk to Flora. We post stuff on Twitter. I posted a picture of her last night! I figured people might want to know about the other quaran-teen. I mean, other people besides me. I mean, other people should know who she is and what she looks like."

Kelsey lets me ramble, but I feel like she's only half listening. She says, "Cool."

There is an awkward silence, and I hear Flora clear her throat.

"Are you sure she's not sick?"

"What? No, of course not."

"Okay, then."

Another awkward silence. I don't understand how we had so much to text about but now in person have so little to say to each other. And I also don't understand how we're going to get through three visiting hours a day.

"How long are you staying?"

"Jeez, Oliver, thanks. Trying to get rid of me already."

"No! It's not that at all. I'm just . . . trying to figure out how much time you'll be here. How much time I'll have you, I mean." I feel my face heating up.

Kelsey grins at me. "Mrs. Guise said I could count my time here toward research for my biology project. Because of that and 'unique exten-uating circumstances,' I'm here as long as you need me." She touches my face with her hazmat hand again, this time much more gently.

# 40. FLORA

Part of me wants to laugh listening to Oliver and Kelsey. He's adorably nervous with her. I know I've never made any guy that nervous before, even Oliver. The other part of me wants to throw up.

The curtain opens, and I guess Kelsey's visiting hour is over. Though I look at the clock on the wall and see there is still another half hour left. Kelsey is beaming at Oliver, and his face is bright red.

"Leaving already?" I say in a voice I don't recognize.

"Yeah, I want to grab some food. Ugh, I had the worst omelet this morning at a diner. I'll see you at the next visiting hour before bed!"

"Yep!" I say, still in the weird voice.

"Um, can you take a picture of me? I can't use my phone with these darn gloves!" I don't know why she's asking me and not Oliver, but she hands the phone to me gingerly, like she's afraid of breaking me. I think she wants a picture with Oliver, but she doesn't make a move to get any closer to him. She's got her hand on her hip, head cocked, and I'll give her credit, she does look cute in a hazmat suit. I look at Oliver, and I can tell from the look on his face that he's thinking the same thing.

I wait until she blinks and snap a picture.

I hold the phone up for her, and she looks at the picture. "Oh! I'm blinking! Can you take another? Maybe take a few this time, just to be on the safe side."

"Yep!" I click away, and I hate how photogenic she is. "Do you want one with Oliver?" I ask half-heartedly. Oliver blushes as Kelsey looks at him.

"Yes, of course!" She swings her arm over Oliver's waist easily, and I hope he doesn't pass out from the excitement.

I snap a few pictures. They look like a couple. I remind myself that this is what I want, that this is what Oliver wants. And it's what I promised him. I owe him.

I show Kelsey the pictures, and she squeals. "Posting this immediately! Hashtag quaranteen!"

Hearing her use the hashtag I came up with makes me want to listen to a punk song and punch walls again. Instead I smile and say, "It's trending!"

Kelsey says, "Oh, I know! I practically have a celebrity boyfriend!"

"Boyfriend?" Oliver squeaks.

"Oh, you know what I mean," Kelsey scoffs.

"Right, of course." Oliver looks confused.

I point to my eyes, then to Kelsey, and Oliver stares at her, trying to look her in the eyes, but Kelsey has her head down on her way out of the room. Oliver helplessly shrugs at me just as Kelsey turns around again, about to walk through the antechamber.

"I'll see you this evening. Will anyone else be here then?"

"My mom," Oliver says, the color draining from his face.

"Great! I can't wait to meet her!"

"Yeah, me too," Oliver says, though the expression on his face says otherwise.

Kelsey scoots out the antechamber, and a nurse is there showing her how to dispose of her hazmat suit. Oliver and I watch her take another quick selfie, then tap at her phone some more, and then she's off.

"Well!" I say. "That was Kelsey."

"It sure was," he says.

A few minutes later, Patty arrives. She's ranting to Oliver about how her cab driver got lost, which is so ridiculous given the technology today, when my mom shows up. She looks a little more refreshed than last time I saw her. She apologizes for being late, says she was on the phone with my uncle.

"Is everything okay?" I ask, alarmed.

"It is. Randy keeps thinking he's sick too, keeps wanting to get his temperature taken. I never should have told him that's what they're doing to you in the hospital."

I miss my cousin.

"Can I meet Oliver?" she says quietly.

"Shh! Mom!" But Patty drones on, and if Oliver has heard my mom, I have no way of knowing.

"What! I want to meet the boy who you kissed for the first time."

"Mom!" I say louder.

"It wasn't your first kiss?"

"MOM!"

"I'm your mother! We talk about these things," she whispers.

She's right, we do. Well, we usually do anyway. She knew about my crush on Damon Cook, about how he sat behind me in biology class, about how sometimes if he leaned forward I felt his breath on the back of my neck. I used to worry that he could see the goose bumps on my arms. But with Oliver it's different. And I don't have a crush on him. I'm helping him win the girl *he* has a crush on.

"It's . . . complicated," I finally whisper back.

She looks at me, waiting for me to elaborate.

"I'll explain when he's not two feet away from me!" I hiss.

"Fair enough," she whispers. "So, as I was saying, I want to meet your roommate," she says, louder.

Patty is oblivious, though, talking to Oliver about another neighbor in their building, and how she counts how many times a day her neighbors flush the toilet.

My mom tries again. "Flora, can you introduce me to Oliver?"

Patty doesn't stop talking.

"This is silly." My mom opens the curtain to reveal Patty and a bored Oliver.

Both look surprised, but Patty also looks annoyed. "Visiting hour isn't over yet," she says.

"What? No, I'm not a nurse or a doctor. I'm Peg, Flora's mom."

Patty's face is blank for a second, and then she looks at me. "Oh, right, how silly of me not to make the connection! You both have the same beautiful hair. Patty, nice to meet you."

But my mom is looking past her, at Oliver. "Oliver, it's so nice to meet you."

Oliver hops out of bed, brushes off his hands, and shakes my mom's hand. "It's really nice to meet you too," he says quietly.

"And you two have the same beautiful eyes," my mom says.

Oliver blushes. He looks up at me, and I suddenly really want to be alone with him. Like actually alone. Not in a hospital room with doctors watching over us constantly, where we seem to have an endless stream of visitors. Actually alone. Somewhere I could talk to him without worrying about someone barging in. It's such a strong urge I almost grab his hand and pull him out of the room with me.

I make myself look away from him for a second, but he's still looking at me. I don't believe in telepathy or mind reading or anything like that, but I swear he's thinking the exact same thing as me. As our moms talk about where they grew up in Brooklyn, we keep looking at each other, wanting to run away and be alone together.

Though at this moment, gazing into those cool-breeze eyes, I feel like we already are.

# 41. OLIVER

It's weird, but I don't feel nervous looking at Flora. Just thinking about Kelsey makes me want to blush, but something about Flora is so calming, soothing. Comfortable.

And another weird thing, but it's almost like I can feel what she's thinking. The feeling is so strong, but I make myself break eye contact with her.

Joey comes in to get our moms, but I'm distracted. So distracted that I forget to remind my mom that Kelsey is here too and they'll get to meet later tonight.

They step out of the antechamber, then actually walk down the hall-way together after they change out of their hazmat suits. I think I even hear them laughing.

We're finally alone, but then my phone beeps, and beeps again, and beeps a third time.

Flora says, "You detonating a bomb over there? What's going on?"

Kelsey has tagged me in the photo she took earlier. She used Flora's hashtag, but she also added her own: #myquaranteen. The photo is getting all kinds of notifications and likes. I skim them, see one from Lucy: **You're practically dating a celebrity.**

Celebrity. That word again. And dating. I'm dating Kelsey?

Flora is looking at her phone too. "Wow, look at Kelsey go," she says. "Told you the hashtag would work. She's bragging about you on social media!"

But she's got that same tired look on her face she had earlier in the day. "Are you sure you're feeling okay?" I ask.

"Why wouldn't I be? I told you, I'm just tired."

As if on cue, a nurse comes in for vitals checks. When Flora's thermometer beeps, she says, "Finally! It's going back up!"

"What is?" Flora asks.

"Your temperature. We couldn't figure out how you had a fever and then it just magically disappeared. This all makes much more sense."

"Wait, Flora has a fever?" I say, unable to restrain myself.

"She does. Just like she did at the warehouse. I'm not sure why this is so surprising?"

I laugh nervously. "I thought maybe it was a spring break miracle!"

The nurse gives me a funny look, then comes to take my vitals. I don't think I breathe the entire time the thermometer is in my mouth. "Your temp is still normal," she says when it finally beeps ten years later.

The nurse leaves, and Flora and I look at each other again. This time I don't have any idea what she's thinking. Finally she asks, "Oliver, what's happening?"

# 42. FLORA

Oliver is looking at me just like the last time a thermometer showed I had a fever. Baffled. Scared. The temperature had to have been a mistake. The thermometer has been wrong before. Granted, I *made* it wrong before. But still. The things aren't error-proof. Mistakes happen in hospitals all the time. People get gloves left in their stomachs after surgery; lab results get lost; babies get switched and go home with the wrong families.

"I'm sure it's a mistake," Oliver says. "A faulty reading." But I can tell he doesn't believe what he's saying.

"I don't understand. They said it was passed only through direct contact with someone. Kissing someone. I haven't kissed anyone. Except you. Did you get it from someone and give it to me? How many girls did you make out with on spring break?" Even as I'm saying the words, I'm not sure I believe them. But I'm scared, and I don't *get* scared—I get mad.

"What? None!" Oliver sputters.

"Have you just been stringing me along? Pretending you need my help when you don't? A girl handbook, I'm such an idiot. You don't need any help from me at all. You're doing just fine on your own." I know I'm grasping at straws, but I hear the punk song starting in my head again. I get up, and Oliver crosses over to my side of the room.

"Flora, listen to me."

He's standing in my way, and I just need him to move so I can punch a wall, kick a door. I try to push past him but he's too fast and he's still blocking me. "Flora, please listen to me," he says again.

"Why? So you can tell me all the names of the girls you kissed? Have you told Kelsey about all of them?"

"Flora, please," he begs.

I keep thinking of the way he looked at me after I kissed him, and for some reason I'm crying, and I just want to hit something, but he still won't get out of my way, so I beat my arms against his chest.

He gently grabs my arms. "You're even stronger than you look."

Which makes me really cry, and I want to stop touching him, especially since I really am diseased, but I can't make myself pull away from him. I rest my arms against his chest, then my head. I feel his hand on my head, his fingers running through my hair. How did I forget to tell him that girls love having their hair played with? Or, at least, this one does.

"You're the only one," he says quickly.

"What?" I pull away, look up at him, but he's looking at the ceiling and won't make eye contact with me, like he's embarrassed.

"It's only you," he says.

"Only me what?"

"You're the only girl I've kissed—the first girl I've kissed. No one else. Just you."

"So you haven't been kissing random girls on spring break?"

"No. Definitely not. Well, it was pretty random that we sat next to each other on the plane. I mean, literally speaking and all." He finally looks down at me and grins.

I sniffle, the tears drying on my face. And just like that I'm looking out the window on a cool spring day, and even if I have a fever caused by a potentially serious disease, I feel like everything is going to be okay somehow.

# 43. OLIVER

"Hey, quaranteens! No kissing!"

Flora and I pull apart from each other. We didn't notice Joey suiting up and walking into the antechamber, and now he's in our room. But he's got that same look he always seems to have on his face. Smug. Like he knows he's better than me. It's a look I've seen from other guys my entire life.

Flora giggles, and her cheeks are flushed.

"I heard your fever came back," Joey says. "Can you sit back on your bed? Do you need help?" He walks over to her and puts his hand on her arm, the same arm I was just holding.

"She's fine," I say before I can stop myself.

"Oh, you're a doctor now, Romeo?" Joey says. He chuckles, shaking his head.

"I *am* fine," Flora says. But she lets him guide her to her bed, and she sits down.

Joey sees me watching, gives me a dirty look, and pulls the curtain closed. He's talking to her, and for once I can't hear what he's saying. I hear the thermometer beep.

Flora anxiously says, "What is it?"

"Still 100.5. Not terrible. But definitely a fever. And remember: If it gets up to 101.5, it's time for isolation. Now, we need to talk about how this happened, which means I need to know more about who you were hanging out with in the Dominican Republic. If this is something you got there, or if it's from the gentleman on the plane." I swear he sounds excited. Delighted, even.

I look at my phone. All the notifications I'm getting from the picture that Kelsey posted. She posted another one of just herself in her hazmat suit, with the caption, On the way back from visiting #myquaranteen.

*My.* I've never been anyone's *my.*

I look at the picture of us again. More comments: aww, u look so happy with him, you 2 are such a cute couple. Comments that even last week would have made my entire life. But that was before Flora. Flora, who cried against my chest—whose arms I held.

I scroll through, read more comments: cute.

And then: I think the #quaranteens are a cuter couple.

I want to see a picture of the #quaranteens together.

I feel that same niggling sense of guilt. Maybe Kelsey won't see them? But I can't really think about that now. Because Flora might be sick.

"I barely left my dad's place—my dad and Goldy's place." Flora sounds embarrassed. "I mean, it rained a lot."

"And what do your dad and Goldy do for a living? Are they out in the general population a lot, interacting with lots of people?"

Flora laughs. "Ha, Goldy doesn't work. She doesn't leave the house unless she's getting her hair or nails done." She pauses. "But she's not a bad person. She loves my dad. He loves her." But I don't think she's talking to Joey anymore. I think she's talking to herself, convincing herself.

"Okay, got it. Sounds like a run-of-the-mill stepmom to me."

"Yeah. No. She's not. She's different. I think." Flora sounds tired again.

"Doesn't matter from a medical perspective," Joey says. He's probably trying to make a joke, but it also sounds like he's brushing her off.

"Well, it matters from a *person* perspective. From a *stepdaughter* perspective," Flora insists.

"Whatever you say. So, tell me about your pops. What's his deal with work?"

"He works from home. His company is based in the States. He leaves the house even less than Goldy."

"And sounds like a run-of-the-mill midlife crisis dad to me."

"Hey! That's my dad!"

"Hey! I'm just teasing. Trying to take your mind off things." Joey's voice sounds kinder again.

"Do they have lots of visitors? Lots of wild parties?"

"Nah, they keep to themselves. Someone cleans their house, but she was on vacation while I was there."

"Hmm, okay. And from my understanding, they haven't shown any symptoms yet."

"They didn't mention anything when I talked to them."

Joey sounds surprised. "No, I mean, someone from our medical staff is in touch with them too."

"Really?" Now Flora sounds surprised.

"Yeah. We can't exactly just let this run its course."

"They didn't tell me they were talking to doctors."

"Oh, yeah, Silver, or whatever her name is, said not to tell you unless it came up, that you had enough to worry about. That she just wants you to get better."

"But I'm not actually sick. Or wasn't actually sick." She still sounds tired, but she also sounds . . . happy? I knew Goldy wasn't all bad.

They keep talking, and I keep thinking how I want him to leave. How I want to be the one to take care of her. He says, "Now, you buzz if you need anything. Let's see what happens with this fever. And no kissing Romeo!"

Joey opens the curtain, and he's got the smug look on his face again. I give him a dirty look, but he just rolls his eyes at me as he jabs the thermometer in my mouth and puts the cuff on my arm. The thermometer beeps; he looks at it and jots something down on his clipboard.

"Can you tell me what it was, please?"

I can tell that he loves that I'm asking. "What what was?" he says sweetly.

"My temperature," I say through gritted teeth.

"Why? Worried you might be sick?"

"Oliver's not sick, is he?" Flora asks. She sounds so tired.

Joey calls over, "Don't worry about him. Just worry about getting better."

"I *am* going to worry about him."

Now I give Joey a smug look.

"It's normal," Joey says. Then, under his breath, "Maybe the only normal thing about him."

"What was that last part?" Flora asks.

"Nothing, just teasing our little Romeo." He nudges me again, harder than he needs to, like always.

Joey leaves, and soon my mom and Peg are back. I listen to the worry in Flora's mom's voice and try to pretend that everything is okay.

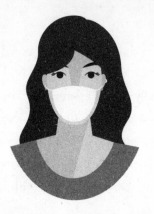

# 44. FLORA

"Are you sure I can't get you anything else?" My mom is wringing her hands looking at me.

"Mom," I protest. "I'm fine."

"I'll bring some of that sore throat tea when I come tomorrow. And cough drops. And some better tissues. The ones here are like Styrofoam." She's talking more to herself than me as she tries to make a list in her phone. "These darn gloves!" she mutters. She digs around in her purse and pulls out a pen and a crumpled-up receipt.

She's writing and doesn't see Kelsey suiting up in the hallway.

Kelsey has a doctor with her again, and she hands the phone to the doctor. I can see she's gesturing to the doctor that she wants her to take a picture. The doctor gives the phone back without taking a picture, and Kelsey pouts her lip.

My mom looks up from her list and out into the hallway. "Who's that? Oliver's sister?"

"That'd be creepy," I say before I can stop myself.

"Huh?"

"It's not his sister."

"Oh. Cousin?"

"Still creepy."

My mom looks at me, and I rub my head. "Remember when I said it was complicated?" I whisper.

She raises an eyebrow, and Kelsey walks through to Oliver's side of the room.

"Oliver! Our hashtag is still trending!" Kelsey says.

Oliver's mom has just been talking about Mrs. Thompson again, and I hear the shock in her voice at being interrupted. "Well, hello. You must be Kelsey."

"That's me," she says.

Everyone is quiet, then everyone starts talking at once. "Kelsey, this is my mom, Patty."

"I'm Oliver's mom, Patty."

"I came down to visit Oliver and take care of him."

Everyone is quiet again, then Oliver's mom asks, "How do you know each other? You have classes together?"

"Yeah, from school. We've had history class together for a while."

"Math!" I hear Oliver squeak.

My mom looks at me again, eyebrow still raised.

I wave my hand, try to make her stop listening. "Want to watch TV? I think *Seinfeld* is on now."

But she's still listening to Oliver telling Kelsey which classes they've had together over the years.

"Mom," I say.

"Hmm, what?" she says.

"TV?"

"How haven't I met you yet after you've had so many classes with my Oliver?" Oliver's mom asks.

"We didn't really talk much until recently," Kelsey says.

My mom looks at me, whispers, "I don't like this girl."

"Mom, shush!" I hiss.

But Kelsey is oblivious as usual, and she's telling Patty how annoying her flight was.

Patty doesn't seem to care and adds the requisite "hmm" here and there.

Then, suddenly, Oliver says, "Flora's fever came back," and everyone stops talking.

# 45. OLIVER

Kelsey and my mom are staring at me, both with completely different looks on their faces. My mom looks angry, worried, and Kelsey looks . . . delighted?

"Oh, Oliver, I'm so scared!" my mom says, rushing forward to hug me.

"Me too!" Kelsey says, peeking over my mom's shoulder. But I swear that she looks like she's trying to hide a smile.

Flora's mom opens the curtain, and I see Flora in bed. She still looks so tired. "Hi!" her mom says, walking over to Kelsey. "I'm Flora's mom. You're one of Oliver's classmates? So nice of you to come all the way from Brooklyn to visit him. I can't imagine this is a fun trip for you."

I can hear the sarcasm in her voice, but Kelsey doesn't seem to notice as she reaches out her left hand to shake. Peg looks down at it and says, "Wrong hand."

Kelsey looks at Peg. "Right, sorry." She sticks out her right hand.

"If anyone is concerned, Flora is feeling okay, even with the return of the fever," Peg says. For some reason her voice seems really loud.

My mom finally pulls away from hugging me. "Well, maybe now Flora and Oliver will think twice about kissing when they're sick."

Kelsey looks like she got slapped. "Wait, what? I'm confused. Oliver and Flora kissed?!" She looks at me, and I wish I could sink so far back in the bed I'd disappear.

I look around and realize everyone in the room is staring at me. Including Flora. I lock eyes with her, wish again I could be alone with her.

But then Kelsey snaps me out of my trance. "What is everyone talking about?"

I laugh nervously and look at Flora again.

"Oliver!" Now Kelsey is shouting.

"Please don't raise your voice at my son!" my mom says loudly.

I look at Flora's mom, and now she's the one who looks like she's trying to hide a smile, then look back at Flora again, who has a blank look on her face.

"Oliver! Look at me!" Kelsey says. I force myself to break eye contact with Flora as Kelsey stomps her foot. "When. Did. You. Kiss?" She says each word louder than the one before.

"I told you to stop yelling at my son!" My mom is on her feet now, getting closer to Kelsey.

"Tell me!" Kelsey screams.

I look at Flora helplessly. We didn't cover any of this in the girl handbook. She shrugs.

My mom grabs Kelsey by the arm and whips her around so they're face-to-face. "Don't yell at my—"

"Assault! Assault! Let go of me!" Kelsey screeches.

Suddenly the room is full of people in hazmat suits, including Joey, and everyone is shouting, and I watch in horror as my mom and Kelsey are escorted out of my room.

My mom screams, "You don't know the first thing about my son!"

"Yes I do. He's my boyfriend!" Kelsey whips her head around to make sure Flora hears her. I don't hear what my mom says, or if Kelsey says anything else, because they're gone.

For a minute, we sit in silence. Then Flora gets out of bed slowly, walks over to the bathroom door, and kicks the door again and again, until her mom and Joey pull her away.

# 46. FLORA

My eyes close. I'm falling, falling, falling, and no one is going to catch me. The darkness never ends, and no one cares.

# 47. OLIVER

I listen to Joey and Flora's mom talking to Flora, and I feel completely and utterly helpless. Joey is giving Flora medicine, and I know it's to calm her down, but I want to run over there and stop him, to tell him she's upset, to let her be upset. Why do we always have to bury all our emotions?

But as much as I dislike Joey, I know he's also a doctor, or sort of a doctor, and he doesn't want Flora to get sicker.

Joey and Peg talk in hushed tones, and I realize I don't hear Flora talking, that she must be asleep. Then Joey and Peg leave, and Flora and I are finally, finally alone. But when she and I were looking at each other before, and all I wanted was to be alone with her, this wasn't what I had in mind.

A few minutes later, Dr. Demarko stops by. She's sympathetic but firm. Kelsey and my mom are not to visit at the same time. My mom will get two visits a day since she's my legal guardian, and she is allowing Kelsey one visit a day. But if my mom feels the visits are too much for me, she'll revoke the visitations, and Kelsey will have to go back to New York. If there are any further altercations between either one of them or anyone else, my own visiting rights will be taken away. While she's talking, my phone lights up with texts from my mom.

"I know this is hard on everyone. I know for a fact it's hard on your mom, and maybe she's not showing it in the best way possible." As if on cue, my mom tries calling.

Dr. Demarko watches me. "Do you need to get that?"

"No, it's fine." I turn the phone over so it's facedown on my bed.

"I hope you're not upset with your mom. Sometimes parents don't always act like parents. Seeing our kids uncomfortable in any way is never easy. You should have seen how I was when my Rachel had to get her tonsils out. And I'm a doctor."

"Me too." I realize that doesn't make any sense, so I nod.

Dr. Demarko continues, "But I know this is especially hard on you. And now with Flora being sick—"

"Yep!" I say, trying to be cheerful.

"Well, if you need anything else, need anyone to talk to, just buzz."

I nod again, hating how transparent my anxiety is.

She waits for me to say something else, but when I don't, she leaves.

I flip my phone back over, look through the novel of texts from my mom. I skim them, and she seems to be saying that she's sorry, but. But. Does it really count as an apology if "but" follows? But she's worried about me, but this is hard on her, but she's a single parent, but Kelsey was rude to her, but Kelsey was a little rude to me too.

I start replying with "It's okay," when she calls again.

"Mom, it's okay," I say right away, and then she basically talks through the novel of texts and I interject "Mmm-hmm" and "I know" when it seems appropriate.

"I don't like that Kelsey girl. I'm not sure what you see in her."

I sigh. "She's nice, Mom. She came all the way from New York to take care of me."

My mom is quiet for the first time, so I keep talking. "We've had classes together for years. She's always been fun. She makes me laugh. I thought her visit would help cheer me up. You want me to rest and not get sick, don't you?"

But it all feels half-hearted. Maybe Kelsey *should* just go back to New York. But then I think about ice-skating a few months ago in Prospect Park, the way the snowflakes stuck to her blue knit hat. How fast she was on her skates, the sound her blades made as she zipped past me. The way she stopped when she saw me clutching the rink wall, skated backward in front of me, trying to show me how to do it. I was nervous on my skates to begin with and her attention made me even more nervous, but the last thing I wanted was for her to skate away.

A snowflake stuck in her eyelashes as I pulled myself away from the rink wall and clumsily put one skate in front of the other. "That's it!" she squealed. I felt like a deer learning to walk on new legs, but she skated with me a little longer, until she was satisfied with her work. "Good job!" she said, and she was off.

Later, I fell, of course. She was across the rink, and when I looked up she saw me and laughed. But I took it as a joking laugh, a laugh we were both in on, like she thought it was funny her skating lessons hadn't worked.

But I don't tell my mom any of this, and she's already talking again anyway. "Please tell me you're still feeling okay?"

"I'm fine, Mom. Flora is the one with the fever." I look at the curtain dividing our room. It seems so quiet in here.

"Yes, but you two kissed. We're talking about you kissing people! Weren't you just in diapers?" And she launches into some story I hear at least once a week: The first time I climbed out of my crib, I set up all my stuffed animals like we were going to have a tea party, and my mom found me asleep on the floor with a stuffed Elmo doll in one hand and a little plastic tea saucer in the other.

Finally, I interrupt my mom again, tell her I'm feeling tired after all the excitement, that I should really get some sleep. We say good night and I hang up.

I notice again how quiet it is in the room. I listen to Flora's deep breaths, wonder what she's dreaming about. I feel like I miss her even though she's right here.

My phone vibrates around 10:30 p.m., and it's a text from Kelsey: I don't care who you kissed. Past is past. I'm here now to make you feel better. Tell ur mom sorry. C u tomorrow.

I have no idea how to respond. I don't know if she's seen what people have said about Flora. She hasn't said anything, to me or online, so maybe she hasn't? Or maybe she's waiting for me to say something? I hate that I can't ask Flora what to say. I hate that I can't ask her anything right now. I hate that she got so upset. I hate that she has a fever. I hate that everything feels so hard and confusing.

I write a few different drafts of messages to Kelsey and finally settle on: It's okay. She forgives you. Can't wait to see you tomorrow afternoon!

I think almost all of that is a lie.

# 48. FLORA

When I wake up in the morning, the first thing I notice is that my throat feels funny. Not sore, exactly, not scratchy, just funny. Sort of like I swallowed something and it's stuck in the wrong tube. My nose is runny too. Maybe it wasn't the feathers in the pillows at my dad's place that were bugging me. Maybe I didn't tamper with the thermometer after all . . .

I'm so groggy. I don't even remember any vitals checks.

I stretch in bed and notice that my foot hurts. Then everything comes rushing back to me. The shouting between Oliver's mom and Kelsey. My sudden fever. Kelsey knowing that Oliver and I kissed. The way Oliver looked at me when I kissed him. I really am diseased and disgusting. Everything my mom told me about Goldy. It was Goldy's idea for me to visit them, not my own dad's. The way I finally got to kick the door. The way Joey and my mom pulled me back to my bed. And then Joey giving me pills, telling me they were to help me sleep.

I shudder. I hate taking medicine. I barely ever even take Advil.

I get out of bed, hobble to the bathroom, and jump when I look in the mirror. I have huge circles under my eyes, and something about my face looks sunken. Sick. I splash some water on my face, brush my teeth, then put my hair up in different ways, but nothing I do takes away the purple under my eyes. I suppose if I wore makeup I could try covering up the circles, but I've never been able to figure the stuff out. Maybe I should try finding a manual on how to be a girl. Which reminds me of the girl handbook. Of how I'm supposed to be helping Oliver. I need to ask him if he's okay, if Kelsey is mad at him. I hope he's not mad at me. I've made a mess out of everything again. But I can fix it. I always do. I just need to think. I wish my foot didn't hurt. I wish I didn't feel so spaced out.

I take a deep breath. I'll go over to his side of the room, make sure he's okay, that Kelsey isn't mad at him. If she is, I'll tell him how to fix it. I'm good at fixing things—at solving problems. I've spent my entire life doing it. Randy's entire life doing it.

I open the door, look at the closed curtain. It's so quiet on his side of the room. Maybe he's still sleeping? I hope it's not because he's feeling sick.

"Oliver?" I say hesitantly.

No answer.

I walk closer to the curtain. "Oliver?"

Still no answer. I find an opening in the curtain, peer through, and he's . . . gone.

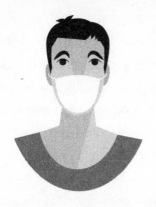

# 49. OLIVER

It's really hard to open my eyes. It must still be the middle of the night. But I feel light hitting my eyelids, so I force them open. Something about my room looks different, but I can't figure out what it is. I sit up, realize how quiet it is. I don't hear Flora moving around. I don't hear Flora breathing.

Suddenly wide awake, I shoot out of bed and yell, "Flora!"

No answer. I look around my side of the room. The window looks out onto the hallway, not the outside world. I feel like I'm trapped in some parallel universe.

"Flora!" I yell again.

I open the curtain. Flora's bed is empty and she isn't there. It must be a dream. I rub my eyes really hard, slap my cheek a little. *Wake up, Oliver!*

Then the door opens and I see someone in a hazmat suit, but they're in a shadow. Then I hear, "So, what do you think of your new digs, Romeo?"

"Joey?" I say carefully. It could still be a bad dream. I still can't see his face.

Joey slowly steps out of the shadow. Or, at least, it looks like Joey. He stares at me quietly for a second, then yells, "Boo!"

I shriek, and he laughs hysterically, clutching his belly.

"What's going on?" I say over his laughter. "Where is Flora? Is she okay? Why does my room look different?"

"Wow, you really are a lightweight, Romeo. We gave you sleeping medicine during one of your vitals checks in the middle of the night and moved you. Dr. Demarko knew if we told you the plans when you were awake, you wouldn't agree to it."

"Wait, what plans? You still haven't told me if Flora is okay!"

"Take a look for yourself. She's just across the hall," he says, bored.

I run to the window and look into the room across the hallway—the room Flora and I were sharing. Flora is sitting on her bed. She turns her head toward me, waves weakly, and smiles.

"What happened?" I ask, slightly relieved I'm not trapped in a parallel universe.

"Her fever spiked overnight," Joey tells me. "We knew it'd be less risky to move you rather than Flora. Less chance of spreading any germs."

"So you guys just drugged me and moved me . . . while I was asleep?" I say sarcastically.

"Yep."

"Um, how is that legal?"

"Um, because you're a minor, and your mom agreed to it," Joey says sweetly. He checks my temperature, blood pressure, pulse, and writes down the results.

"Joey!" I call as he's leaving. He turns around, still looking bored. "Tell her I said hi?"

Joey smirks but doesn't say anything, and leaves.

# 50. FLORA

Oliver and I look at each other across the hallway. He gives me a thumbs-up, which is kind of weird, but endearing. It's so nice to see him, yet strange to be so far away. I suddenly realize how accustomed I've become to having Oliver near me.

I scroll through my text messages and find the picture of Oliver I used for the very first #quaranteen post. I look at his picture, his cool-breeze eyes. I remember how soft his hair was when I brushed it away from his face.

It feels like a lifetime ago.

I text him: I'm sorry. I hope things are okay with Kelsey.

Oliver jumps when he gets my text. He looks at the message, then looks at me, confused. He writes back: Yeah, it's fine. Are you okay?

Never been better, I write back. I start a message about how I want to help him with the girl handbook stuff, this is all just a minor setback, when my phone buzzes with notifications. I close out of my texts, then see that I've been tagged in a video, and so has Oliver.

A video? I certainly haven't been anywhere for anyone to take a video of me. And it's not like my mom or Oliver's mom has been taking videos of me while I'm asleep. I click on the video, and it starts playing. There isn't much to see, though, because it was taken inside Kelsey's purse during her visit yesterday.

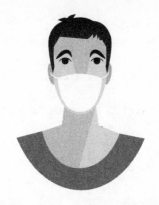

# 51. OLIVER

I watch the video, confused at first. I hear a conversation that sounds familiar, then realize it's familiar because it's a conversation that happened yesterday. I stop the video, feeling a little sick, and it's not because I'm in a hospital room.

I close out of the video, look up at Flora, but her head is down, looking at her phone. I watch all the comments roll in.

The #quaranteens kissed!

We know the #quaranteen names! Flora and Oliver.

Maybe Oliver's mom should be in #quaranteen to get her temper under control.

Poor Kelsey! #quaranteen

Kelsey should break up with Oliver. His mom is psycho and he clearly likes Flora. #quaranteen

Is Oliver going to kiss Kelsey and get her sick? #quaranteen

Oliver can give me a kissing disease #quaranteen

One of the #quaranteens is sick!

Flora deserves to be sick for trying to mess up Kelsey and Oliver. #quaranteen

#TeamKelser #quaranteen

#TeamFloriver #quaranteen

Flora finally looks up, disbelief on her face. She's still shaking her head when her mom walks into her room, her arms full of cough drops, tissues, and tea. A few minutes later, Kelsey waltzes down the hallway and into my room.

Kelsey grins, and the knowing look on her face takes me right back to the skating rink in Prospect Park. "Hello, Oliver," she says calmly, formally. She holds out her arms, and I slowly get out of bed and give her a hug, but something about the way she's hugging me seems familiar, reminds me of the way someone else has hugged me before.

I pull back quickly. She's got a sympathetic look on her face, and I think of her hug—the way people hugged me at my dad's funeral. It's . . . comforting. She squeezes my shoulder, and I remember my great-aunt Bertha doing the same thing.

"It must be so hard on you that Flora is sick," she says in the same calm voice.

"It is," I say. I shake my head, trying to snap out of the trance she's put me in. "But why did you do it? *How* could you do it? All these strangers are saying things about me, about you, about Flora, about our lives. I just . . . ugh! My mom is going to be so mad!" I realize I sound like a whiny six-year-old, but I don't care.

She looks surprised. "Do what?"

"Put that video online!" I practically bellow. I didn't know I knew how to bellow.

"Oh, that?" she says, waving her hand dismissively. "What's the big deal? I wanted to get a video of me meeting my boyfriend's mom for the first time."

"What's the big *deal*?" I snap. "It makes my mom look crazy! It makes it sound like she's attacking you. It tells people, strangers, that Flora is sick. It tells people things about me that—"

"Well, maybe it sounds like she's attacking me because that's what happened," Kelsey interrupts.

I keep waiting for the punch line. She's making me feel . . . crazy. "And Team Kelser? Team Floriver? Really?"

"Oh, that? It's so funny, but people think there's some kind of love triangle between the three of us. But that's so silly, because we're the ones dating! It doesn't bother me because the drama is just for show. Everyone knows we belong together," she says nonchalantly.

She doesn't wait for me to respond. I'm still too in shock that people are bored enough to mash up my name with anyone else's. Too in shock that people think I could be involved in any kind of love triangle.

Am *I* Team Floriver or Team Kelser?

"Don't you think the world deserves to know how hard it is for us?" she says.

"For us?" I'm trying to focus on what she's saying.

"All the things we have working against us. You're in quarantine. Your mom disapproves of our relationship. Your roommate is a threat to your health. It's the perfect story line, isn't it?"

"Huh?" I say, confused.

"I bet Romeo and Juliet wish they could have told people how unfair their parents were. They couldn't," she says with a knowing grin, "but we can."

Her saying Romeo makes me think of Joey, which makes me think of Flora. I look across the hallway, but she's talking to her mom.

"Past is past, Oliver," Kelsey says. She squeezes my shoulder again. "But I can see it's really bothering you. I'll take the video down." She fiddles with her phone, then says, "All gone!"

"Really? That's it? But what about all the people who saw it already?"

"I can't imagine it was that many people."

"I don't know. It seems like a lot of people commented on it."

"Really?" Kelsey's eyes light up. She pauses and says, "I mean, I'm just excited that you'll have so many people to support you. If you change your mind and want me to put it up again, just let me know. Now, what else can I do to make things better?"

"Um, I'm not sure. I wish Flora wasn't sick."

Kelsey flinches a bit when I say Flora's name. "That reminds me, you should probably post an update about her soon. People are worried. Something to think about. Is there anything else you need in the meantime? Anything I can get you?"

I wish she could bring in a carton of fresh air. I wish she could bring in the smell of newly cut grass, of flowers, of garlic cooking at a restaurant. At this point I'd even take the smell of summertime New York City streets when it's trash pickup day. I wish she could bring in a car, and I could be on a road trip somewhere, anywhere. Finally, I say, "Well . . . this is lame, but I've been craving gumdrops. I used to eat them on road trips with my parents when I was a kid. I know I could ask my mom to get them, but then she'll lecture me about staying healthy and whatnot."

"Sure, Oliver, I can do that," she says.

"Really?" I never thought the idea of gumdrops could make me so happy.

"Absolutely." She smiles warmly. "I think it's time for a quaranteen picture!"

"Oh, right, that thing."

"That thing, you silly!" Kelsey scoffs.

Before I realize what's happening, Kelsey gets up from her chair and throws her arms around my neck. Her sudden closeness inadvertently makes me grin as she snaps a picture on her phone. She shows it to me, and I look so happy. We look so happy. If I were an outsider, I would never guess the picture had been taken in a hospital room, with someone with a rare form of mono just a few feet away. At the thought of Flora, I feel the smile leave my face. But Kelsey is already uploading the picture.

She taps the screen a few times. "There!" She looks at me. "This could be our most liked post yet!"

"Right, yeah, maybe," I say uneasily.

"What's wrong?"

"It just feels . . . kind of bad."

"What does?"

"Social media. Likes. I don't know. Flora is sick. Other people could get sick."

"And the perfect thing to do when you're feeling upset or worried or scared is to reach out to others on social media. Share your story with others. Let others take away your pain."

"Yeah, I guess," I say uncertainly.

She looks down at her phone and squeals, "Ohhh! Forty-eight likes already!"

I pick up my phone and look at the post: Taking care of #mybravequaranteen. Hope I can make him feel better! #quaranteen

But somehow . . . I feel even worse than I did before.

# 52. FLORA

I wake up, which is weird because I don't even remember falling asleep. My curtain is closed around my bed, so I can't look out the window to see if it's day or night. It reminds me of all the times I've fallen asleep doing my homework, how I wake up in my bed, but my pillow is a heavy textbook, and I'm still in my clothes from the previous day.

But at home when this happens, I usually bolt out of bed in a panic, run to my desk, and see how much homework is left—how much I can fit in before I have to get ready to go to school. Now the thought of getting out of bed seems impossible, and my legs feel like lead. So do my eyelids.

I open my eyes again, and I think I've just blinked, but I'm not sure.

I blink again. My mom is here now, and I can't figure out why she looks so worried. I look at her, try to swallow. My throat feels like there's lava in it. I finally manage to ask, "Is Randy okay?"

My mom laughs, but then looks like she's going to cry. "That's my Flora, always thinking about someone else, even when she's sick."

*Sick.* That word again.

"What . . . what day is it?" Each word feels harder to get out than the one before it.

My mom looks at me like she doesn't understand what I've said, but I'm too tired to repeat myself.

Joey appears next to my bed, smiling his usual smile. "It's Friday."

I realize that's not the question I meant to ask, and as if he's read my mind, he says, "It's morning. A little after nine. You slept through your mom's visit last night."

I nod. My throat hurts too much to say anything else.

I see a gleam in Joey's eye that I haven't seen before. He takes my temperature and writes on his clipboard. "Similar symptoms as the man on your flight, same timeline. This is all great."

"Great?" my mom says sharply. "My daughter is sick and you think this is great?"

He grins. "Relatively speaking, yes. Medically speaking, definitely."

My mom narrows her eyes at him and says through her teeth, "When is she going to get better?"

Joey flips through his clipboard and taps his pen against it. "Who can say for sure? We don't know much about this disease, after all. But based on what we've seen so far, it's a fast and furious illness, so she should expect to be feeling better in a week, maybe two. But we'll see. That's what makes this all so exciting!"

"Exciting?" my mom yells. "My daughter is not your guinea pig!"

"No, of course not," Joey says, but he's already writing something down on his clipboard again. He looks up at me again, taps my foot, but I can tell he's distracted.

I take another long blink, and when I open my eyes, my mom is gone and once again I have no idea what day it is.

# 53. OLIVER

I look across the hallway to Flora. I can't believe how much she's sleeping. I can't believe how much I miss talking to her. I want to do something to help her, like she helped me on the flight when I had my panic attack. But what?

I've never taken care of anyone sick before. Never even taken care of a sick pet. When I see someone sneeze on the subway, I hold my breath, and whenever I see anyone puke on TV, I have to close my eyes. Blood makes me light-headed, and just hearing the word *wound* nauseates me.

No one I've ever cared about has been seriously sick. I realize Flora is someone I care about. And now she's sick.

Flora's hair is almost entirely swept away from her face, and I notice her ears for the first time. How have I never noticed how small and cute they are? There is one loose strand of hair across her cheek. She has one hand close to her mouth, and her fingers twitch in her sleep, like she's trying to move the hair. I wish I could walk out my door, across the hall, and brush the hair away from her face.

Then I think about the germs, about getting sick. I think about the man from the flight. I look at my hand, run to the bathroom, and wash it under water as hot as I can stand. When I get out of the bathroom, Kelsey is on my side of the room, sitting in a chair.

"I was wondering where you were!" She smiles.

"I was out for a walk," I say sarcastically.

The color drains from her face for a second. "Really? Is that safe?"

"Oh, I was kidding," I say. "Lame quarantine joke."

"Ha, right."

There is the awkward pause that still surprises me and still makes me wonder why it exists as she looks at me.

I absentmindedly swing my arms and clap my hands, and the sound makes Kelsey jump.

"Oh, I finally remembered your candy!" She digs through a plastic bag and pulls out a box of candy. "Here you go!" she says triumphantly.

It's a box of Mike and Ikes. "Oh, tropical!" I say. "How . . . exotic."

"Right? I figured since you were coming back from the Dominican Republic and all."

"Did you get gumdrops too?" I feel embarrassed, though I don't know why.

"No? Didn't you say Mike and Ikes? I think my grandmother likes gumdrops."

"Err, yeah, I probably said the wrong thing," I lie. "Quarantine brain and all."

Kelsey is on her phone again. She's really good at using it in her thick hazmat suit gloves. "Now that I gave them to you, I can finally post this picture!" she says.

"What picture?"

She doesn't answer, so I pick up my phone, and the number of notifications that pop up still surprises me. I scroll through until I find Kelsey's post. It's a picture of the box of candy: Sweets for my sweets. He loves these! #mysweetquaranteen #quaranteen

#TeamKelser all the way. #quaranteen

They're the cutest. #quaranteen

Um, can we get an update about Flora please? #quaranteen

I open the box and take out a piece of candy. It's bright blue, and I'm not sure what flavor it'll be. I pop it in my mouth, and I'm still not sure what flavor it actually is, but I know it's not a gumdrop. I'm not sure why I think this, but I know that Flora would have gotten me the right kind of candy. She seems like she's good at taking care of people. Actually, I *know* she's good at taking care of people after she helped me through my panic attack.

I dig through the candy box, pull out a yellow piece, and stick it in my mouth. I'm trying to figure out if it's mango, pineapple, or lemon when Kelsey jumps up from her chair and runs over to me, waving her phone. She's so excited she can barely speak.

"Reddit wants to do an AMA with us!"

"A what?"

"Ask Me Anything. It's where people ask someone famous questions on Reddit. Like anything. You should see the stuff people asked Daniel Radcliffe."

"But we're not famous?" I blurt out.

Kelsey looks offended for a second, then playfully jabs me. "Why do you like messing with me so much? We totally are! How many other people are dating in quarantine?"

*Dating.* How did that happen? I'm not sure if I'm more surprised that I'm supposedly famous or that I'm supposedly dating someone. I don't know how to clarify either with Kelsey, so I eat another Mike and Ike. Lime? Watermelon? To be honest, I'm not sure I care anymore.

# 54. FLORA

I have another dream about falling, but this time Oliver is going to catch me. I jolt awake before I land in his arms.

I look around the room, look out the window into the hallway, look at Oliver's room. I fall asleep again.

Another dream. This time I'm in an elevator. Someone else is with me, but I don't recognize her. The doors open, but all we see are stars in the night sky. The doors close again, and we're floating away.

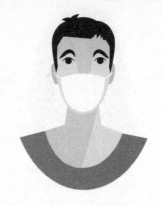

# 55. OLIVER

Somehow, there has been an actual routine, a schedule to my days. I hate that the routine includes just watching Flora sleep but not talking to her. The days pass slowly, predictably. My mom visits in the morning and talks at me about herself, then Kelsey visits and we both spend a lot of time on our phones. My mom visits again in the afternoon, and then it's nighttime. Somewhere in all of that are a million visits from doctors and nurses.

And not talking to Flora. I hate that part of my days the most.

Kelsey and I do talk a little, but mostly about the hashtag. She convinces me to post an update about Flora, says that people are worried. She practically writes the post herself. **Flora is a fighter and getting stronger by the day! Thanks for the good thoughts! #quaranteen**

I want to post how much I miss her, how worried I am.

And the #quaranteen posts keep coming in. Strangers think that Kelsey is an awesome girlfriend or a terrible girlfriend. That Flora isn't really sick or is sicker than I've posted. That we're not really in quarantine. And everyone wants to know more about the kiss.

Except Kelsey.

# 56. FLORA

I'm not sure if I'm awake or asleep. I want to move, to turn over, but my legs feel like they weigh at least six hundred pounds. Then I'm trying to run, but I can't pick up my lead legs, and someone is chasing me, but I can't see their face. They're getting closer and closer to me, and all of a sudden, my legs turn into water and I drift down myself, a river flowing away from my pursuer.

I listen to the water, and then I'm awake, no longer flowing, but stuck in my bed in my hospital room.

I move my arm to look at my watch: 8:36 a.m. It's a Sunday. I've been in the hospital for two weeks. I'm so happy to be awake long enough to move my arm that I become giddy. I play with the buttons on my watch, find one that makes the screen light up so I can see what time it is, day it is, even in the dark. I lift up my blanket over my head, push the button, and even under there I can see that it's now 8:39 a.m. And it's still Sunday. It's cozy under the blanket, and it makes me think of the forts I make with Randy. I close my eyes. Just for a second.

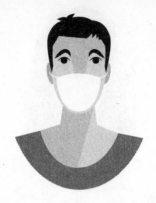

# 57. OLIVER

Something feels different when I get out of the shower, but I'm not sure what. I look across the hallway and see that Flora has pulled the blanket over her head. The blanket is thin, though, and I can see the light-up face of her watch.

Does this mean she's awake? Does this mean she's feeling better? Maybe I should text her.

The light-up face on the watch turns off.

# 58. FLORA

I feel really hot and like I'm trapped in a cave. My breath feels really close to my face. I feel like the cave is falling in on me, and then I'm awake and trying to push the blanket off me. But I'm too tired and it hurts too much to move.

Then I feel the blanket being pulled from my face and someone is there, peering down at me, worried. I feel my hair stuck to my sweaty face, but whoever it is leans over and carefully brushes it away.

"Girl handbook," I croak, trying to smile. "You've been studying."

A laugh. I know that laugh. "What are you talking about?" It's Joey.

"Playing with girls' hair. Never mind."

I want to text Oliver, see Oliver. I want to ask him how things are with Kelsey, how things are with him. I want to know what's going on with the hashtag. What happened with the video Kelsey posted. If the Internet is interested in him and Kelsey . . . or him and me.

I've been sleeping so long and I miss talking to him.

I miss him.

Then I see Kelsey in the hallway. She practically skips to Oliver's room. I wonder how she has so much energy, if I ever had that much energy, if I'll ever have that much energy again. She runs her hands through her hair. I bet Kelsey's hair doesn't feel oily like mine. She puts on her hazmat suit, and she looks even cuter in it than I remember.

Just watching her is exhausting, and my eyes close.

# 59. OLIVER

"What is it like dating in quarantine? Is a hazmat suit comfortable? Where will you go on your first real date?" Kelsey is reading me questions from the Ask Me Anything thing on Reddit.

"Ohhh, here's a good one!" Kelsey looks at me coyly. "What is it like dating someone you can't kiss?"

I'm taking a sip of water and I choke when I hear the word *kiss*.

"I'm going to say it will be worth the wait," Kelsey says, looking out the window dreamily. She looks back at me. "Right, Oliver? What are you going to say?"

*I have a girlfriend, I have a girlfriend, I have a girlfriend*, I think. *My girlfriend is Kelsey, my girlfriend is Kelsey, my girlfriend is Kelsey.*

Once again, I try to think about the Kelsey from Prospect Park, ice-skating in front of me, the way she looked into my eyes, helped me skate. All the times over the last few years when we had math class together, the feeling I'd get in my stomach every time she walked into the classroom, the feeling every time she'd look anywhere even close to my direction.

But the snow has melted, and that version of her seems further and further away, less and less like the Kelsey beside me.

I never actually asked her to be my girlfriend, and she never actually asked me to be her boyfriend. It's weird how we are just suddenly dating.

Does this mean I want to break up with her? How do you break up with someone you never really asked to be your girlfriend in the first place? I've never even had the courage to ask a girl out on a date, much less be my girlfriend, and now, somehow, I might have to break up with someone. Maybe. What would I even say? I wish I could ask Flora.

Plus, airline tickets are expensive. And she's risking her own health to take care of me. Things she likes to remind me of. But for good reason.

I wish again that Flora was awake for longer, was in the same room. She and I were still only a few chapters into the girl handbook, and I already need to know how the epilogue goes.

I look at Kelsey again, her hair hanging a bit in her face, and I'm reminded of how I wanted to brush Flora's hair away from her face, and the thought makes me smile. Kelsey looks up at me, sees me smiling, and her eyes light up.

"You've just helped me figure out how to answer one of the questions!"

"I have?"

"Yeah. What's your favorite thing about dating Oliver? His smile. It's *contagious*," she says with a wink.

Again, I have nothing clever to say right away. Everything I'm thinking feels too awkward to say out loud.

But Kelsey's head is down again, and she's looking at her phone.

"Um, yours too." She doesn't hear me. "Yours too!" I say louder.

"Mine too what?" Kelsey looks up, confused.

"Your smile. It's contagious too."

Her eyes light up again. "He's sweet. That's my other favorite part of dating Oliver."

"You too," I say. Once again, she doesn't hear me, but this time I don't bother repeating myself.

# 60. FLORA

When I open my eyes, my mom is staring at me again, and she looks so worried. "Hi, sweetheart!"

I swallow carefully. Still burns, but it feels less like lava and more like I drank hot cocoa too fast. "Hi, Mom," I say slowly.

"Are you feeling better? You look like you're feeling a little better! Should we get Joey in here?"

But she doesn't need to do anything, because suddenly he's there, and he's grinning at me, like he's happy to see me.

"She's awake!" he proclaims. "We missed you, kid."

I swallow again. "How's Oliver?" I ask.

Joey is holding his clipboard and writing something down, but I still see him make a face. "Oh, Romeo is fine. His girlfriend has been keeping him company, that's for sure."

"Right, girl—" But I pause to swallow, my throat feeling hotter and more lavalike.

"Your followers and fans are pretty worried about you too," he says.

"Who?"

"Oh, right, you probably haven't been checking your phone," Joey says.

"Oliver let everyone know that you got sick. But that you're doing better," my mom chimes in. "He asked me if it was okay first. I told him it was. I hope that's all right?"

I'm so confused, but it hurts too much to ask all the questions I want to ask.

"So, your illness is running about the same course as the man on the flight's. That's good," Joey continues.

"Why is that good?" my mom snaps.

Joey says, "Your virus seems to be concentrated in your throat. Also a good thing."

My mom is looking at Joey, waiting for him to go on, but he's writing again. "And why are these good things? It seems like it's incredibly painful for my daughter to swallow, much less speak."

"Oh, well, it's a good thing for everyone else she's been exposed to. The man on the flight was sneezing and coughing, which is a faster way to spread an illness. Flora hasn't developed those symptoms yet, so luckily she's keeping the germs to herself."

"Yeah, luckily," my mom says sarcastically.

Joey looks up from his notes at me. "You do look more like yourself; the color is returning to your cheeks. We've kept you hydrated with that IV in your arm, but I'm going to get you some Jell-O too. Should feel good on the throat. Any questions for me?"

I open my mouth, but he interrupts. "Sorry, bad joke. I know your throat hurts. I'll be back."

My mom watches him walk down the hall, then turns to me. "Flora, I'm so happy to see you awake!" She squeezes my hands hard.

I open my mouth again, but she says, "You don't have to say anything. Just know that I'm so happy." She squeezes my hands harder.

I nod, smile. I want to ask about Oliver but I don't even know what to say. My mom won't be able to tell me what Oliver has been thinking, doing, while I've been asleep. And I want to ask about these supposed fans and followers that Joey was talking about.

She leans forward. "Oliver—"

But then Joey is back in the room, handing me Jell-O and pudding. Maybe he doesn't think I'm disgusting and germ-ridden like Oliver did, like he must again now that I'm sick for real.

But even chewing squishy Jell-O is exhausting, and by the time I've finished half a cup, I feel my eyes closing. I feel my spoon dropping out of my hand as I doze off, but someone must catch it because I don't hear it hit the floor.

# 61. OLIVER

I think one of the things I miss most about my apartment is how it feels in the middle of the night. Not that it's quiet, because there is always a floor creaking or a pipe clanking somewhere in our old prewar building. I miss the feeling of it being the middle of the night and knowing that everyone else in the building is asleep, or should be asleep. The feeling of waking up at 2:42 a.m. and walking across my apartment and feeling like I've snuck into a party.

Not like the 2:42 a.m. at the hospital, which doesn't differentiate night from day, where there are always people working, people coming in and out of my room. I can at least look outside and see that it's dark, but it doesn't really make much difference.

I'm looking out the window now, and even though Miami is a big city, I can still see more stars here than in Brooklyn.

I wonder what Flora is dreaming about, wonder if she's dreaming about me.

*I have a girlfriend*, I think to myself again. *My girlfriend is Kelsey.* In all my fantasies and daydreams over the years about Kelsey being my girlfriend, I always envisioned me asking her out in some grand, exciting, romantic way, and I always envisioned our first date being the kind that other girls would be jealous of, that other guys would be jealous of for not thinking of themselves.

My favorite date idea was watching the fireworks on the Wonder Wheel in Coney Island, our little cart swinging back and forth gently in the cool night breeze. In my fantasy, I was able to overlook my fear of heights as I slipped my arm over her shoulder to keep her warm. We'd get off the ride together and my arm would still be over her shoulders, and then I'd win her a teddy bear from one of the games and she'd be laughing at something funny I said.

Why would I ever think I'd want to break up with her?

When I see her in the afternoon I should ask if she wants to go on a first date to Coney Island when we get back from quarantine. When we get back from quarantine . . . Sometimes I forget that I won't be in the hospital room forever, that I will go back to school, back to Brooklyn, that this will all be one of those things someday I'll forget the details of. Like my dad's funeral. I can't remember who I talked to, I can't remember what I ate, I can't remember what suit I wore, and I can't remember any of the readings from the service. The only thing I remember is that I didn't cry.

But unlike my dad's funeral, I don't want to forget all the details of quarantine. I'd even be okay with remembering every single vitals check, every single middle-of-the-night wake-up call if it means that all my memories of Flora will stay in my brain forever.

I look out the window onto the hallway, see Flora sigh in her sleep, and file the memory away in my brain, pack it away carefully in a box that I know I'll handle with the utmost care.

# 62. FLORA

I wake up on my own, not because someone is waking me up, and it's a lovely feeling. I wiggle my toes, my fingers, and knowing I don't need a nap after makes me feel like I can do anything. I stretch my arms overhead, then look at my watch. It's 8:37 a.m. Maybe I'll climb a mountain by 8:37 p.m.

Joey walks in, and I smile at him. "Hey, you," he says. He seems happy to see me, and his happiness makes me wiggle my fingers and toes all over again. He sits down on the edge of my bed, and I'm acutely aware of how close my foot is to his butt. He doesn't seem to think I'm poisonous. I look up at his face, and his eyes are watching mine.

I feel myself blush a little. I'm suddenly self-conscious of my hair, of what I must look like. Hopefully the hazmat suit blocks out some of the stench that has to be coming from my mouth.

He says, "Your color really is returning."

I nod, and I think my throat feels okay enough that I could actually speak, but I don't trust the words that might come out of my mouth.

"Let me check your vitals." He takes my temperature, pulse, and blood pressure.

He furrows his brow at the thermometer and says, "This really *is* interesting." But he seems to be talking to himself more than to me as he jots notes down on his clipboard.

"Interesting?" I finally say, with some effort. I'm surprised at how much my throat still hurts. "Good interesting? Bad interesting?"

"You still have a fever. I was hoping by now it'd be going down."

"I still have a fever?"

"Aye."

"It's been over a week."

"This is a new and unpredictable disease."

"Right." I'm glad my mom isn't here for this conversation.

I look at him in his hazmat suit. I look around the room, to the antechamber that separates my room from the rest of the hospital. I think of the way the guy who brought me the gift basket looked at me, like I was poisonous. Disgusting.

I think of the way Oliver looked at me after I kissed him.

I feel tears well up in my eyes.

But Joey has his head down, making notes on his clipboard, and doesn't notice.

"I'll see you later. Someone will bring you breakfast soon." He leaves the room, head still down, writing. He looks up in the hallway and waves, but doesn't see me wiping away tears.

I wonder why it's "someone" and not him, but I don't need to wonder long because I feel my eyes closing.

When I open my eyes again, my breakfast is on the tray next to my bed and my mom is dozing off in her chair. I look at my wrist. Now it's 10:42. Darn it. Two hours gone, just like that, and I almost slept through my mom's visit again. I miss being awake for longer than five minutes. I miss being able to remember my life, to live my life.

# 63. OLIVER

All through my mom's morning visit I rehearse in my head what I want to say to Kelsey. How I want to take her to Coney Island, to the Wonder Wheel. How I'll win her the biggest stuffed animal in all Luna Park.

You'd think my mom would notice I'm not listening to her, but as usual she doesn't and as usual I'm amazed at how long she can talk. Like how does her brain think of so many things to say?

My mom ends her visit the same as always, telling me that she'll see me soon, but to call or text if I need anything before then. She gives me a hug, and touches my nose with her index finger. I think she must have seen the nose thing on a TV show or something because she only started doing it a few days ago.

"Love you, my Oliver!" she says over her shoulder as she leaves.

I look across the hallway, out of habit, but Flora's curtain is drawn.

I miss her.

# 64. FLORA

I wake up just in time to see Kelsey go into Oliver's room, and in my half-awake state I think that one nice thing about being in isolation and being sick is that I don't have to talk to anyone. Not that I could stay awake long enough to have a normal conversation anyway. I really want to know what's going on with them, with the hashtag. I know they're dating, but I don't know how much advice Oliver has followed from the girl handbook. I wonder if he's played with her hair yet. I remember what it felt like when Oliver ran his fingers through my hair. But he's got a girlfriend now, I remind myself. And I'm not the kind of girl who flirts with other girls' boyfriends. That's not my thing.

I look across the hallway again, but someone, probably Kelsey, closed the curtain. I wonder what they're doing. Maybe they're watching a movie together. Maybe they're playing a really intense card game. Or maybe they're staring longingly into each other's eyes, just like I told Oliver to do.

There is a part of me that hopes he isn't taking my advice.

I fall asleep trying to think of the last movie I watched.

# 65. OLIVER

I'm watching Kelsey on her phone, like usual, trying to make myself say the words I've been rehearsing all morning. I don't know why it's so hard for me to talk to her. She's my girlfriend.

She looks up from her phone. "Everyone really liked that last picture of us together."

"Which picture again?"

Kelsey looks shocked, and slightly annoyed. "Um, the one from yesterday, where I posted and said it's our ten-day anniversary."

"Right." She can't see it, but I'm mentally rolling my eyes.

"Oliver, that picture is a huge deal. Did you seriously not know what I was talking about?"

"I did! I was just joking," I lie.

I can tell Kelsey doesn't believe me, but she says, "Right. A joke."

*Ask her out, Oliver. Open your mouth and say the words already.*

"We should go out," I blurt.

"We already are?" Kelsey looks annoyed again.

"No, I mean, when we get back to Brooklyn. Like out. Like on a date. Somewhere. Together." This isn't coming out the way I rehearsed it in my head at all.

Kelsey's face relaxes. "That'd be nice. Where do you want to take me? Wait, hold on, I want to record this." She lifts her phone to take a video.

"Coney Island," I say.

"Wait, I wasn't recording yet. Can you say that again? But maybe say a whole sentence?"

"Right. Um, Kelsey, let's go to Coney Island."

Kelsey puts down her phone, looking disappointed. "Maybe a little more romantic? Think of our audience!"

"Audience? We're not in a play."

"I know. I meant audience as a metaphor."

"A metaphor for what?"

"Or a figure of speech. I don't know. Do you want to say it again?" She's lifting her phone again.

I clear my throat. "Kelsey, when we get back to Coney Island, I want to take you to Brooklyn."

Kelsey's face falls as she looks at me.

I realize what I've said. "Sorry," I say in a small voice. "Let me try again. Kelsey, when we get back to Brooklyn, I want to take you to Coney Island. On a date."

Kelsey beams. "Perfect." She taps her phone. "Aaand . . . posted." She's quiet for a minute, then says, "Wow, those tweets sure do show up quickly."

I watch her for a bit, then say, "Do you want to know where I want to take you?" I don't know why I feel so embarrassed. It's normal to take your girlfriend on a date.

"You already said Coney Island."

"Yeah, but it's a big boardwalk."

"Oh, okay. Sure, where do you want to take me?"

She lifts her phone to record, but I say, "We don't need to record this, do we?"

"Why wouldn't we?"

"It might be cool to have some privacy. Some things just between us."

Kelsey grins slyly as she puts her phone down. "You're so romantic. Tell me about our date."

Even though she's not recording me, I still feel embarrassed, and I hear my voice shaking as I say, "We could go on the Wonder Wheel and watch fireworks."

Kelsey waits for me to say more.

"I'd win you the biggest stuffed animal at the ring toss. And we could have hot dogs." I thought there was more, because as I'm saying the words out loud, I realize how lame the date sounds.

Kelsey smiles. "Sounds good. Except the hot dogs. They gross me out."

I don't know why I feel disappointed by her reaction, but I don't think she notices my disappointment. She's back on her phone.

I wonder if Flora is awake yet. If she'd be proud of me for saying something romantic. Logically, I know she *should* be happy for me—I'm following her advice from the girl handbook, after all.

But part of me wonders if I should have taken the advice.

Because nothing about quarantine is logical.

# 66. FLORA

When I wake up, I don't feel like I'm dragging myself out of quicksand. It feels more like the day after pulling an all-nighter for school. Like every single muscle in my body is tired, and like every single inch of my body slept hard. But at least I don't feel like I'm trying to pull myself out of a bottomless pit.

I look at my watch. Only 8:10 on Friday morning. The earliest I've woken up on my own since I got sick. *I'm sick, in a hospital, in quarantine*, I think. Now that I'm feeling a little more awake, I can actually string together more complex thoughts.

*Oliver* is my next thought. Though he was never far from my mind, even when I was in the bottomless pit of being more tired than I ever knew was possible. Like I didn't know the cells in my body could create a feeling of pure exhaustion like I've been feeling.

I look out at the hallway. He's still sleeping.

I stretch, and I'm surprised at how sore I am. Who knew sleeping could be so painful. I run my tongue over my teeth, and I swear it feels like algae is growing on them. Gross. I can't remember the last time I brushed them. I want to get my toothbrush, but the bathroom seems so far away.

A nurse comes in for a vitals check and looks startled when she sees that I'm awake. She puts the thermometer in my mouth, straps on the blood pressure cuff. The thermometer beeps first. "Ninety-eight-point-six. It's normal." She smiles at me.

"Normal? Are you sure? Can't these things give false readings?"

"Sometimes. That's one of the reasons we do so many vitals checks throughout the day and night. We'll keep an eye on you, like we have for the last sixteen days."

"Sixteen days," I repeat to myself.

"What's that, dear?"

"Nothing, just doing some math in my head."

"Okay. Joey will be right in."

"Could I take a shower first?"

"Sure, but I'll need to help you. It's been a long time since you've been out of bed on your own."

"Help me shower?" I'm not used to people helping me; it's supposed to be the other way around. I'm supposed to be the helper. I always have been.

"Yes, dear. Hospital policy. Don't worry, you don't have anything I haven't already seen a million times."

"No, it's not that," I say quickly. "I'm . . . not used to asking for help." It's hard to even say *help* out loud.

"Well, you don't have to say it. Let's get you cleaned up and get a fresh set of sheets on this bed."

And with that I'm escorted to the shower, and when I leave I feel like a whole new person. I even get to brush and floss my teeth.

But by the time I get back to bed I'm exhausted, and I celebrate my cleanliness by promptly falling asleep.

# 67. OLIVER

"Everyone really likes your first-date idea!" Kelsey says. She looks up from her phone at me. Sometimes I feel like the phone is a part of her body, like she's holding it so much it's going to fuse to her hand.

"Who is everyone?"

"You're so funny, Oliver. *Everyone!*"

I must still look confused, because she says, "Everyone on social media! Are you messing with me again? Sometimes I can't tell when you're messing with me." She lightly pokes my shoulder with her free hand.

"Why would you think that?" Flora didn't give me this tip, but my fifth-grade teacher, Mrs. Robinson, did. When someone asks you a question and you don't understand what they are talking about, ask them a question back.

"You're so funny, Oliver," Kelsey says again, shaking her head. She looks back down at her phone.

*My girlfriend is looking at her phone. My girlfriend is posting about her boyfriend on social media. I am Kelsey's boyfriend.*

I could watch the video she took of me asking her out on a date again, but I don't feel like being reminded of what a fidgety dork I am. I read through comments.

Kelser 4ever #quaranteen

Oliver should take Kelsey on the Tunnel of Love #quaranteen

Aww, Oliver is so sweet. #quaranteen

What a lame date idea. #quaranteen

Wake up, Flora! #quaranteen

IS KELSEY EVER GOING TO TALK ABOUT OLIVER AND FLORA KISSING sorry for yelling #quaranteen

I look from Kelsey to Flora's room through the window. I'm so used to seeing her asleep, but when I look closer, I see that her eyes are open. She sees me looking at her and grins.

Kelsey laughs at something on her phone, and I look at her. When I look back at Flora, she's turned over, and her back is to me.

Kelsey looks up from her phone and smiles at me. The late-afternoon sun lights up her hair, her face, and I want to tell her she's beautiful, but I'm too distracted thinking about Flora.

She looks down, and I think, *Next time.*

# 68. FLORA

"Your fever is gone, just like that! Do you think it will come back?" my mom says.

"I'm not a doctor, but I don't think so," I say. I don't know why I say it so sarcastically.

I've taken a shower, my fever is gone, but I'm grumpy. Then Joey comes in, and I feel a little less annoyed about everything.

"You heard the good news about our quaranteen?" he says to my mom.

"Yes, of course." She sniffles.

"Now that she's finally better, you can probably head back to Brooklyn soon like we talked about. I know you need to get back to your brother and nephew."

"Wait, what?" I say. "You're leaving already? And when did you guys talk about this?"

"Well, we've certainly had ample time to talk while you've been asleep." Joey winks at me.

The wink reminds me of my dad, and now I feel even more annoyed. "You know about Randy too? What else did you guys talk about while

I was asleep? Or were you just plotting your escape the entire time?" I look at my mom.

My mom is still sniffling, and she closes her eyes. "Flora, I can't tell you how hard this has been on me."

I don't know why I'm being a pill.

"We were thinking your dad and Goldy could come," my mom is saying.

"Come where?" I ask, distracted.

"Camp Quarantine!" Joey says. "Or should I say, Camp Hashtag Quaranteen. They're looking at tickets, just waiting on the okay from us—from you—to buy them."

"Right, because of course you've been in touch with them too," I say.

Joey either doesn't notice or doesn't care about my sarcastic tone, because he says, "Sure have. They're both so relieved your fever is gone."

"I wish I could stay, Flora, I do," my mom says.

"I know, I'm sorry," I say, and I mean it. "Just . . . do you think *they* need to come?"

"He's your father. She's your . . . stepmom." She tries to smile, but I can still see the grimace.

"I think I'm mad at him," I confess.

"You'll have plenty of time to talk about it when they visit." Joey's cheerfulness usually makes me feel better, but now I feel like I don't want him to know anything else about my family. "And you can find out if they're Team Kelser or Team Floriver."

I have no clue what he's talking about, and I don't feel like finding out. "When are you planning on heading back?" I ask my mom, changing the subject.

"The day after tomorrow."

"Not wasting any time, are you?"

My mom studies my face, and I quickly say "Sorry" again.

"You'll be back in Brooklyn, back home with me, in no time!"

I haven't been awake long enough to think about Brooklyn, about my life outside this hospital room. Nothing could be further from my mind. "Back in Brooklyn?"

"I know we do have deluxe accommodations and gourmet food, but you can't stay forever," Joey jokes.

"I know. I just . . . I don't need to stay longer even though I got sick?"

"You were sick already, that's why you came to the hospital, remember?" Joey says. "Unless you were faking because you wanted to spend more time with Oliver." I look at him, shocked, but he laughs. "I'm kidding. Speaking of, when you've been fever-free for twenty-four hours, we're going to put you guys back in the same room again."

"Really?!" I say, more excitedly than I expected. "I mean . . . that soon?"

"Yep. Since your biggest symptoms were fatigue and a fever and a sore throat with no cough, you have a low risk of spreading any germs."

"We'll be roommates again?" I say, still letting the news sink in.

"Together again," Joey sings, loud and off-key. "Oh, one thing: You'll have to wear a face mask for the first forty-eight hours you're in the same room again. But it'll be long gone by the time you go home in fourteen days."

"Wow, you're already counting down the days?" I try to sound like I'm joking, but I know Joey must hear the hurt in my voice.

"Not at all. I'm a numbers kind of guy, especially with my patients."

*His patients. I'm his patient.*

"But, hey, still—no kissing Romeo again while you're here. Not that you would, since he's spoken for and all." He winks.

"Right," I say with tight lips.

"See you later." He salutes me, then leaves the room.

"Isn't it great news?" my mom says eagerly. "You'll be back in your own bedroom before you know it."

"Yeah, great," I say, distracted. I'm looking in Oliver's room.

My mom is watching my face, and I think maybe it *will* be good to have my mostly oblivious dad and Goldy here.

"So what time is your flight?"

"In the late afternoon, after your second visiting hour. Then your dad and Goldy will be here the next morning!"

I can tell she's trying to muster some enthusiasm, which I know can't be easy, so I say, "Cool."

"You might want to think about looking at your phone, checking out stuff online," my mom says hesitantly.

"Why?" I'm feeling grumpy again.

"There's . . . a lot to catch up on."

"With what?"

"Well, that hashtag thing of yours really took off!"

"It did? People are still talking about that?"

"Why don't you see for yourself?" She hands me my phone, and I look at it for the first time in almost two weeks.

She wasn't kidding.

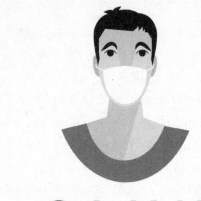

# 69. OLIVER

Flora's mom leaves her room, and my mom leaves a minute later. They change out of their hazmat suits and walk down the hallway together.

It's kind of cool how our moms have become friends. Maybe they'll hang out when we all get back to Brooklyn. Maybe we'll all hang out together. Go to Prospect Park together, go to our favorite restaurants together. It's a weird *Brady Bunch* thing to think.

I think about the fluffy blueberry pancakes at the diner down the street from my apartment. How one time I found a hair in my food, but I pulled it out and ate the rest of the pancakes—that's how good they are.

I feel my stomach rumble. Now I'm craving hairy pancakes.

I look across the hallway, and Flora is still awake. She's sitting up in bed, with her phone in her hand.

I wonder if she's catching up on the hashtag. I hope she's not mad that I told people how she was doing. It was probably a stupid thing to do. I wonder if it's too late to delete the post. I wonder if she's seen what everyone is saying about the kiss. Our kiss.

I'm fiddling with my phone, feeling embarrassed for posting stuff about her, when Joey suits up and walks in.

"Enjoy your last day in solitary confinement," he says as he does his vitals checks.

"Huh?"

"You and Flora will be reunited tomorrow," he says, writing down the results.

"Really? How?"

"The same way we took you out. On a stretcher."

"That's not what I meant." I'm not sure what I meant. "I just, I didn't know we'd be roommates again."

"Well, now you do. You'll be roommates again tomorrow."

"I wonder what Kelsey will think about that," I say, mostly to myself.

But of course Joey overhears. "I do too." He grins evilly. "*Hasta luego*. That means—"

"I know what it means! I'm half Mexican!" I snap.

But he's already out the door.

I look across the hall again to Flora, who is still on her phone. Does she know that we'll be roommates again?

Roommates again. Quaranteens together again. Oh god. Does this mean Flora and I will be expected to post stuff? The followers are ruthless. So far I've been letting Kelsey do most of the work. Even the update about Flora was mostly written by Kelsey. Team Kelser. What about when I'm part of Team Floriver again?

I start a text to Flora, but don't know what to say. I never know what to say.

# 70. FLORA

Even though Oliver is only getting moved across the hall, it's quite the process to transfer him. He's in the same kind of stretcher that we came to the hospital in, and his eyes look just as bugged out as they did then.

I watch from my bed as the nurses and doctors wheel him in past me over to the window, and unzip him. He starts to get off the stretcher himself, but one of the nurses pushes him back down. He says, "Oh, sorry, right," and lies down again, blushing.

They transfer him to the bed, and one of the nurses makes a few notes, then they wheel the stretcher out of the room.

We're alone.

He hops off the bed. He's smiling at me, and his face crinkles up, and looking into his eyes, I somehow feel safe. He looks so healthy and . . . awake. Even though I'm not sick anymore and I'm showered, I still feel self-conscious of my hair, which looks weird and flat. I gingerly touch the mask on my face.

I don't have a fever, but I still feel poisonous.

It's so good to see him. I missed him so much.

He has a girlfriend. Who I helped him win over.

He's still looking at me.

"Um . . . hi," I finally say. "You new here?"

He chuckles. "I am! Can you show me around?"

I smile at him. Resist the urge to hug him, touch him in any way. The distance between us feels like it's buzzing with electricity.

He has a girlfriend.

"I'm sure you're tired of everyone asking you how you're feeling . . ."

"Ha, tired," I say.

"What? Oh, ha."

He's looking into my eyes, and I think of that thing I told him from the girl handbook—about looking into girls' eyes—and wonder if he's following that advice with Kelsey.

"How's Kelsey?" I ask at the same time that he asks, "I'm so sorry you got sick."

There's an awkwardness, a tension, that I don't remember from before, and it's so weird to be in the same room as him again.

We both look at each other, waiting for the other person to speak.

"How's your *girlfriend*?" I finally say.

I hate that he blushes. "She's good. That hashtag was pretty genius, by the way. Did you catch up on all the posts? Probably helps that Kelsey updates all the time. All the time!" His voice gets a bit loud. "I put up some stuff about you too. I hope that was okay. People were worried. Oh, and you really knew what you were talking about with that girl hand-book thing. That stuff worked." He's talking really fast.

"I'm sorry I wasn't able to give you more tips before I got sick. I'm sure I'll be able to think of more now that I can stay awake for longer than five minutes. Though it sounds like you don't need any more tips and are doing fine without me."

"I'm not," Oliver says quickly.

"Not what?"

"Doing fine."

"Oh? Why is that?"

"I've been worried about you," he says.

I wasn't expecting that, and clearly Oliver wasn't either, judging by the look on his face.

I'm surprised, but also annoyed. He wasn't the sick one. He has no idea what this is like. He's got a girlfriend, and I was stuck in bed with algae mouth.

"I'm sorry this has been hard on you," I say more sarcastically than I mean to.

His face crumples. "It has been—"

"I hope you didn't lose any sleep over it. I got enough sleep for the both of us."

"What are you talking—"

"But at least you have your *girlfriend* to take care of you."

"Why do you keep saying that word like that?"

"What, *girlfriend*?" I can't keep the venom from dripping out of my mouth.

Oliver looks hurt, and his face reminds me of our first day in quarantine, back in the warehouse, when quarantine just seemed like it would be like a fancy camping trip. Before I kissed him.

"I thought you'd be happy for me, that I have a girlfriend. I followed the advice you gave me. You're the one who came up with the idea for the girl handbook, the hashtag!" Oliver sputters.

"I know," I say quietly.

"I finally get the girl I've been crushing on for years, and you seem mad about it or something," Oliver says, exasperated.

A reminder of the history he has with Kelsey. All the shared classes, shared teachers, shared hallways. It's a history I'll never be able to have with him.

"Why did you come up with the hashtag? With the idea for the girl handbook? Why did you want to help me?" Oliver asks me, almost accusingly.

The question catches me off guard. "I don't know."

"Just like you don't know why you kissed me?" he says. "Flora, *why* did you kiss me? Not sure if you noticed, but even strangers on the Internet want to know why."

It's the first time he's asked me about the kiss.

I look at him, look right into his eyes. "I wanted to do something nice," I admit.

I don't know if I mean the kiss or the girl handbook or the hashtag or what I mean, but it feels too scary to clarify. And too exhausting.

But just like before, just like always, our conversation is interrupted by a visitor. Kelsey.

"Honey, I'm home!" she says, breezing in, only looking at Oliver. "Just like old times, being back in this room." She finally looks at me. "And Sleeping Beauty is awake!"

I'm thinking what I should say to her, but I feel like my brain has turned to molasses. Everything feels so slow, so sluggish.

I finally decide I should try to laugh, but it's too late; she's pulling Oliver to his side of the room. "I need to keep my patient healthy!" she says over her shoulder. "My *boyfriend*, that is." She smiles at me, but there's nothing genuine about the smile at all. She pulls the curtain closed. Then I hear her spray something in the air, and I realize by the smell that it's disinfectant spray.

She's talking to Oliver about the hashtag, about all the attention they're getting online, and there is a tiny part of me that wonders if Kelsey actually likes Oliver, or if she likes the attention. I squash the thought down in my brain, though, and remind myself I did the right thing, that Oliver has the girl of his dreams.

# 71. OLIVER

"I think we should live-tweet our date to Coney Island," Kelsey says.

"Yeah, sure."

"And don't worry if you don't win me any stuffed animals. I know those things are rigged."

"Yeah, sure."

"Maybe we should do the Wonder Wheel a few times, just to make sure we get really good pictures. What if we do it thirty times to commemorate how long you're in quarantine?"

"Yeah, sure."

"Oliver, are you listening to me?"

I am. Sort of.

I keep thinking about the way Flora said the word *girlfriend*. It was like she tasted something gross and was spitting it out.

I keep thinking about what she meant by *something nice*. Was she talking about kissing me? Why would she think that'd be a nice thing to do? It *was* a nice kiss, even if it wasn't what I ever would have guessed in a million years my first kiss would be like. Memorable, that's for sure. Just like Flora is. Memorable. Unforgettable. Like no one I've ever met before . . .

"Oliver?" I realize Kelsey is talking.

"Err, sorry, can you say that last part again?"

"What last part? I just said like a million things."

I laugh nervously. Busted.

"Well, the *most* recent thing I said was that thirty trips around the Wonder Wheel will cost two hundred and forty dollars. That's expensive."

"Expensive?"

"I mean, we can split it maybe. This is the twenty-first century, after all. Or maybe we could do a crowd-funding thing."

"Um, let's think about it. It's still a while away."

"Um, not really! You're getting out of quarantine in less than two weeks. We should go on this first date as soon as possible, don't you think? Before interest in the quaranteens dies down."

Less than two weeks. It feels like an eternity and like no time at all. I've just gotten put in the same room as Flora again, and already I need to start counting down the nights until I'm not sleeping next to her every night, listening to her breathe.

Though, based on our last conversation, I bet she's counting down the seconds until she gets to go home—and gets to run away from me.

# 72. FLORA

It's weird to have a roommate again. It's weird that Oliver is my roommate again. It's weird that things already feel weird with us. Again. Still.

But I'm still really tired and fall asleep fast that night without talking to Oliver again. When I wake up the next morning, my watch says it's almost 9:00 a.m. I slept twelve hours. I wonder if this is how I'll feel for the rest of my life. Always completely exhausted and like I can sleep for half a day and still be tired.

I feel my eyes close again and then my mom is here. "Morning, Flora. You still feeling okay?" she asks, a worried look on her face.

"Yeah," I say. "Just tired."

"Okay. Joey had said you probably would be for a few days. I wish I could stay longer. You understand I need to get back to your uncle and Randy, right? He's never been alone with Randy for this long. I'm not sure what I was thinking."

"You were thinking about me," I say. "You were thinking about getting to your sick daughter in quarantine. Mom, cut yourself some slack."

My mom smiles. "I can tell you're feeling better. You're making *me* feel better."

I brush it off. "Well, it's true. Randy will be okay. Will *you* be okay? I think you should get a massage. Or have brunch with your friends." For some odd reason, I almost suggest that she have brunch with Oliver's mom sometime, but I have no clue where that idea comes from.

She laughs. "Yes, *Mom*."

"Can't pour from an empty cup," I say, grinning at her. My mom loves saying hokey old clichés just to annoy me.

"Don't look a gift horse in the mouth," she says.

"The grass is always greener on the other side."

"It's definitely greener outside quarantine. Especially since there is no grass in here to begin with," Joey says, stepping into the room.

I forgot about Joey's dimples. The butterflies that I was too exhausted and sick to feel before are back.

"That's a dad joke," I say.

"I'm not a dad," Joey says.

"No, I know. I just . . . it's so cheesy, I meant it's a dad joke. Because dads always tell cheesy jokes."

I hear Oliver laughing on the other side of the curtain, but Joey just stares at me.

"Never mind," I say. "Let's make sure my temperature is still normal."

"Good idea," Joey agrees, moving on.

He puts the thermometer in my mouth and it beeps. "You're good," he says, looking at the results.

My mom beams. "Thank you." She tries to clasp Joey's hand, but he's writing on his ever-present clipboard.

He looks up, distracted. "No need to thank me. Thank the virus for getting out of your daughter's body. That was a wild ride, huh?"

"So wild," I say. How could I have forgotten about his dimples?

"See you on the flip side. Or in a couple hours."

"That's another dad joke!" I say.

He looks confused again, and I hear Oliver laugh a second time. Joey salutes me, then opens the curtain to Oliver's side of the room. "What's so funny, Romeo?" But I can tell he's trying to be lighthearted, buddy-buddy, since Oliver's mom is there.

I don't hear a response, and then realize Joey must have put the thermometer in his mouth when I hear beeping.

"Well, what does it say?" Oliver's mom says impatiently.

"Your son remains healthy. Normal temperature. See ya later."

Joey leaves, and I hear his mom say, "I don't like him. I don't care if he's a doctor."

My mom whispers to me, "I don't either." Though I don't know why she's whispering. And I don't know why she doesn't like Joey. She must not have noticed his dimples.

# 73. OLIVER

I hear Flora take a shower after her mom leaves. I smell coconut and mint. It's amazing she can take a shower by herself. A few days ago, I saw a nurse helping her into the bathroom. She's so strong. I wonder if she remembers me telling my mom that I think she's strong right before she got sick. I wonder if she'd be insulted if I told her how strong she is again. I wonder if she'd be insulted if I told her a lot of the things I like about her.

I hate that our conversation from yesterday wasn't finished. I hate that I can't figure out why she was being weird about Kelsey. I hate that I have a girlfriend and I feel more confused about girls than ever.

I hear Flora go back to her bed and flip on the TV. I want to talk to her. I *need* to talk to her.

Two soap operas later, I finally say timidly, "Uh, Flora?"

She doesn't say anything. Maybe she's asleep? Maybe she's ignoring me? Maybe she has earbuds in?

I pick up my phone and fiddle with it nervously. I see all the notifications about Kelsey's latest post on her #favquaranteen, her #untouchableboyfriend.

And all the #quaranteen posts.

**I thought Flora was better. Where is she? #quaranteen**

**Enough of Kelser, I want Floriver! #quaranteen**

I send her a text: r u awake?

She writes back: No. Sound asleep.

I laugh.

Then wait.

Finally, I type: can I come over?

If you want.

My mom ordered some new clothes for me online. But after wearing hospital gowns for so long, it feels weird to be wearing normal clothes again. There's so much more to worry about, keeping buttons buttoned, zippers zipped, everything unwrinkled.

I stand up, smooth my jeans, zip up my hoodie halfway, then unzip it again. Even when I'm in a hospital room, I can't pull off the loungey casual look without looking and feeling like a doofus.

I open the curtain a little bit, start to walk through, realize I need to open it more, and step back to my side of the room. I pull on the curtain, but too hard, and I accidentally fling it open.

Flora looks up at me from her bed. "Well, that was dramatic," she says.

The curtain is still swinging behind me and I put a hand on it to stop the swaying.

"So, what's up?" I try to say casually, but there is nothing casual about me.

"I dunno. You texted me."

"Oh, right." *Ask her why she was being weird about Kelsey*, I tell myself.

It's just like my fantasies and daydreams about Kelsey all over again. I've spent all this time imagining how things will be—how I want them to be—and now she's awake and it's different from what I thought and the girl of my daydreams is different from the girl in front of me. Except this is Flora, not Kelsey.

"You're really feeling better?" I ask.

"That's the word on the street," she says.

I want to talk to her about Kelsey, tell her I'm confused about Kelsey, and maybe she is too and that's why she got weird about her yesterday.

She feels so unreachable, though. She looks at me expectantly. I stare into her eyes, following the advice she gave me about looking into girls' eyes.

"What are you doing?" Flora jumps and looks away.

I'm confused. "Just looking at you?"

"Well, it's creepy."

I want to tell her that looking into her eyes was one of the things she told me girls love, but she's giving me a dirty look.

"You're still doing it."

"I just wanted you to know I was listening to you."

"Well, I wasn't saying anything. And you looked like you wanted to eat my soul."

Just then, Joey comes in, and I'm half-relieved to see him, to put an end to this awkwardness that I can't figure out.

He gives me a side-eye, but I see Flora blushing while she looks at him. "Hi," she says to him warmly. Much more warmly than she's been speaking to me.

"Don't let your girlfriend see you over here. Rumor is that she's the jealous type."

They both laugh, and I say, "No she's not! Wait, who told you that?"

"Uh, just look at the Internet, dude," Joey says. "She's obsessed with you! And your relationship."

He sits on Flora's bed and I stand there, sputtering, not sure what I should do. Should I stay? He's only going to check her vitals. But he is a doctor. Or sort of a doctor or whatever. Maybe I should leave. Do you say bye if you're only walking back to your side of the room, which is separated by a curtain? Forget the girl handbook, I need a quarantine etiquette handbook.

Joey makes the decision for me and says, "Do you mind, Romeo? A little patient confidentiality."

"Right." I go back to my side of the room. This time I don't have any problems with the curtain.

It's only after I sit on my bed while I hear them talking and laughing that I realize there really isn't such a thing as patient confidentiality when we're sharing a hospital room in quarantine. I also realize they're talking about pizza, and not about anything medical.

He stays with Flora until her mom arrives, and I remember that her mom is leaving tonight and her dad and Goldy are coming tomorrow. I should have talked to Flora about that. Be a listening ear or whatever, because as much as my mom drives me nuts, I know I'd be sad if she had to leave. Maybe I can talk to her again after Kelsey leaves. Not that I'll feel any more comfortable around her then.

I don't understand why it's suddenly so hard for me to talk to her.

Kelsey is only a couple of minutes late this time, so she doesn't apologize. Based on my calculations, I've noticed that if she's less than five minutes late, she doesn't apologize. Six minutes and seven minutes are questionable, but anything eight and over she'll apologize for profusely. Sometimes her cab drivers get lost, sometimes the elevator is slow. Sometimes she "loses track of time" at her uncle's house, or on the beach.

I miss worrying about being late for things. Actually *going* somewhere—going outside.

"How are you?" Kelsey says. "How's my boyfriend? Can I get you anything?"

She says the same thing every time now, so I say the same thing every time now too. "I'm good, thanks."

Then she looks at her phone, and I look at my phone, and I try not to think about Flora and what Flora is thinking about, which seems impossible.

# 74. FLORA

"So I've been in touch with your teachers. They said they want to work with you on a schedule that supports your health needs," my mom tells me during her next visit. Her last visit.

I think that my health needs include not having schoolwork mentioned while I'm still in the hospital, but I keep my mouth shut.

"And maybe we should think about hiring a babysitter for Randy while you get back on your feet."

Randy. I miss my cousin. I miss taking care of him.

"Can I think about it, Mom? I feel like taking care of him again would probably be the thing that makes me feel the most normal."

"Sure, of course, honey."

"Thanks, Mom," I say. "For everything."

My mom hugs me. I still haven't gotten used to hugging someone in a hazmat suit. I kind of feel like I'm hugging a giant pillow.

She pulls back, looks at me, hugs me again. "I'm going to miss you so much," she says.

"Me too." I'm trying and failing not to cry.

She tries to brush my tears away, but her giant gloves feel clumsy against my face.

"I'm so sorry," I say.

"Honey, I told you, don't apologize for getting sick. It's not your fault. *I'm* the one who still feels guilty."

"Please, please don't feel guilty anymore, Mom," I beg. *"Please."* The guilt I feel for everything I've put her through bubbles up my body and hurts more than any of the aches I had while I was sick.

My mom gives me a worried look. "Are you sure it's okay that I'm going back?"

"Yes," I say, fighting the tears. I feel my bottom lip quivering and I bite it so hard I'm afraid I'll taste blood.

I hear Kelsey leave, which means my mom will be leaving soon, leaving me in quarantine. And I'm going to see my dad's new wife, who I supposedly shouldn't hate. Because she invited me to visit them, not my own father. Who basically ignored me the entire time I visited him. And somehow when they leave I'll just go back to Brooklyn and back to school like none of this ever happened, like I'm the same Flora I always have been and always will be. Except now I'm diseased and poisonous and no one will want to touch me with a ten-foot pole.

And Oliver will be here through it all, with his girlfriend by his side. His girlfriend, whose intentions I'm still having my doubts about.

I bite my lip again, think I actually taste blood.

My mom is wrapping her pillow arms around me again, and I don't know why we're both trying not to cry. We're doing a terrible job at the "trying" part.

"I love you so much. I'll talk to you every day. Every day! You'll be sick of me by the time you get home."

"Never," I say, and I mean it.

"Remember everything we talked about with your dad and Goldy, okay?"

I nod, wiping my tears.

She gives me one last huge hug, and then she leaves. She removes her hazmat suit and throws it in the bin. Then she comes around to my window and puts her hand on the glass.

I put my hand on the glass too, but already she is so far away from me.

# 75. OLIVER

I hear sniffling on Flora's side of the room. She sounded so upset saying bye to her mom.

I want to comfort her, but she also seems like the kind of girl who doesn't want to be comforted when she's crying. Though I don't know why I think that. I could send her a text again, but even that seems too invasive, too much of a reminder of what tight quarters we're in, how little privacy we have. I bet she misses having a room to herself. The last thing I need to remind her of is how close she is to me. And yet I can't help but resent how far away she feels.

I decide to give her what little bit of privacy I can offer, and I take a really long shower. It's quiet on Flora's side of the room again when I get out, and this time I'm pretty sure she's asleep.

She wakes up and clicks on the TV just before my mom arrives.

"My Oliver!" she says. I feel guilty that she's here.

"Hi, Mom."

"How's she doing?" I can tell my mom is trying to speak quietly, but quiet isn't a volume that really exists for her, so I'm sure Flora can still hear her.

"Um, she's okay." Though I actually have no idea how she's doing.

"I can't imagine how lonely she must be, poor girl," she says loudly.

"Mom!" I hiss.

"I mean, can you imagine if I left you? And you weren't even sick!"

"MOM!"

"Poor girl," she says again, shaking her head.

"She's healthy now, and she's strong. She's always been strong."

My mom looks at me, surprised. "I don't doubt that one bit. She and her mom have not been dealt an easy hand. If anyone can go through everything she's been through and come out on top, it's that girl." She jabs her finger at the curtain.

Now I'm the surprised one. Usually my mom spends her visits gossiping about our neighbors in our building.

She looks at my surprised face and laughs. "I'm a mom. I notice these things. But I can't say the same thing about your social media girlfriend."

I should shush her, but I don't.

My mom looks at me expectantly. I wonder if she's asked me a question and I totally spaced out while she was talking. Wouldn't be the first time. "Well?" she finally says.

"Well what?"

"Aren't you going to defend your girlfriend the way you defended Flora?"

"Oh, right. Kelsey is strong too. I know it can't be easy dating someone in quarantine," I say half-heartedly.

"Uh-huh," she says, unconvinced. Finally she says, "Follow your heart."

"What does that mean?"

She just smiles at me and says vaguely, "You'll see."

My mom moves on, going back to building gossip, and I listen to Flora flipping channels. And I keep wondering how she really is doing.

After my mom leaves, I pace around my side of the room, my phone in my hand. Finally, I type, Are u ok?

Then I promptly stick my phone under my pillow so I don't have to feel how it's not vibrating a response.

I pace more, then give in and grab my phone. I have a text, but it's from Kelsey, my girlfriend. Which should make me happy. Thrilled. But it doesn't.

We text back and forth, and I keep hiding my phone, and then I finally have a message from the person I want to hear from, but it's not the message I'm hoping for. Just Yep, fine. Good night.

Except she doesn't go to sleep. Because she posts for the first time.

**Feeling much better. Thanks for the support, everyone. #quaranteen**

She includes a selfie too, with her mask on her face, and I can see our curtain off to the side. I have the feeling of being in a parallel universe again.

There's a link to her Instagram, and I slap my palm to my head so hard that it hurts. I had no clue she had an Instagram account, which is dumb, because of course she does.

I don't know why, but I feel nervous when I click on her Instagram link. I look away, look down at my phone again, and my phone screen is filled with pictures Flora took.

She feels so close but I miss her. There are pictures of the friends I saw on FaceTime, pictures of who I guess must be Randy. And so many pictures of a little garden in her neighborhood. I feel like I'm invading

her privacy for some reason, like she'd be annoyed if she knew I was looking at pictures of her, so I go back to her post.

She's back! #quaranteen

#TeamFloriver at last! #quaranteen

Flora! We need to know about the kiss! #quaranteen

I still don't think she was ever sick. #quaranteen

WHY/WHEN/HOW DID YOU KISS? #quaranteen

# 76. FLORA

I toss and turn all night. Maybe I've overdosed on sleep from being sick, or maybe I miss my mom. Maybe I feel icky about my post. When I post on Instagram, I usually stick to pictures of things. Things that aren't my face. Even though the mask covers most of my face and I'm feeling better, I'm still self-conscious. I remember all too well what I looked like when I first got sick and I feel like I will forever have dark circles under my eyes. Like I'll always look and feel diseased. Poisonous.

And it just feels so . . . fake. Not real. Even though it *is* real. But how can I possibly convey the smell of the hospital room, the sound of Oliver rustling around in his sleep, the urge to breathe fresh air, in a post online that a bunch of strangers are going to look at? I came up with the idea for the quaranteen hashtag because I wanted to help Oliver get the girl of his dreams. I didn't expect so many people to be interested. I didn't expect Kelsey would get so much attention—*enjoy* so much attention.

And I didn't expect anyone to find out about our kiss. Our kiss that I can't stop thinking about. Our kiss that I bet Oliver wishes had never happened.

Or maybe I can't sleep I because I have no idea what I'm going to say to my dad or Goldy in the morning. I'm still mad at Dad. I still don't understand him. I still don't know what I think about Goldy.

Why didn't he invite me to come see him? Why did my mom and Goldy have to be the ones to think of it? What if they *hadn't*? Would he have just gone on with his life until one day he didn't even remember me anymore? Until that part of his brain, those brain cells, just died, and I might never have even existed?

When I wake up in the morning, my eyes feel sandy like they do when I've stayed up too late studying.

I look at my phone, feel creeped out by all the strangers talking about me, analyzing me, analyzing my face, asking me questions. Creeped out and still . . . fake. These people don't know anything about me. The real me. They don't know that my favorite food is grilled cheese, that I hate raisins, that I broke my wrist in second grade, that I'm afraid of swimming in the ocean. I don't know how to channel any of this me-ness into a picture, but I also don't think I want to anyway.

I put my phone down, feeling itchy and restless again, and I head to the bathroom. I play with my hair, make faces at myself, see what my mad face looks like. Oliver's right, my nose does wrinkle when I get mad. How have I never noticed that in sixteen years?

Oliver.

I really miss talking to him. I shouldn't have been so mean to him in the text last night. It's not his fault my parental situation is confusing and weird. Not like his is exactly easy either. I did miss a lot when I was sick and sleeping, but I still don't know where his other parent is. If he has another parent. He said something about it being just his mom when we were at the warehouse, but there's been no other mention of anyone, almost like a second parent doesn't exist or never existed.

I wonder if my dad wishes I didn't exist.

I go back to my bed, and see Goldy—not my dad—texted a little while ago to say they're at the airport, about to head over to the hospital. Because my stepmom should be the one to tell me that my dad is on his way to visit his daughter in quarantine.

I text Oliver: Sorry. Tough night.

It's only a little after 8:00, and it's quiet on his side of the room, but he writes back: No worries.

I'm thinking about what to write back to him, but then: Here if you want to talk.

I feel my heart flutter a little in my chest. Then I remember, that was something I wanted to put in the girl handbook. *Make yourself available to girls, tell them they can talk to you. And mean it.*

Is he practicing a move from his *own* girl handbook on me? *He has a girlfriend*, I remind myself.

I let go of the thought quickly, because I see my dad and Goldy suiting up in the hallway. They both look scared. And not like Kelsey, posing scared, but actually scared. Joey is with them, showing them how to put their hazmat suits on, and my dad keeps missing his armhole.

He wipes his head, and I see that he's sweating.

Finally, he gets the suit on, and Goldy gets hers on too. Joey walks through the antechamber with my dad and Goldy close behind, and then they're in my room.

"Flora!" my dad exclaims. "Is it okay to touch her?" he asks Joey.

"Of course it's okay to touch me," I snap. "Why do you think you're wearing the hazmat suits?"

"There's my Flora Cracker," my dad says, smiling. It's the nickname he gave me when I was in fourth grade and I got in a fight at the playground with some bigger kids who had been making fun of Randy.

He bends down to hug me, but it's the kind of hug you give someone you don't know very well, a friend of a friend after a big group dinner.

Goldy is still standing next to Joey. "You can hug me too," I say in the same hot tone. Everything my mom has told me about her has been relocated to another part of my brain.

Goldy walks over to my bed, and as she gets closer I see she has tears running down her face. She leans over to give me a hug, a real hug.

When she pulls away she says, "We're so glad you're feeling better."

Of course the first thing she says to me is *we*.

"Thanks, me too," I say with tight lips. "Hey, feel free to take a picture. I only have to wear this face mask a few more hours. We're still trending. Maybe you can trend too!"

Goldy looks at me, confused. "I don't want to trend? I posted stuff before because I was worried. Am worried. And I thought maybe you'd feel better knowing how many people cared."

I don't feel like telling her how flawed her logic is, so I don't say anything at all.

Then we all just stand and look at one another. Finally, Joey steps in with the trusty thermometer and blood pressure cuff.

"What does it say?" my dad asks nervously.

"One hundred five."

"What?!" my dad roars.

"Bad hospital joke," Joey says. "Still normal. Enjoy your visit." I want him to stay, to rescue me from Goldy and my dad, but he's already on Oliver's side of the room.

"How's the food here?" Goldy asks. "Did you get the gift basket I sent you? I know you're not gluten free, but it was the only 'healthy' kind I found that could deliver here."

I'm too shocked to say anything, so I don't.

"I think there were chips in there. Healthy chips. I always want salty things when I'm not feeling well," Goldy tries again.

"Thank you," I say.

We look at one another some more. Oliver's mom arrived during Joey's visit, and I hear her telling Oliver about a new orzo recipe she read about online.

"Oh, I love orzo!" Goldy says. "I make it with grilled peppers and feta cheese when I'm feeling especially naughty."

*Because feta cheese is living life on the edge,* I think cruelly. But I don't say anything.

Oliver's mom either doesn't hear or doesn't want to acknowledge what Goldy says because she keeps talking to Oliver.

But Oliver pipes up, "Feta cheese is my favorite kind of cheese."

"Whose favorite cheese is feta?" I say before I can stop myself. Oliver's mom stops talking, and my dad and Goldy are looking at me.

I stomp out of bed, open the curtain, and Oliver and his mom both look startled. "Sorry," I say. "But, seriously, Oliver, feta?"

Oliver smiles. "Yes."

He leans forward, looks through the curtain at my dad and Goldy. "Hello. I'm Oliver."

*When did he get so polite?*

"Kenneth," my dad says, standing up. He sticks his hand through the curtain, shakes hands with Oliver. "This is my wife, Goldy."

"Well, good, everyone has had a chance to meet each other!" I say shrilly, pulling the curtain shut again.

"Um, Flora, did you forget about me?" Oliver's mom says from the other side of the curtain.

Everyone laughs, but I just want to put in my earbuds and dance around and try not to kick a door again.

"Nice to meet you!" Goldy says, tilting her head back to angle her voice over the curtain.

"Likewise!" Oliver's mom says.

Everyone laughs again, and even though I'm still annoyed, somehow the tension in the room is gone because of feta cheese.

And Oliver.

# 77.OLIVER

"What's your favorite kind of cheese?" I ask Kelsey later, during her daily visit.

She's been in my room for almost twenty minutes, and it's the first thing I've said to her in almost as long.

At first, I think she doesn't hear me because she doesn't look up from her phone and doesn't say anything.

I open my mouth to ask her again when she asks, "Who has a favorite kind of cheese? Are you talking about to go on a pizza? A sandwich? What's the context?"

"Oh, there is no context. I was just wondering if you had a favorite kind of cheese."

"Oh, okay." She looks disappointed. But she finally glances up from her phone. "I thought it was related to our date. Or maybe a game you wanted to play."

"A game about cheese?"

"I don't know."

"Yeah, me neither."

We both go back to our phones again.

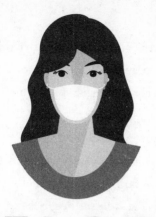

# 78. FLORA

My dad and Goldy have only been here for one whole day—three visits—and it already feels like three hundred. They don't have tickets home yet, "just in case," they say, but I want to tell them to just go home already. I can't imagine another ten days of visits with them.

After everything my mom told me, there is so much I want to say to both of them, especially my dad, but I don't, and it feels like my spring break all over again with us watching TV and talking but not about anything important. I feel like I'm intruding on them, like I'm an outsider in my own family, like I don't fit in.

I'd almost rather listen to Oliver and his girlfriend. Almost.

Visiting hours are over for the day, so I turn on the TV, flip through the channels, but everything seems too loud, even with the volume off. I keep the news channel on for a bit, and there is a shot of a hospital, and I realize it's the hospital we're in. I turn the TV off. I don't feel like hearing any more strangers talk about me.

I touch my face, feel how naked it is without the mask. It's weird how I got used to feeling it on my face.

I pick up my phone, and it's more strangers taunting me, asking about the kiss. Floriver. They really couldn't think of a better name? Not that it matters, because Kelsey has made sure the entire Internet knows that Oliver is her boyfriend. I look under my curtain and see Oliver's socked feet pacing the room.

I text him, What are you doing?

A few minutes later, he responds, Not much. You?

Which doesn't necessarily make sense, but I'll take it. I pull open the curtain, and Oliver has the same startled look on his face as when my dad and Goldy met him and his mom.

Before he can say anything, I plop myself down in the chair on his side of the room. "Are you busy?" I ask.

He looks around. "I think I can fit you in."

I laugh. "You sure? You sure you don't need to track down some feta?"

He laughs now. "It's a good cheese!"

"Why are we still talking about cheese?"

"You brought it up," he reminds me.

"Actually, *you* brought it up the first time," I tell him.

He scratches his chin. "You sure about that? It might have been—"

"God, she's just such a bimbo . . . and she's my stepmom," I interrupt.

"Goldy," Oliver finishes.

"Just don't say her name."

"Whose?" Oliver says, grinning at me.

I almost answer him, then close my mouth again. "She's awful, isn't she?"

"Actually . . . I didn't think so at all. I mean, I only talked to her for a few seconds, but she seems—"

"Please don't say nice."

"Well, I was going to say sweet. But nice too, yeah."

I groan. "Great. You too?"

"Me too what?"

"Another straight male species member won over by my stepmom. Please don't ask me how much older than me she is because it's gross."

"What? No, it's not like that at all."

"What is it like, then?" I realize I'm suddenly getting tired of the conversation.

"Remember what your mom said, though? About it being Goldy's idea for you to visit?"

"How do you know about that?" I say, ice dripping from my voice.

"It was one of the first conversations you and your mom had when she came to visit. Before you got sick."

"You were listening?" I ask, trying to keep my voice from shaking.

"Yeah, I was. I was following your advice. You said being a good listener was important."

"I did? When? What are you talking about?"

"In the girl handbook."

He looks so confused, so earnest, and I finally say, "There's a difference between listening and eavesdropping. I said being a good listener is important. I meant when the girl is talking to you, when she *wants* to talk to you, wants you to know things. Not when you're stuck in quarantine together and you're eavesdropping on a deeply personal family conversation."

His face falls, and I can tell I've hurt him. "I was just trying to help," he says softly.

I'm reminded of when my mom told me everything about my dad and Goldy, and I had the odd sensation of wanting to know that Oliver was listening, of wanting him to know all these things about me. And he did listen, and I didn't even tell him to, and now his feelings are hurt. Again. Because of me.

"Thank you," I say, touching his arm.

"For what? Being lousy at following instructions? For messing up the girl handbook, even when the author is my roommate?"

"Wait, messing up the girl handbook? What are you talking about?"

Oliver's face turns red. "Um, nothing."

"I don't think you need any more help. You've got it pretty well memorized, judging by social media. It's super clear to everyone that you have a girlfriend!" I wonder if my voice sounds as loud to Oliver as it does to me. I'm trying really hard again to squash the voice in the back of my head that is telling me maybe Kelsey likes the attention more than Oliver.

"Err, that's right," Oliver says. But his face is getting redder.

"Why did you bring up the girl handbook?" I ask.

"Nothing! I just . . . forgot."

"Forgot what?"

"It's nothing."

"You already said that. It's obviously something. Not nothing." I realize how ridiculous I sound.

"Can you let it go, please?" Oliver begs.

"What am I letting go?"

Oliver's face is getting redder by the second, and he wipes his forehead. He crosses his arms over his chest. I'm stressing him out, and I don't know why it's all bugging me so much.

"I'm going to bed," I say abruptly, getting up.

"Um, it's only nine o'clock. Are you feeling okay?" But Oliver looks relieved.

"I'm *fine*!" I say more forcefully than I intend to. "I mean, thank you."

"You're welcome."

But I can tell he doesn't know what I'm thanking him for, and I'm not entirely sure either.

He fans his face, and I go back to my side of the room. I wonder why after talking with Oliver I feel both better and more confused about everything.

# 79. OLIVER

Kelsey texted to say she would be late, and she doesn't get to my room until 2:25.

"I'm so sorry I'm late!" she says when she arrives. "The appointment took forever!"

"Appointment? For what?" I'm confused.

"Um, my hair! I cut off like six inches!"

Now that she mentions it, her hair does look a little different. "Oh, it's just hard to see under the hazmat suit," I say.

"Gee, Oliver, you sure know how to make a girl feel special!"

"No, I'm sorry. It looks . . . nice."

"Nice, great," she says. "I didn't even put anything up on Instagram because I wanted to show you first. I can tell *that* was a waste."

"I'm sorry," I say lamely.

Flora is talking to her dad and stepmom about tacos, but I wonder if she's listening to what we're saying.

I rack my brain to think of any tips Flora gave me that can make this any better, but then I think about the girl handbook and what I said to

Flora last night. I feel my face getting hot just thinking about almost telling her I'm trying the girl handbook out on her.

I look out the window, and when I look back at Kelsey she's glaring at me.

"I'm sorry," I say again. "I think I need to get my vision tested. Or maybe my brain tested. It really does look . . . cute."

I must have said the right word, because Kelsey doesn't look so mad anymore. "I forgive you," she says. "But don't you want to know why I got my hair cut in the first place?"

I figured she got her hair cut because it was too long, but something tells me I shouldn't say that. "I would love to hear why you got your hair cut."

"For you! For us! It's our sixteen-day anniversary! Since we're both sixteen years old it's a really special anniversary."

And then she's next to me with her phone in her hand, taking a selfie. She looks at the picture, looks at me, says, "Maybe you could post the picture? Seems like I'm always posting everything, doesn't it?"

It *seems* that way because it *is* that way. But I say, "Good idea."

She texts me the picture of my doofusy face, and I try to write a post but I don't know what to say. I know I shouldn't ask Kelsey, though, whose eyes I can feel searing into my head. Finally I write **Happy sixteen-day anniversary. #quaranteen** and hit TWEET.

Kelsey's phone dings, and she smiles, looking satisfied. I'm relieved that I passed her test. The Internet's test. We watch the comments roll in.

**Kelser Forever. #quaranteen**

**Sixteen days? Who celebrates sixteen days? #quaranteen**

Cute hair! #quaranteen

Totally, totally getting my hair cut like that tomorrow. #quaranteen

Oliver is surrounded by two beauties. Can I go to #quaranteen too?

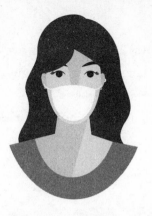

# 80. FLORA

My dad and Goldy are going on and on about a new juice they want to try, and I'm listening to Oliver and Kelsey, thinking I need to give him more girl handbook tips. Though I'm still so confused about what he said last night about messing up the girl handbook. He hasn't messed it up with Kelsey at all, that's for sure. I can hear their phones going off, and I'm sure she's posted a cute picture of them that the Internet is loving.

So what was he talking about? What does he think he messed up? And why was I so mad that he listened to the conversation I had with my mom, when at the time I *wanted* him to hear it?

He was probably confused. Kind of like I'm confused now.

I look at my phone while my dad and Goldy talk. Oliver posted something. I'm surprised. Surprised and . . . something feels weird in my stomach. I look more closely at the picture. How did Oliver not notice her haircut right away? And did Kelsey only get the haircut for Oliver . . . or for all her followers?

I run my fingers through my hair, pick at my split ends. The last time I got my hair cut was just before Halloween. I wonder if the hospital has a hair stylist they can send in a hazmat suit. Though would I trust someone to use scissors in those gloves?

I pick at more split ends. Not like I need to impress anyone, anyway.

# 81. OLIVER

We still have ten minutes left in our visit, but Kelsey is packing up.

"Where are you going?" I ask.

"Oh, I need to take care of some things," she says.

"Okay."

There's the awkward pause again, but then she smiles and says, "Happy sixteen-day anniversary."

I can't believe we're celebrating a sixteen-day anniversary, but I say, "You too. And I'll make it up to you. For forgetting."

She smiles again. "Oh yeah? How?"

"It'll be a surprise." A surprise. Every time my dad would skip one of his custody weekends with me he'd tell me that next time he saw me he'd have a surprise for me. I never knew if he meant it'd be a gift, or something special we were doing. Because whenever I finally saw him again, he'd never bring it up.

"I like surprises," Kelsey says, and I feel guilty when she smiles even more. She squeezes my hand. "See you tomorrow."

She leaves, and then I hear Flora's dad and Goldy leave, and it's just Flora and me.

It seems so quiet in the room that I think I hear my heartbeat in my ears.

Then Flora's phone makes a video chat ring. I hear her groan, wait a second, then say, "Hi!"

There is a bunch of giggling on the phone, and Flora says "Hi" again, and then the giggling stops and a girl says, "Flora! We thought you were dead!" Followed by more giggling.

"Wow, thanks," Flora says, and the girls keep laughing.

"Sorry," one of them says. "We just ate a bunch of cookie dough and are super hyper."

"Maybe if we get sick we can come to your hospital and stay with you!"

"That doesn't even make sense," Flora says, but the girls are laughing too hard to hear her.

"Why did you call me?"

One of the girls says, "Shut up, I can't hear Flora! What did you say, Flora?"

But there is more giggling, and then it sounds like the phone drops, and then one of the girls says, "She put cookie dough down my shirt!"

There is some more scuffling, then it sounds like running, and the other girl says, out of breath, "Flora, we're so happy you're feeling better. We were going to make these cookies for you as a welcome-home present but we ate all the dough!"

Then there is screaming.

"Sorry we haven't been able to raise you more money. I guess people aren't interested in helping cure a new disease. Maybe because it doesn't make your face look gross or anything."

"Hey, can you kiss me when you get back? I want mono! I'd love to sleep for a few weeks and skip school. That sounds awesome."

Flora sighs. "I have to go now. My doctor will be here soon."

"Ohhh, your doctor. Is he hot?"

"That's such a weird thing to ask. Who cares if her doctor is hot? And why do you assume her doctor is a man?"

"Fair point. But is he? She?"

Another eruption of giggles, but this time they end abruptly, and the call is over.

Flora takes a deep breath, then I see her feet on the floor by the curtain, and then she says, "Sorry, Oliver."

"It's okay," I say quickly. But I don't know why she's apologizing. She told me being a good listener is important, that girls like that, so I say, "Do you want to talk?"

She opens the curtain. "You have no idea."

Her hair is piled on top of her head in one of those crazy bun things that girls seem to know how to do instinctively and that seem super confusing to me. She's in yoga pants and a hoodie and she looks . . . effortlessly beautiful.

I must be looking at her too closely because she plays with the zipper on her hoodie and says, "I can come back later if now isn't a good time."

"No, no, it is. Stay!" I pat my bed. It feels too close, too intimate, but she sits down next to me. Her leg rests against mine.

I look at our legs, feel the warmth.

Flora exhales, and her breath is on my cheek. "I'm sorry my friends are idiots."

"You don't need to apologize to me. I mean, it's not your fault. I mean—"

"No, I just feel bad. They were being so loud and stupid. I wasn't sure if you were trying to . . . rest or anything."

"I'm good. Thank you, though."

"You're welcome."

"Um, are *you* good?" I ask.

Flora exhales again, and I'm so aware of how close her mouth is to me, of her leg still pressing against mine. "Quarantine isn't all I thought it was cracked up to be," she finally says.

"Oh?" I say carefully.

"I thought some distance from my friends, from my family, would be good. But it's just made everything harder, worse." She pauses for a moment. "Oliver, I can't tell you how sorry I am for dragging you into this." She grabs my hand, then lets go quickly.

"You didn't drag me into anything."

Flora laughs. "You are a terrible liar. I one thousand percent dragged you into this. You wouldn't be sitting here in a hospital room if it weren't for me. If it weren't for me . . ." She trails off, her eyes searing into mine. "But look, it got you a girlfriend!" She nudges my arm gently.

"Right, my girlfriend."

It's quiet for a few seconds. My mind is going a million directions, but I say, "Your friends aren't idiots, they're just clueless. There's a difference. They're worried about you but don't know how to tell you, and they have no idea what you've gone through. My friends acted like idiots too after my dad died."

It's the first time I've talked about my dad with Flora. With anyone, actually, besides my mom.

"I'm sorry, Oliver," Flora says quietly.

"It's okay. He was a jerk."

Flora doesn't say anything; she just waits for me to go on. "But I still miss him," I say. "Isn't that stupid?"

"No. Absolutely not. My dad is a jerk sometimes too and I still miss him."

"He doesn't seem like it. My dad really *was* a huge jerk. Like really. Like didn't visit me or keep in touch with me kind of jerk."

I should feel embarrassed to be telling her all this, but I don't.

"I mean, what kind of dad doesn't even call his own son?" I feel tears in my eyes, but I will not cry in front of Flora.

"A jerk. You're right. But you know it's because *he's* a jerk and not because *you're* a jerk, right?"

I nod, afraid that if I speak I really will cry.

"Good. Because you're the opposite of a jerk. You're pretty awesome, actually."

She moves her leg away, and immediately I miss feeling her body so close to mine. My leg is warm from where she was resting against me. *She called me awesome.*

"Thank you," I say carefully, not trusting my own voice. "But we were supposed to be talking about you! Isn't that why you came over?"

"Was it? I don't even know anymore. Maybe we should stop talking about people like my idiot friends and your jerk dad and start talking about awesome people."

"Like me?" I say before I can stop myself.

"Works for me." She smiles.

*She thinks I'm awesome.* "I bet you say that to all the boys you're in quarantine with."

She laughs, throws her head back, and her hair tickles my neck. "Kelsey is one lucky girl," Flora says. She stands up suddenly. "Speaking of, since I'm the author of the handbook, I also think we should probably remind everyone on the Internet that she is your girlfriend. Just in case. Team Kelser, right?"

"Um, right, good idea." But I think that's the last thing I feel like doing. "How do you think we should do that?"

"We could make a video."

"A video?"

"Just to show everyone that we're just roommates. That Kelsey is your girlfriend. How silly Floriver is," Flora says.

"Right. It's silly."

"Totally silly!"

"Right," I say again. "So what kind of video?"

"Oh, *I* have to think of it?" But she's smiling.

"Yeah, aren't you the hashtag manager?"

She wrinkles her nose at me and I laugh, and she just looks madder and wrinkles her nose more. I want so badly to tell her how cute she is.

"So glad you're taking this so seriously, Oliver," she says. But then she smiles at me again. "Well, since we're roommates, why don't we make a video showing our room?"

"That's deep."

"Hey, I don't see you coming up with anything better! Anyway, we can do it tomorrow. I'm sure you probably need to text or chat with Kelsey now. It is your sixteen-day anniversary, after all."

"You heard that?" I say, suddenly feeling embarrassed. Flora smirks at me, and I say, "Girl handbook says to listen, not eavesdrop."

She says, "Touché," and closes the curtain. I hear her laughing on her side of the room. I touch the part of my leg that rested against hers. It's still warm.

# 82. FLORA

I wonder if I can call in sick for my dad and Goldy's visit. It feels like so much is unresolved, and there is so much I want to say and we just talk about stupid things like tacos and juice. Not that I really feel like opening up to Goldy. Even if my mom said she wasn't horrible, it still doesn't mean I suddenly feel comfortable with her or want to bare my soul to her.

So I'm surprised when my dad shows up for a visit alone.

"Where's Goldy?" I ask.

"She thought maybe we could use some alone time."

"Alone time? Why?"

"She feels like we didn't have enough of it when you visited. She wants to spend as much time with you as possible, but she also knows you need time with me too."

"Oh, so you're following her advice again? Doing what she wants? Otherwise she'd be here, and you wouldn't want to spend any alone time with me?"

"Flora, be nice." My dad looks hurt.

I finally explode. "I just don't understand why you didn't invite me to visit you!"

"What are you talking about?"

"It took two different women nagging you to get you to invite your own daughter to see you. And one of them is a woman I don't even like. Didn't even like. I don't know."

"So your mom told you."

"Of course she told me!"

"It's complicated," he says.

"Try me," I challenge him. "I still have eight days here. I think I'll be able to understand this quantum physics by then."

My dad puffs up his cheeks, exhales. "I guess I was scared."

"Scared? Of what?"

"Of your disappointment."

"Why would I be disappointed?"

My dad sighs. "I let you down, Flora. I let your mother down. I said vows in front of family and friends and I broke my promise. And I let myself down."

"Let us down how?"

"I should have tried harder to make it work. I should have given it my everything."

"You think?" I say sarcastically.

My dad shakes his head sadly. "I'm so sorry for any pain I've put you through."

"Well, marrying a blond hottie half your age sure didn't help things any."

My dad looks up at me sharply. "She's your stepmother. She loves you. I know what it looks like, but just give her a chance. You'll see how big her heart is."

"That's not the only thing about her that's big," I mutter.

"What was that, Flora?"

"Nothing."

"Anyway, I was afraid that you'd be disappointed. I felt like such a cliché, such a stereotype. I see other men just like me and their young new wives all the time in our neighborhood, and I realize how pathetic we look. But please trust me, Goldy is different. She loves you. You have no idea how hard this has all been on me."

"Hard on *you*? I swear to god if one more person tells me how hard things have been on them I will flip OUT."

"I'm sorry, Flora. I'm still a dad—still *your* dad—and I'm still allowed to worry."

"You've been worried? I doubt it," I say hotly.

"Of course I have."

"Well, you're also my dad who barely texted me while I've been in quarantine. I heard from Goldy more than I did my own father!"

"I didn't want to bug you. And I thought if Goldy was in charge of being in touch with you, it'd bring you guys closer."

"Well, I'm so glad that Goldy's needs are what's most important to you." Suddenly I'm aware of just how loudly I'm speaking, how quiet it is on Oliver's side of the room. He and Kelsey are both probably on their phones, but still, I bet anything Kelsey is listening to every word and eating it all up. If she records anything about my personal life and puts it on social media . . .

"It's okay, Dad," I say abruptly.

"It is?" He looks confused.

"Yeah, sort of. Maybe we can talk about it later." I gesture to the curtain next to my bed and my dad looks at it, still confused.

"Later as in before you go back to Brooklyn?"

"Yeah, that works. That's still not for a bit."

"It's a little over a week away."

"I know," I say impatiently. "In the meantime, Dad, just—"

He looks at me hopefully. I'm tired of being angry at him, at Goldy, at the world. I might as well make the best of the time I have with him in quarantine.

"I forgot what I was going to say." Which is probably for the best.

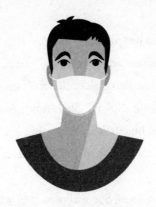

# 83. OLIVER

Kelsey is staring at the curtain between our beds, listening to Flora talk to her dad, and she looks like she wants to stick some popcorn in a microwave.

"So I was thinking more about Coney Island," I mention loudly. But it's useless, she can't tear her ears away.

"I think maybe she's jealous of us," Kelsey whispers.

I give her a horrified look, put my fingers to my lip to shush her. "I don't think she is. I mean, I know she isn't."

"Whatever you say," Kelsey says, not looking away from the curtain.

"It *is* what I say!" I stand up from my bed. "Why do you think that?"

"She seems really mad at her dad and stepmom. Do you think maybe it's misdirected anger at you, at me? She's jealous because we're happy and she's taking it out on them?"

"What are you *talking* about?"

"I dunno, it was just a thought. One of my friends suggested it."

"One of your friends? Or someone on social media?"

"Um, same thing?"

"Right."

Kelsey goes back to her phone.

"She's got a lot going on, you know," I tell her. "And she's been through a lot, besides just being sick. But she's tough and she's strong."

Kelsey looks up at me. "Okay." She sounds bored.

I want to say more, but she's standing up.

"Anyway, it's time for our picture. Come here, boyfriend."

But I don't move.

"All right, I'll go to you!" She walks over to where I'm standing. She puts her arm around me, but I still don't budge.

She snaps some pictures, then walks back to her chair. "Oh, these are perfect!" she says more to herself than to me. She taps her screen, then looks up at me. I still haven't moved.

Kelsey goes back to her phone, and curiosity finally gets the better of me. I check her post: #grumpyquaranteen #socutewhenmad #quaranteen

*She called me cute. Kelsey called me cute. Kelsey is my girlfriend. My girlfriend thinks I'm cute.*

I feel warmth spreading to my cheeks as I look up from my phone, and Kelsey is smiling at me.

"You don't look so grumpy anymore. Still cute, though."

My face feels like it might actually catch on fire. I try to drink water to cool myself down, but my hand is shaking and I spill all over my shirt.

Luckily Kelsey is back on her phone again and doesn't notice.

As the heat leaves my face and I get my hands to stop shaking, I keep repeating in my head, *My girlfriend thinks I'm cute. My girlfriend thinks I'm cute.*

*My girlfriend thinks Flora is jealous of us.*

Flora *did* sound angry, but she also sounded like she had every reason to be.

Still, I can't help but wonder . . . what if Kelsey is right?

# 84. FLORA

My dad and I are watching *The Big Bang Theory*, but all I can think about is who Oliver was talking about when he said "she" is tough and strong.

Maybe his mom? Maybe he was talking about Kelsey in the third person? That would make sense, because then she called him cute. His girlfriend.

*I don't like boys with girlfriends*, I remind myself.

I try to erase my conversation with him last night from my brain. Sitting next to him on his bed, our legs touching, smelling his clean-laundry smell. He has a girlfriend.

I will give him advice on how to be a better boyfriend, but I will not be the girl who listens when he wants to complain about his girlfriend. Not that he needs to complain about her. I will not tell him I'm worried she might be using him, because that is not true. It can't be true. Oliver wouldn't like someone so shallow. I'm being paranoid. And we will make a video that will show everyone on the Internet we are only roommates. That there is no Floriver.

I pick up my phone and look at Kelsey's latest posts. Oliver looks so mad in the recent picture. It's weird that I have no idea why, especially since he's only a few feet away from me.

When we go back to Brooklyn, he's going to get mad and I won't know why then either. I won't know when he showers, brushes his teeth, or when Kelsey visits him.

I won't know anything at all.

# 85. OLIVER

I'm pacing my room again. It's 7:00 p.m.—a time when families are having dinner together, talking about their days together, all the things they did and places they went together. A time when I'm reminded yet again that I haven't left this hospital room, much less the hospital. That I haven't done . . . anything, really.

My phone buzzes, and I have a text from Flora. Want to play Crazy 8s?

Crazy what? I write back.

"Please tell me you've heard of Crazy Eights," Flora says, opening the curtain.

"I have now."

She scowls at me. "I'll deal."

Flora hands me the cards, explains the super simple rules, and we play for two hours. She beats me every single time.

We don't talk much during our games, but the silence feels so much different from the silence I have with Kelsey. It feels . . . comfortable.

At one point, I look up at her and she's brushing her hair from her face, and I remember how I wanted to move a strand of hair off her face when she was sick. I remember how soft her hair is.

I know I have a girlfriend, but looking at Flora, I suddenly feel like it's time to brush up on my girl handbook skills. And it's dumb, but maybe hearing something nice about herself will help after that conversation with her dad.

I look at her as she lays down a two of hearts on my two of clubs.

"What is it?" she asks.

"What is what?"

"You're looking at me funny again."

"Your . . . your teeth are just so big!" I blurt out.

Flora looks at me so coldly I feel the blood drain out of my face. That didn't come out right at all. "What did you just say to me?"

"I meant that—"

"I have buck teeth, right? That's what you meant?"

"No, Flora, not at—"

"Thanks so much for reminding me what I dealt with all throughout elementary school, Oliver. Kids called me Bugs Bunny. But then I got braces in middle school and kids made fun of that, because kids make fun of everything." She jabs at her eyes like she's trying to push tears back in. "Then my mouth finally looked normal in high school, but it doesn't matter because I still go to school with so many of those same stupid kids." She takes a breath, looks at me with tears in her eyes. "And then other stupid kids who didn't even know me have to remind me about it all over again—make me feel ugly all over again."

"Flora, that's not what I meant, I promise!" I spit it out as quickly as I can. "I just meant that your smile is so pretty, it makes your face look big." I didn't say that right either.

"So now my face looks fat too?" Her voice is shaking. "Wow, Oliver, you really know how to make a girl feel special."

Kelsey said the same thing to me. "Wait, I said that wrong!" I say quickly.

"I don't think I want to know what you'd say if you had said it right."

She's got tears in her eyes, and they look like they're about to spill over, and I'm panicking. I wanted to make her feel better, and I've made her feel worse. I've made everything worse. Like I always do.

I exhale loudly. "I meant to say that your smile is really pretty. So pretty that when you're smiling it fills not just your entire face, but your entire body. The entire room, actually. Your smile fills the entire room. Especially when you smile at me."

Flora's mouth drops open.

Just then our door opens and a nurse comes in for a vitals check. She goes to Flora's side of the room and calls for her.

But Flora is still looking at me.

The nurse walks over to my side of the room. "There you are." She rolls her eyes. "Let me get your stats."

She takes Flora's temperature and blood pressure and pulse, and even though I know Flora is recovered I still don't breathe properly while the thermometer is in her mouth. She doesn't tell us the results, so I say, "Well, what was it?"

She rolls her eyes again. "It's normal, just like it has been for the last six days."

"Just making sure," I say defensively.

"Well, thank you, Doctor," she snaps. "Only a teenager and already a man is checking my work," she mutters.

"He didn't mean anything," Flora says kindly. "Neither one of us could do your job. I'd been too sick to say it before, but thank you for taking care of me."

The nurse studies her face, waiting for a punch line, but when there isn't one, she says gruffly, "You're welcome. Glad you're feeling better."

"Thank you," Flora says.

The nurse takes my vitals. When she's done, she starts to walk away, then turns and says, "Your temperature is normal too."

She doesn't wait for either of us to say anything else before she leaves.

"That was nice of you to say that," I tell Flora.

She shrugs. "It's true. I couldn't do her job. A lot of people couldn't do her job. A lot of *doctors* couldn't do her job."

"I guess I haven't really thought what it must be like to be in her shoes. I've seen all these doctors and nurses, and sometimes I almost forget they have a life outside this hospital. Like they have an existence outside these halls. That sounds dumb."

"No, it doesn't," Flora says. "I get it."

"You do? You thanked her. That's not even a thought that has crossed my mind. Then again, you are Flora."

"What does that mean?" She tries to give me a dirty look, but she wrinkles her nose and looks adorable, and I laugh.

Just like before, she tries to give me an even meaner look, but her nose just wrinkles more, and she looks even more adorable, and I laugh even harder.

"Great, now he's laughing at me," Flora says, but she's laughing too.

We laugh together like we've been laughing together forever. And in some ways, in all we've gone through together, it *has* been forever.

And I can't think of anyone I'd rather go through this forever with.

It's not until I go to bed that I realize that we didn't mention anything about the hashtag, about the video we're going to make, about Kelsey.

Not once.

# 86. FLORA

When my eyes pop open, my first thought is that we need to make a video. I owe Oliver, I remind myself. After our usual rounds of morning visits, I text Oliver, Let's make our video, roommate.

He opens the curtain, his cool-breeze eyes are sparkling, and he's smiling. He's probably excited to make it clear to everyone once and for all that we're just roommates. "I'm ready!" he says.

"Great!" I say. "Start filming."

He looks alarmed. "I thought you were going to film."

"Right." I sigh. "And direct. And choreograph. And score. And edit."

"Sounds only fair to me. You're the hashtag creator and girl hand-book author, aren't you?"

"Yeah, but you're my student. Consider this your first test."

"But you didn't give me a chance to study!"

"Then this will be even better. More natural. Less forced. Let it flow, Oliver!"

"Um, let what flow?"

"Your creative genius!" I gesture around the room. "You can show off the marvelous view we have of a parking lot out this window." I swoop my arm to the other side of the room. "And on this side of the room we have a view of the hallway, where we are able to see our approaching guests."

Oliver is recording me on his phone. "Don't forget about our bespoke curtain," I say, pointing. "What it lacks in acoustic protection, it makes up for in beauty, don't you think?"

He nods. "Wait, why do you need acoustic protection?"

"One of us snores," I say in a stage whisper.

Oliver looks shocked. "You should get that checked out! Good thing you're in a hospital."

I go on, "To match our top-of-the line curtain, we also have these high-thread-count sheets. Which you can see very well on Oliver's bed since it isn't made."

Oliver aims his phone at his bed, then quickly picks it up. "Hey! That's supposed to be a secret!" But he's grinning, and my face hurts from grinning too.

He points his phone at my bed. "Oh, come on, that isn't real!"

"Pretty sure it's hard to fake a made bed, Oliver."

"I mean, you don't really make your bed like that! You just did that for the video! I mean, fine, maybe, yeah your bed kinda always looks like that."

He's still got his phone recording my bed, but he's throwing his sheets around on his bed. "There! Much better." He points his phone at his bed again. It's a mess.

I burst out laughing, and he does too.

"What else do you think people want to see?" Oliver says, looking at me.

"Assuming anyone is still watching the video, I think we probably should stop now while we're ahead," I say.

"Good point," Oliver says. "Okay, signing off. The roommates. The quaranteens." He points the phone at me, still recording. "You should probably say something too," he says, looking at me.

"What should I say?"

"I thought you were the director?"

"I thought *you* were the director!" I say back.

He flips the phone so he's recording himself. "Flora says bye. And thanks for watching. Quaranteens signing off."

"You already said that!" I say, just as he stops recording.

"Said what?"

"That quaranteens signing off thing."

"Oh, so should we do it again?" He has an evil twinkle in his eye.

"Definitely not!"

"Okay, well, I'll post this." He taps at his phone.

"Thanks. Everyone will forget that Floriver even existed."

"Right," he says, looking at me.

"Right."

After a few seconds, he says, "Thanks. That was a good idea."

"It's the least I can do." Another pause. "After everyone watches the video, they'll see what great . . . roommates we are."

"Right," he says again.

I've disabled all the alerts on my phone, so I only hear Oliver's going off.

He's still looking at me. "I think something is happening to your phone," I say.

He looks down at his screen but doesn't say anything.

"Did it work? Is everyone saying what good roommates we are?" I ask, trying to sound enthusiastic. He doesn't say anything, just keeps scrolling. "Oliver?"

He finally looks up, looking alarmed. "Um, not quite?"

"What? What do you mean?"

But he doesn't answer me. I pick up my phone to see for myself.

Oh god. The video might have been an even worse idea than the hashtag.

# 87. OLIVER

The notifications are filling up my screen.

They're so in love! #TeamFloriver #quaranteen

Kelsey is going to be mad! #TeamFloriver #quaranteen

TEAM FLORIVER! #quaranteen

I'm still reading the posts when Kelsey calls me. She never calls me.

I pick up, but it's loud in the background. I hear birds squawking. "Hello?" I say hesitantly.

"Oliver!" Kelsey's voice sounds a little shrill.

"Where are you?" I ask. "Is everything okay?"

"I'm at the beach," she says. I can hear the waves hitting the sand.

"Oh, cool." I'm not a big beach person, but suddenly the thought of having sand between my toes sounds like the best thing in the world.

"I saw the video!" Her voice is shrill again.

"Oh, yeah, isn't it great? Flora thought of it."

"Thought of what, exactly? How to make me look like a fool?" she says angrily.

"A fool? What are you talking about?"

"The video. You guys are so . . ."

"Such good roommates," I say.

"That's not what people online think!"

I try to play dumb. "Really?"

"Yes, really. Everyone is saying how cute you two are together. How well you get along. How *we* shouldn't be together."

"Well, that's . . . that's—"

"Stupid? Not true? Fake news?" she fills in.

I look at Flora and realize she's waving at me madly. "Um, hold on one second."

"Tell her you're going to delete the video! You'll make a new one just for her! You'll make it up to her!" Flora says quickly.

"Um, Kelsey, I should go," I say. "I think I have some work to do."

"Work?" she says incredulously. "You're in quarantine. What kind of work could you possibly need to do?"

"It's, uh, it's work for you. To make it up to you. A new video kind of work."

"Don't make any more videos!" she orders. "That will just make things even worse."

I look at Flora helplessly. "Okay. We will think of something."

"*We?*"

"I mean me. I mean I. *I* will think of something."

"Just . . . just forget it," Kelsey says, sounding calmer. "Just take the video down. I'm sorry. I'm just ready for you to be out of quarantine!"

"Yeah, me too," I say, but then I look at Flora and think I might be lying.

"Well, I should go. I think I'm going swimming," Kelsey says.

"Me too."

"What?"

"I mean, I should go too."

"Okay, bye."

"Bye."

I hang up, rub my head as I delete the video.

"I'm sorry, Oliver," Flora says quietly. "I thought the video was such a good idea."

"Yeah, so did I."

"We'll figure out a way to fix it."

"No, it's okay, Kelsey said not to bother."

"Really?" Flora looks surprised. "Did she say why?"

"I think she thinks it'll make things worse. So weird that people mashed up our names, isn't it?" I say, trying to change the subject.

Flora is looking at her phone and doesn't answer me.

"Flora?"

She finally looks up, worried. "Did you say something?"

"I did, but what's wrong?"

"It's nothing!" she says quickly. "Well, it's just . . . since that video went up, people are talking about Kelsey. Guys are offering to take her out on dates if you . . . break up."

"Wait, for real?"

"People are so creepy! The Internet is so weird!" She's trying to sound lighthearted but she still looks worried.

I want to ask more, but Joey arrives with food and for vitals checks, and then my mom and Flora's dad and Goldy show up. Even though we're roommates, I still feel like we're never alone.

# 88. FLORA

And just like that, our days in quarantine wind down.

> The #quaranteens are almost quaran-free!

> Will Floriver survive outside of a hospital? #quaranteen

> Finally, Kelser can go on a real date and get away from Flora.
> #quaranteen

> I still think they're not really in #quaranteen

But even with the online attention, I feel a little bit of the same disappointment that I did when we came in. I don't know what I'm expecting exactly, except more hubbub, more sirens. There should be some kind of countdown clock somewhere in our hospital room. Like Times Square on New Year's. Or maybe a doomsday clock?

Five days left, then four, then three.

Like everything in my life, even quarantine settled into a routine for me.

My dad and Goldy visit, we watch TV, talk a little. Interspersed in there are vitals checks, doctors' visits, and the canned sitcom laughter coming from either my TV or Oliver's.

Oliver. At least there's Oliver. He keeps quarantine interesting. We play cards, watch soap operas and bad daytime talk shows. We avoid watching the news. We look out my window and take bets on who is going to walk by next. He thinks the dragon tattoo on the woman's fore-arm should be named Saphira.

We don't talk about what is going to happen outside quarantine, in the real world. He doesn't ask me about school, how I'm going to make up all the missed assignments and papers and tests, and I don't ask him about his school either.

And there's his girlfriend. The video seems to have brought us even more followers, more attention, and Kelsey seems to keep getting more and more popular on social media. And more guys are talking about asking her out if Kelser falls apart.

I can't keep ignoring the bad feeling—the really bad feeling—that she might be using Oliver. Maybe she's trying to make everyone focus on her again after my failed roommates video, but all she ever wants to talk about with Oliver is hashtag this, hashtag that, and I'm kicking myself for ever thinking of it in the first place. Sure, it got him the girl, but it also got the girl social media fame, which I worry she enjoys more than Oliver.

I'm listening to them talk, and I swear she says the word *hashtag* fifty times in five minutes.

When she finally leaves, I text Oliver: Hey, you busy?

I hear him laugh, then he texts back: Terribly.

I slide the curtain open, and he grins at me, his blue eyes sparkling.

"What's up?" he asks.

"Nothing, just saying hi."

"Um, hi."

I'm starting to lose my nerve, but Oliver's phone lights up in his hand with social media notifications.

It's now or never.

"Has she always been this active on social media?" I blurt out.

"What? Who?"

"Your girlfriend. Kelsey." I try not to make a face when I say her name, but I'm not sure I'm successful.

"Yeah, I think so. Why?"

"I guess I'm just worried about her intentions," I say honestly.

"Intentions? What do you mean?"

"I mean, what's your history? You never dated before, right? Never asked her out before all of this?"

"No. She's just always been a crush." Oliver looks a little dreamy for a second. But then he snaps back to reality. "Why are you asking all these questions?"

I choose my words carefully. "I'm just a little . . . concerned."

"Why? Spit it out, Flora." He's got his arms crossed over his chest.

"Fine." I sigh. "It's just . . . she posts, like, constantly on social media, and she uses the hashtag—"

"That *you* came up with!"

"Yes, that I came up with. But she's taken it and gone with it and added to it, and she seems to really like the attention, the fame, and now all these guys are talking about asking her out—"

"She's doing it for me," Oliver snaps. "She's doing it because she wants me to know that I'm not alone. That other people care about me, are worried about me."

"Are you sure that's why she's doing it?" I ask.

"I wish you would stop hinting at whatever it is and just come out with it already."

"I think she's using you for the attention," I say quickly, then slap my hand over my mouth.

We stand there, looking at each other in silence for a few seconds.

Oliver's face turns white. "How *dare* you," he spits. "A girl finally likes me and you accuse her of using me? Do you think I'm *that* awful that no girl would want to date me? That no girl would come all the way to Miami from New York and expose herself to all this craziness unless it was for a little attention?"

"I . . . I don't think you're awful," I say quietly.

Oliver says, "Well, you must, because otherwise you wouldn't say these awful things to me. But you know what? *She* doesn't. Look, Flora, I don't know what it is I did to you, why you kissed me and dragged me into quarantine—this mess—in the first place. My mom was right: What kind of person kisses someone when they're sick? I'm sorry your life back home is hard. Truly. But I didn't make it hard. I've never wanted anything but good things for you, but it seems you've never wanted anything but bad things for me."

"Oliver, listen—"

"Are you jealous? Is that what it is?" Oliver interrupts.

"What?" I ask, flustered. "What are you talking about?"

"Kelsey said you probably were, but I didn't want to believe her. Now I know she's been right all along. I'm sorry I took your advice and got the girl. We only have a few more days left in quarantine. Maybe we just shouldn't talk anymore. Sometimes it seems like every time we do, it ends like this."

Not talking to Oliver is the last thing I want, but I'm used to not getting what I want, so I say, "Okay," in a calm, quiet voice.

Oliver gets up from the chair on my side of the room, walks over to his side, and has his hand on the curtain. He opens his mouth to say something, but he just shakes his head and closes the curtain.

I wish more than anything I could kick another door, punch a wall. But I don't. Instead I picture the garden in my neighborhood, think about the statue of the girl with her head up. Think about how I can keep my head up just like her.

I turn on the TV and try to forget that Oliver ever existed.

# 89. OLIVER

I'm listening to the *Jeopardy!* music coming from Flora's side of the room and am absolutely seething. How could she just so casually say that Kelsey might be using me?

I pull up Twitter and look through our hashtag, all our pictures together. I love how happy we look. You can't fake that kind of happiness, right?

I scroll through more pictures, more posts. Kelsey in her hazmat suit, Kelsey on her flight to Miami, Kelsey in her hotel room with the hashtag #missingmyquaranteen. Kelsey on the beach, Kelsey on the beach again. She sure doesn't look like this is too hard on her.

I look at the picture of the Mike and Ikes. *Who really does like gumdrops, anyway?* I think.

But there is a tiny little voice in the corner of my mind that keeps getting louder and louder the more pictures and posts I look at.

*She's right.*

# 90. FLORA

I toss and turn all night, and there is a part of me that almost misses being sick, when I could sleep so easily. At that point I was too tired to be mad, to think of all the things I wanted to say to Oliver.

I want to tell him that I said all those things about Kelsey because I don't want him to get hurt. Because I care about him. That he deserves better than someone who doesn't appreciate how awesome he is. I think of how awesome he is. How much he makes me laugh even when he's not trying—especially when he's not trying. I think about his cool-breeze eyes. I think about kissing him.

I pick up my phone, even though I don't know why. I scroll through all Kelsey's posts, but I'm not looking at her, I'm looking at Oliver. Which is ridiculous since he's a few feet away from me and I could easily open the curtain and see him. Though I know I'm the last person he'd want to look at.

I keep scrolling. Why do his blue-green eyes have to be so stupid and pretty anyway?

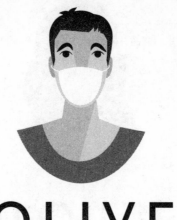

# 91. OLIVER

Kelsey is only five minutes late, so she doesn't apologize when she comes in. "Can you believe it? Only two days left in quarantine! We get to go on our first date soon! Our followers can't wait," she says.

"Followers, right."

"Isn't it amazing how many we have?"

I don't say anything, but she doesn't notice, and says, "I've been thinking about our first kiss. We should definitely make sure we get a video of it."

Kelsey is talking about kissing me, and I'm still replaying my conversation with Flora in my brain.

"Oliver? Aren't you excited? Isn't this what you've been looking forward to? I know you've had a crush on me since forever," she whispers, eyes on her phone.

I don't know if it's the mention of the crush I used to have, or the sudden mental image of Kelsey laughing when I fell ice-skating, but I blurt out, "Sometimes it feels like you like me because I'm in the hospital. In quarantine."

"What?" Kelsey glances up from her phone. She looks as shocked as I feel.

"No, it's nothing," I say, trying to smooth things over.

"Okay," she says skeptically, looking back down at her phone.

"Actually, no!" I shout with a force that surprises even me. "We need to talk about this."

Kelsey cocks an eyebrow at me, but her thumb is still scrolling on her phone even as she looks at me.

"God, can you please just put your phone down for a second?"

"Jeez Louise," she mutters, putting her phone down.

But then she looks at me, with her full attention, and I feel my nerve slowly dissipating.

The silence stretches out awkwardly between us, like it always does, and she reaches out her arm to pick up her phone again, like she always does.

"No!" I yelp.

"Oliver, what is your deal?" None of the kindness that I've seen for the past three weeks is on her face, though, and I remember again how she laughed when I fell ice-skating. It suddenly occurs to me that she wasn't laughing with me, because I wasn't laughing. She was laughing *at* me.

"You didn't even bring the right candy!" I say.

"Huh?"

"I asked you to bring gumdrops and you brought Mike and Ikes."

"Yeah, because my grandma eats gumdrops."

"And so do I! And I don't care if that makes me old or boring or weird or whatever."

"O . . . kaaaay," she says.

"And you bought them for social media!"

"Bought who?" Kelsey says, rubbing her head. I hate how crazy she's making me feel.

I want to look at my phone, to send a desperate text to Flora asking what I should say, but I hear her watching TV with her dad and Goldy and I know that'd make me a hypocrite. And I know this is a conversation I want to have on my own. I need to have on my own. I can't follow any more advice from the girl handbook. I need to write my *own* girl handbook.

"Look, Oliver, if this is about candy, I can buy you the stupid gum-drops, it's not a big deal."

"They're not stupid! And neither am I."

"I never said you were?"

"But you make me feel that way."

"Why? Because I didn't get you the right candy?"

"Because you didn't get the right candy *on purpose*. Because you wanted to do what was cute and fun. For attention. For you."

Kelsey gasps. "So this is the thanks I get? I risk my life by coming down here and exposing myself to something that could kill me just to take care of you, and this is how you show your gratitude?"

"What have you done to take care of me?" I say before I can stop myself.

Kelsey's eyes bug out of her head. "Are you kidding me right now? You have to be kidding me right now. Someone is going to jump out from a corner of this room any second and tell me this is all a big joke, right? I'm in a freaking hazmat suit and I'm accused of being selfish. A hazmat suit! Do you know how scary this has been for me?"

I've heard that last sentence, that same sentiment, so many times from my mom. And Flora's parents. So many times, and I'm so tired of having to worry about how scary this is when I'm the one in the hospital bed, when I'm the one who really cares about someone who really was sick. Flora is the one I care about, not Kelsey. And social media is what Kelsey cares about, not me.

"I think maybe you should leave."

Kelsey picks up her phone. "Yeah, I think that's a good idea. I think you need to cool off a bit. I'll post something on your hashtag so you can see how much other people care about you. How much *I* care about you. How selfish I'm not."

"No! No more social media. And no more visits. I think you should leave this room, leave this hospital. Leave this state." I take a deep breath. "Go back to Brooklyn."

"Okay, now I know you're messing with me. Joke's over, Oliver. It was funny, you had me going. I'm ready for things to go back to normal with us."

"Normal? We've never had a normal, Kelsey."

"How can you say that? We've been in the same English class for two years."

"Three years! And it was math class."

"Right, that's what I meant." She's rubbing her head again. "Listen, I'll see you tomorrow, okay?"

"No!" I say.

"No?"

"No. I don't want you to come back tomorrow."

"Um, what are you talking about? What about our date to Coney Island?"

I shake my head. "No."

"Oliver, we have our own hashtags. We're like a celebrity couple! People have expectations for us!"

"Well," I say, "I have expectations for myself."

"You don't know what you're doing, Oliver!" she says angrily.

"That's the thing, Kelsey, I know exactly what I'm doing, even if it took me a while to realize it. And I know I'm doing the right thing."

"Just wait until social media hears about this. Everyone will be on my side. They'll see how awful you really are."

"What's awful about me?"

"Um, you're breaking up with me!"

"How can I break up with you if I never even asked you out in the first place?"

Kelsey opens and closes her mouth a few times, then says very quietly, "I'll make you sorry for this, just you wait."

"I'm sorry," I say hollowly. I think I've told strangers "bless you" after a sneeze with more emotion.

"Sorry? *Now* you apologize? You're unbelievable."

"I . . . never meant to hurt you. I think things got out of hand. Maybe we can still be friends?"

Kelsey throws her head back and laughs. "I never want to see your face again."

I realize she has her phone in her hand. "Are you recording this?" I ask.

She narrows her eyes at me. "Wouldn't you like to know?"

"I would, actually."

"Good-bye, Oliver."

"Um, bye? Can I give you a hug? A high five?"

She scowls at me.

"Okay. You don't have to. Sorry, that was dumb."

And as usual, we stand there looking at each other awkwardly. Something crosses over Kelsey's face, and she puts her phone in her bag and says, "See you around Brooklyn."

And she leaves the hospital room.

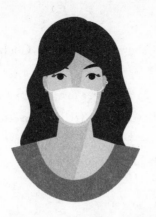

# 92. FLORA

I'm watching an old sitcom from the eighties with my dad and Goldy. My dad turned up the volume when things got really heated with Oliver and Kelsey. Goldy keeps shooting me looks, but I'm keeping my eyes on the TV, trying to keep my face blank, empty of emotion.

I feel like someone in the hallway is looking at me. I turn my head and Kelsey is there.

I wave, but she just glares at me. She has her phone out, and I'm afraid she's taking a picture of me, but then I see she's typing something. She walks over to me with her phone out, and her notebook app is open on her phone, and she's written "U CAN HAVE HIM."

I give her a confused look, and she jabs a pointed finger at the curtain. Oliver.

She's typing on her phone again, this time "JUST DON'T GET HIM SICK."

Right, because that's all I do. Because I'm disgusting and diseased.

I give her a double thumbs-up and a fake smile, and Kelsey leaves.

My dad is still looking at the TV, very interested in a commercial for an extra-strength shower cleaner, but Goldy is watching my face carefully.

I want to tell her to mind her own business, but I am her business now. "The hashtag leaves out a lot. I'll have to tell you all about it sometime."

Goldy smiles and says, "I'd like that."

# 93. OLIVER

I'm pacing around my room again, checking my phone, checking the hashtag. Kelsey hasn't posted anything about our breakup yet, and my stomach feels like it does when I ride the creaky old elevator in my apartment building.

Flora's dad and Goldy say good-bye, and then Flora turns the volume down on her TV.

Now I feel like the cable has broken on the elevator and I'm falling.

"How's it going over there?" Flora finally says.

I throw the curtain open. Flora is sitting on her bed, and the afternoon light from outside lights up her face and hair again. "Kelsey left," I blurt out.

"Well, visiting hour was over, right?"

"No, I mean, she left, left."

"Like left for the day?"

"Like left the state."

Flora bites her lip, and it looks like she's trying to hide a smile. "But we still have a few days of quarantine. What are you going to do without her care?" I think she notices my annoyed reaction because she immediately says, "Okay, I'll stop being mean. What happened? For real."

She looks right at me, in that same direct Flora way she always does. The way that both kind of takes my breath away and completely relaxes me because it's so honest and so pure. She thought of the hashtag thing but she doesn't need to hide behind it.

"You were right," I say.

"Right about what?"

"Kelsey. She was using me." I don't feel upset saying it. I feel . . . numb.

"I'm sorry, Oliver," Flora says. "I really wanted to be wrong."

"Thank you."

And we just look at each other, the afternoon light streaming into our room.

"I need to focus my attention somewhere else too," I finally say.

"Oh? And where is that somewhere else?" She's biting her lip again, but it doesn't work because I see her smile.

"Um, it's kind of a some*one* else."

"Go on." She lets go of her lip, and now she isn't hiding her smile anymore.

"It's you. I want to focus my attention on you, Flora. I wasn't much help taking care of you when you were sick, so I want to take care of you now. Be here for you now." For some reason, my voice almost cracks.

"Oliver," Flora says. I love the way she says my name. I open my mouth to tell her that, but I think by the way she's looking at me, maybe she already knows it.

"Oliver," she says again, smiling even bigger. "You already are."

"Already am what? Go on," I tease.

"Oliver, you already are taking care of me."

She starts to push herself up in bed, and I give her my hand to help her. I know she's not sick anymore, but it's a reflex.

"See?" she says, taking my hand. "You know what to do before I even ask for help. My foot fell asleep and I can't get up!"

I look at our intertwined hands, then up at her face. A strand of hair fell across her face while she moved herself. I push it gently out of her eyes, and she rests her head against my hand. Before I know what I'm doing, I run my fingers through her hair. It's so soft. I smell the coconut and mint that is just her and just so familiar now. I want to kiss her. And I don't need a girl handbook to tell me she wants to kiss me too.

And this time I can tell her wanting to kiss me has nothing to do with wanting to extend her quarantine stay. Our quarantine stay.

But I can't. Because kissing her *will* extend our stay, and now that she is finally better, I just want to get us out of here and back to Brooklyn. A kiss got us here in the first place, and a non-kiss will get us out. Or something.

I feel like she has to know it too, so I'm surprised when she leans forward even farther, her face inches from mine. But unlike twenty-eight days ago, I see the kiss coming and I can pull my head away from hers, let go of her hand, let go of her hair, even though every inch of my body wants to kiss her so bad.

She looks so hurt, so rejected, then quietly says, "Right, I'm poisonous. Disgusting."

"No, Flora, not at all. You know that's not true."

"I do? Remind me how I know that, please?"

"Because you're—"

"Just forget it, Oliver, okay? I've already forgotten it."

"Flora, I—"

She looks at me, more hurt than I've ever seen her, so I just say, "I'm sorry. When we get back to Brooklyn we can hang out."

"Hang out! That'd be great. Good old pals. Maybe we can play Crazy Eights some more."

"Flora, I'm sorry. I mean hang out like—"

"I don't know what you're apologizing for," she says coldly.

She turns the TV on again, pulls the blankets up around her and over her head.

I stand there for a minute, feeling like an idiot, and even more clueless about girls than ever.

Finally, I go back to my side of the room and see that Kelsey has posted a selfie of her in sunglasses, giving the peace sign, with the hospital in the background. Hasta la vista, #quaranteen. Some people don't know how good something is until it's gone.

#TeamKelser is no more? #quaranteen

I always knew she was too good for him. #quaranteen

I'm totally going to ask Kelsey out. #quaranteen

Oliver is an idiot. #quaranteen

None of their comments sting as much as the conversation I just had with Flora.

I keep scrolling.

#TeamFloriver together at last! #quaranteen

I knew this day would finally come. #quaranteen

I can't wait for Floriver to kiss again! #quaranteen

I put my phone down. What do a bunch of strangers on the Internet know, anyway?

# 94. FLORA

I wake up feeling like I can't breathe. I don't hear Oliver snoring, so he must still be awake.

I pick up my phone, and I have texts from him. I delete the texts without reading them. I don't need him to remind me that I'm diseased, that I'm disgusting. I don't know what I was thinking when I tried to kiss him. Just like the first time I kissed him.

I wish I could delete him from my life. It was a mistake to kiss him the first time, and it was an even bigger mistake to try to kiss him the second time.

We only have one day left in quarantine. We went without speaking the first few days of quarantine; I'm sure we can end our time in quarantine the same way.

Then we'll be on our way back to Brooklyn, back to our separate lives, and this will all be in our past.

Just like our kiss.

# 95. OLIVER

I text Flora that I'm sorry. She doesn't respond. I text her that I didn't mean to hurt her—that I want us to get out of quarantine and I don't want to do anything to mess it up. Nothing back.

I want to kiss her when we're not sitting in a hospital room. I want to kiss her outside somewhere, where we can feel the wind in our hair, where we can hear birds chirping. Where we can both see the blue sky. Or watch a sunset. Or maybe even look at the moon together.

I watch the sun come up. I wish I could tell her how beautiful it is. Or even better, watch the sunrise with her.

# 96. FLORA

My mom emails me a link to my boarding pass and tells me what time she'll pick me up tomorrow. This time I'll be flying into Newark, not LaGuardia. Assuming I don't have to go to quarantine again first.

Becca and Jenna video chat me again to let me know they want to have a welcome home party for me, but I tell them not to bother.

Oliver and his mom are talking about their flights back. Through some snafu they're on different flights. She's set to fly back in the morning and Oliver in the afternoon. She makes a lot of calls to a lot of people and Oliver tells her it's not a big deal.

I think he and I might be on the same flight together to Newark. But it doesn't matter because we're never going to talk again.

# 97. OLIVER

My last morning waking up in quarantine. My last morning waking up next to Flora. I bet she can't wait to get back to Brooklyn, to get away from me.

I pull my suitcase out of the wardrobe. There's still some sand in it. My mom asked a hospital worker to do my gross laundry from my spring break, so I pack my newly clean clothes. Such a contrast from when I threw all my dirty, crusty clothes into my suitcase in the Dominican Republic.

In the Dominican Republic, before I met Flora. Before Kelsey was my girlfriend. Ex-girlfriend.

My mom comes in, tugging her giant suitcase behind her. She stops by my bed, but the suitcase topples over and opens the curtain between my bed and Flora's.

Flora looks down at the suitcase, then up at me and my mom. She asks, "Do you need help, Ms. Russell? Maybe redistribute some of the weight?"

"I always overpack. I wasn't sure how long I'd be here, what the weather would be like, plus I picked up a few souvenirs. Oh, Oliver,

I wish we were on the same flight! Flora, you'll take good care of him, right? Just like you did on the way here?"

"Mom, she doesn't need to take care of me." I step in, feeling embarrassed. But I can't help but be happy to see Flora again. Even though she was right next to me, I missed her.

"I'd be happy to, Ms. Russell." She smiles at my mom, then looks at me. Her smile fades a little. "Only if it's okay with Oliver."

"It's more than okay with me," I say. "I mean, sure. I mean, thank you."

Flora smiles again and says, "No problem." She goes back to folding her clothes.

"Next time I see you I won't be wearing a hazmat suit!" my mom says. "Can you believe we'll be home tonight, sleeping under the same roof again?"

I look at Flora. "No, not at all."

I'm still looking at her when my mom gasps. "I'm going to be late! Oh, I can't wait to give you a hug without this suit!" She wraps her arms around me. "I love you, Oliver. Please text me when you're on your way to the airport—"

"And at the airport, on the airplane. Got it, Mom."

She does the weird nose thing again, then hurries out the door, tugging the suitcase behind her. She pulls off her hazmat suit and throws it in the bin. Her suitcase falls again and almost knocks over a doctor. She picks it up, and she's gone.

Flora and I look at each other, the curtain still open.

"Thanks, Flora," I say.

"For what?"

"For . . . everything."

Before she can say anything else, her dad and Goldy arrive.

Is it possible to miss Flora already?

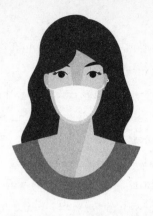

# 98. FLORA

"These are your last few hours here!" my dad says. He pats my leg, makes a strange sound in his throat.

Goldy puts her hand on his shoulder, and I can watch her do it without wanting to punch anything.

"Me neither," I say.

"I'm so happy you're okay, Flora," Goldy says. I'm surprised she didn't say *we*.

But I bite my tongue and say, "Thank you. Thank you for coming to visit me. Both of you."

My dad is nodding, and he makes that throat sound again. It's the same sound he made when he told me about him and Mom divorcing.

"I think you guys should come to New York," I say. "Maybe see Randy. See my friends."

My dad says, "We'd love that."

He looks at Goldy, and she's nodding too. "I haven't been to New York since high school."

My first thought is that was only a few years ago, but I say, "Have you ever been to Brooklyn?"

"Fuhgeddaboudit!" she says, in a really bad, loud Brooklyn accent that makes my eyeballs itch.

I try to smile, but my dad says, "Goldy, that was awful."

They both laugh, and I laugh too.

"So, that's a no?" And we all laugh again.

"You have everything you need for your flight? Your mother has your flight info?" my dad says, looking around my room.

"Yep."

"You're checked in? You have your seat?"

"Kenneth, she's been on an airplane before."

"I know, but this time is different."

"How?" I ask.

"After everything you've gone through," my dad says, waving his hand. I look at him, waiting for him to go on, and he says, "Oh, who am I kidding? You could handle a flight around the world and back and still be cool as a cucumber."

Goldy says, "Cool as a cucumber?"

My dad waves his hand again. "You know, unfazed. Relaxed. *Cooool*."

Goldy and I look at each other and laugh. "You are such a dweeb," I tease.

We watch *The Price Is Right*, like we have for all their morning visits, and then it's time for them to go.

My dad gives me a big hug, and it feels so comfortable and familiar. Last time I hugged him good-bye at the airport in the Dominican Republic, I was so mad at him and Goldy for ruining my spring break. For taking me away from Becca and Jenna. For taking me away from my mom. But now I couldn't be more grateful to them for giving me a chance to meet Oliver. Even if he's grossed out by me and hates me.

I hug Goldy, and this time I let myself relax into her hug.

I don't feel angry anymore, but I don't feel 100 percent happy about everything either. I know that's okay, though. It took time for me to recover from mono, and it's going to take time for me to recover from all the changes my family has been through. That I've been through.

"I love you, Flora Cracker. I don't think any of us will forget this spring break anytime soon."

"I love you, Dad." I look him in the eyes when I say it, and he hugs me again.

He makes the throat noise one more time, and Goldy puts her arm around him as they walk out the door together. They take off their hazmat suits, then stand at the window outside my room blowing kisses at me, my dad dabbing his eyes.

They turn around and walk down the hallway together, holding hands.

# 99. OLIVER

A nurse comes in to do a final vitals check. I wonder how many times my temperature has been taken in the last thirty days.

She turns her back to me for a second, writing something down on her clipboard. I have my hand on the thermometer, and Flora looks at me with horror as I pull it out of my mouth.

I grin, pop the thermometer back in, and the nurse records my temperature as perfectly normal.

Flora glares at me, adorable nose wrinkle and all, but then she smiles. At me.

The nurse goes to her side of the room, and I close my eyes while the thermometer is in her mouth. I hear the beep, hear the nurse say, "You are both cleared to leave quarantine. Congratulations, and I hope we never see you again."

I open my eyes and say, "Thank you." But the nurse is already walking out of the room.

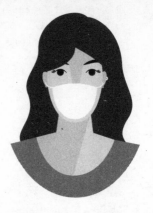

# 100. FLORA

Joey is walking down the hallway. He's got two other men with him, and they're pushing empty wheelchairs. He grins at me, like always. He puts his hazmat suit on, then comes into the room.

"Well, this is it!" he says cheerfully. "Just think, this is the last time you'll be seeing me in this thing."

I should be excited to leave quarantine, to leave the hospital. And part of me is, but part of me is also . . . sad. This room has been my home for the last thirty days. Thirty days of sleeping next to Oliver, being next to Oliver, and once I walk through the antechamber, that phase of my life is over. Though I bet he can't wait.

Joey looks around the room. "You look like you're packed and ready to go! What about Romeo?"

"Um, I'm not sure. We haven't been in touch much these last couple days."

"In touch? Flora, his bed is right next to yours." He laughs.

I force a laugh. "We've been trying to prepare for life outside quarantine again." Which I suppose is sort of true.

"Well, I hope you're both ready, because it's time to go!" Joey opens the curtain. Oliver is sitting on his bed, and he immediately springs up.

"Are we going? Should we get to the airport? You never know how long security will take."

Joey laughs. "Dude, your flight doesn't leave for another four hours."

But Oliver doesn't hear him. He's wheeling his suitcase to the door. He doesn't even look back at the room. Or back at me.

"Well, I guess we're going, then," Joey says. "Hey, Romeo, let me go first."

"Oh, right," Oliver says.

He walks through the antechamber, and Oliver finally looks back at me. He looks like he wants to say something, but then he quickly pulls his suitcase through the chamber.

I follow him, and we're in the hallway I've looked at for the past thirty days. It feels like being on the other side of a camera. Like being in the audience after on the stage.

"Your chariots," Joey says, gesturing to the wheelchairs. "Not quite the souped-up ones you had on the way in."

Oliver tries to climb into one of the chairs, but he trips on a pedal. The man behind the chair catches him just in time, helps him into his chair. "Sorry. Thanks," Oliver says.

Joey lightly touches my arm, and it's the first time I've ever felt his fingers. Even though he's not in a hazmat suit anymore, I'm the one who suddenly feels naked.

He guides me over to the chair, and I feel like I might pass out when he wraps his hand around my arm to help me into it. Are hot interns why this whole thing about patients leaving hospitals in wheelchairs started?

"All right, boys, you take good care of our patients," Joey says.

"You're not coming with?" I say before I can stop myself.

"Ah, I'm afraid this is where our ships part."

"Oh, right," I say, feeling embarrassed. Obviously I knew he wasn't coming to the airport, but I wasn't expecting to say bye to him just yet.

He kneels down in front of my chair. I can smell him. He smells like aftershave and shampoo and I feel dizzy breathing him in. "You take good care of yourself, okay? You're a tough cookie." He puts his hand on my knee, squeezes it, and then stands up.

"*Hasta la vista*, Romeo," he says, saluting.

Oliver just glares at him, but Joey has already started to walk away. He turns around one more time, looks around quickly, and then blows me a kiss.

I gasp, tell myself he's just doing what he saw my dad and Goldy doing. Then I'm moving, and realize the man is pushing my wheelchair.

I look over my shoulder, and Oliver is behind me in his wheelchair, taking in all the new scenery. I don't think he saw Joey's blown kiss.

There is so much to look at, so many people see. I had every inch of my hospital room memorized and my brain can't process how many things I'm being wheeled past. We get in an elevator, and the movement is jarring, but for some weird reason I have that feeling in the back of my mouth like I want to cry.

I look at Oliver again, and he's looking all around too. "I forgot how many buttons there were in elevators!" he says.

"I know the feeling."

We get pushed down another hallway, and then I see the sliding glass doors leading outside.

Oliver and I are leaving the hospital the way we came in—together.

We get closer and closer to the doors, and then we're outside.

Birds are chirping, and cars are honking, and ambulances are pulling in, and there are people everywhere. Everywhere. Crowds of people, and when they see Oliver and me, they all start yelling. It's hard to concentrate on all the faces at once, but I realize they're saying our names and "Floriver" and telling us they love us. A bunch of them are holding up signs that say things like FLORIVER 4EVER. One even has a photo of Kelsey's face with a big X over it. That one's my favorite.

The orderlies pushing our wheelchairs tell the crowds to back off. I turn to Oliver and he looks just as shocked as I feel. Everyone is watching us, yelling, and it's so hard to process this many faces at once, so much sunshine at once.

I look past the crowds of people at a food cart across the street. I gulp in the air. It smells like exhaust and humidity and tacos . . . but it's the best air I've ever smelled.

We're mostly in the shade, but I reach out my arm into the sunshine, and I don't care if I get a sunburn. But then I see the crowds of people are getting closer again, and they all have their phones out, taking pictures.

Oliver is watching me, watching the crowds. "What are all these people doing here? What do they want?" He looks a little scared.

"Kiss! Kiss! Kiss!" they chant.

I watch the huge group of people all say the same word over and over again while they stare at Oliver and me with their phones out, and the last thing I want to do is what they're robotically chanting.

And I know Oliver doesn't want to kiss me anyway.

# 101. OLIVER

A cab shows up, and the guys with the wheelchairs push us over to the car, yelling at the crowds. The driver hops out, and another guy shows up with our luggage on a cart, and they throw our stuff in the trunk. I watch Flora get out of her wheelchair, realize I'm supposed to do the same. Maybe sitting in the wheelchair has suddenly taken away my ability to walk, because I feel like I can't move.

A teenage girl runs over, and suddenly she's right next to me. It's surreal for someone to be standing so close to me and not see them in a hazmat suit, so I'm too in shock to say anything, to do anything.

Flora whips around just as the girl is bending her face close to mine. She screams, "NO! He doesn't want that!" And I snap out of my daze, turn my head away, and hop out of the wheelchair.

Flora is sliding into the cab, and she grabs my hand and yanks me in too. I slam the door shut.

It's so quiet in the car compared with the chaos outside. We just look at each other, breathing heavily.

"We need to get to the consent chapter in the handbook," Flora says.

"Yeah. I think it's an important one," I say.

The driver hops back in the car, looks around at the crowd, and lays on his horn. The crowd scatters, and we're on our way to the airport.

I try to look at everything out the window but we're going too fast for my brain to keep up.

"You going to be okay on the flight?" Flora asks when we get to a stoplight.

At first I think she's making fun of me, but then I see the concerned look on her face. I say, "Why wouldn't I be?"

"No reason. Except that we've been through a lot in the past thirty days, and based on our last flight I don't know if you're the world's best flyer."

"We have, haven't we." I don't know why the word *we* makes me smile.

Flora laughs and goes back to looking out the window.

# 102. FLORA

We pull up to the airport, and my brain is still in overstimulated mode. There are tons of people on the sidewalk, then I realize they're all yelling and chanting and staring at our car. At least this time they're being held back by airport security workers.

Oliver turns to me, looking horrified. "We got this," I say. "Hold my hand, ignore them. They can't follow us past security." I look into his eyes, and even if he doesn't feel calm, his cool-breeze eyes calm me down and I want so much to kiss him. But I don't want to give this crowd of maniacs what they want.

The driver hops out of the car, rolls our luggage to the curbside check-in. "Ready?" I ask Oliver. He offers me his hand, and I squeeze it.

He looks down at our hands, looks up at my face. He nods, squeezes my hand back.

I get out of the car first, and he follows me. People are yelling the same stuff as at the hospital. They chant "Kiss!" again. Maybe since I've heard it before it doesn't bother me as much. Or maybe because I'm holding Oliver's hand nothing bothers me as much.

We meet the driver at the ticket counter and I quickly figure out his tip. I let go of Oliver's hand for a second to give the driver money. Oliver is still reaching for his wallet.

"You can get me later," I say.

He starts to object, then looks around at the crowd of people, quickly nods. "Thanks." I hand the woman at the counter my boarding pass and ID. People are yelling, "Kiss! Kiss! Kiss!" louder, but the woman doesn't even bat an eye as she checks my suitcase. She says loudly, over the chanting, "Have a good flight!"

She quickly checks Oliver in and says, "Next time, be nicer to your girlfriend. Don't string her along like that. Or I'll send your luggage to Alaska." She hands Oliver his ID and boarding pass. "Have a nice flight!"

"Um, thanks," Oliver says.

I grab Oliver's hand again, give one last look to the airport workers holding back the crowd of people, and lead him inside. He looks around, scanning the signs, but I'm already tugging him in the direction of security.

"Don't listen to ticket agents. Or anyone," I say as we walk.

"Anyone?"

"Okay, you can listen to me."

"I like listening to you," he says.

I grin at him. "You mean eavesdropping?"

We get in the security line, and I finally let go of his hand. I look around quickly, but no one is paying any attention to us or seems to recognize us. He says, "Oh, you have no idea." He smiles mischievously.

"Hashtag quaranmean," I say.

"Hashtag quarandramaqueen."

"What? That doesn't even make any sense." I laugh.

"How does it not make sense?" Oliver protests.

"How does it make sense?"

"What we were talking about again?"

"I was just going to ask you the same thing," I say.

Oliver laughs again, and we're almost at the front of the security line. "Hey, this is where I first met you!" he says, then looks embarrassed.

"Sure you don't have a fever? We met on the flight," I remind him. "There was that whole CDC thing when we landed? We went to quarantine?"

"Not ringing any bells," Oliver says.

I lightly jab his stomach with my elbow and he grabs my arm. I'm still not used to feeling bare skin on my bare skin.

I don't think Oliver is either, because he looks embarrassed again. He lets go of my arm as we inch forward in line. "There was a woman on the phone," he says.

"Huh? Where?"

"In the Dominican Republic. At security. You made a face. I made a face. It was a moment."

"Oh my god, that was you!" I say.

"So glad to know I left such a lasting impression," Oliver says jokingly.

"Oh, you have, Oliver Russell," I say seriously.

"What?" The smile leaves his face.

But it's my turn at security, so I step up to the TSA agent. I turn around, and Oliver is still looking at me.

The TSA worker hands me my ID and boarding pass back and I get in the security line. Oliver is sent to a different line. He trips over his shoelaces while taking off his shoes.

My line moves faster, so I'm through the body scanner before him.

He walks through the scanner, forgets to take off his belt, and walks through again. An agent picks up his bag and opens it.

After examining the bag, the agent hands it back and Oliver hurries over to a bench. I sit down next to him and say, "Don't forget to text your mom."

"How did you know that?"

"You're not the only person who knows how to eavesdrop."

He smiles, then looks up at the signs. "Which way to our gate?"

But I'm already up and heading there. "This way," I say, and Oliver follows me.

Our gate isn't very crowded, and we have almost two hours before our flight.

Oliver has his phone out and almost walks into me when I stop. His phone rings, and even without looking we both know it's his mom. "I'll give you some privacy . . . for once." I laugh. "I'll be right back."

I head to the restrooms, and now that I'm not helping Oliver, I'm back to being in overwhelmed mode, taking in all the people around me. The bathroom line is long, but it's so nice to see people who aren't in hazmat suits. I forgot how many colors clothes could be, how many different ways women could wear their hair.

I wash my hands at the sink, and in the reflection of the mirror I see that a woman is staring at me. I quickly leave the bathroom.

I go to one of the stores and buy a bag of chips. And gumdrops.

Oliver is off the phone when I get back to where he's sitting.

"Just in case you get hungry on the flight." I hand him the bag.

He opens the bag, sees the gumdrops, and before he can say anything, I say, "Professional eavesdropper."

"Thank you," he says quietly. "That's one of the nicest things anyone has ever done for me."

"Well, you won't think I'm so nice when I destroy you in Crazy Eights." I pull out the deck of cards, shuffle, and deal out our hands before he can say anything else. Before I can say anything else that will make me think about kissing him again.

We play for a while, and I'm really concentrating on beating him, when I feel eyes on me and I realize the couple sitting across from us is staring at us and talking. Oliver looks up to see what I'm looking at. One of the men says, "You're the quaranteens!"

His husband jabs him. "I told you not to say anything!"

Oliver looks panicked. I grab his hand, and the first man says, "I was rooting for you two all along. And I usually don't like celebrity gossip. Or really anything on social media."

I snort. "You and me both."

We all laugh, and Oliver and I go back to playing cards until it's time to board.

# 103. OLIVER

Flora and I walk down the jet bridge single file. She walks in front of me. It makes sense, her row is farther back on the plane, but at the same time I also know she'd be walking in front of me even if I was sitting in the last row in the plane and she was in the first.

We walk onto the plane, and the smell of recycled air and the dings from the intercom bring me back to thirty days ago.

I take a deep breath just as Flora looks over her shoulder at me. I give her a thumbs-up. If she can handle getting sick in quarantine, I can handle a three-hour plane ride.

We stop in front of row 15. "Here you are, sir," she says to me. She starts to walk down the aisle, and even though the man behind me keeps bumping his duffel bag into my legs, I say, "Flora! Wait!"

She turns around, alarmed. "Everything okay?"

"Yeah, it is. Just . . . bye?"

"I'll see you in Newark, Oliver," she says cheerfully. She ruffles my hair, and it reminds me of when she gave me bedhead for my picture for Kelsey.

"Yeah, in Newark." But that feels like a different world, a different planet.

"Hey, buddy, you need help finding your seat?" the man with the duffel bag asks, jamming it into the back of my legs again.

"Nope, got it, thanks."

I climb into my middle seat, but no one is on either side of me yet. *Maybe they won't show up, and then Flora can sit with me!* I think. Which is dumb, because she's had thirty days of being next to me nonstop, and I'm sure the last thing she wants is to sit next to me on an airplane. Look how well it went last time we sat next to each other on a flight.

Two young frazzled parents with a baby board. The mom is scanning the rows, checking her boarding pass. When she gets close to my row, she looks disappointed.

She says something to her husband, who looks at me, and makes the same disappointed face.

They get to my row and the wife says, "Um, the window seat is mine. The aisle seat is my husband's. But if you don't mind, could we sit together? No one ever buys middle seats!"

"Oh, sure!" I say.

I start to stand up, realize I forgot to unbuckle my seat belt, sit down, unbuckle it, and stand up. I scoot into the aisle, which is hard with the parents and the baby, and there is now a huge line of passengers.

"Hey! Families with young children are supposed to board first!" a man shouts.

The mom is sliding into the aisle, and she looks up. "Don't give him the satisfaction. He's not important," I say before I can stop myself.

She looks at me, and before I know what I'm doing, I grab the baby so the dad can get into his seat. The dad puts their bags under their seats, and I'm holding a squishy little baby who looks just as surprised as I am.

I somehow slide into my aisle seat with the baby and hand the baby back to the dad in one smooth gesture. I don't figure out who was yelling, but like I told the mom: He's not important.

# 104. FLORA

I find my row. Two men in suits with an empty middle seat between them. The man in the aisle gets up, and I scoot into my seat.

He's looking at me out of the corner of his eye, then turns toward me. "You look so familiar. Why do I feel like I've seen you somewhere before? Maybe you go to high school with my daughter?"

"I was on the news for a hot second. Our hashtag got really popular. My . . . friend and I were sent to quarantine together. We're both healthy now, though," I say quickly.

He snaps his fingers. "Aha! I knew I recognized you from somewhere. What were you in quarantine for again?"

"Tropical mono."

"The kissing disease?"

"Yeah, a mutated form."

"And they let you on a plane, just like that?"

"I'm not contagious anymore," I say, annoyed. "In this form, it's only contagious when someone is actively sick. I haven't been actively sick in almost two weeks."

"Mono makes you really tired, right?" he asks.

"So tired. Like you think you'll never be able to stay awake again kind of tired."

"And you got to sleep a lot?"

"I wouldn't say *got* to."

"Hmm, well, I'd love to have an excuse to stay in bed for a few days!"

I don't feel like explaining to him that it was hell to be too tired to even brush my teeth, even look at my phone. "Yep!" I say, with a fake brightness to my voice.

He goes back to his phone, and the man in the window seat ignores me the entire flight, which is fine with me.

# 105. OLIVER

It's gray as we get close to Newark. It's hard to look out the window since I'm on the aisle, but I can see New York City just off in the distance. The parents next to me smile at each other and touch their baby. I hear the mom say, "Home."

Home.

We land, taxi, and pull up to the gate. This time the CDC isn't there to meet us.

There are some more dings, and everyone gets up. It seems so calm after my last flight. I see Flora in the back, and I wave at her. The family next to me stays sitting, so I wait for everyone behind me to go, and then when Flora is next to my row I hop out.

"Good flight?" I ask.

"Better than the last one," she says.

We both laugh. But it's hard to talk much. The flight was crowded and everyone is in a hurry.

And the problem with getting off a flight together is you never really know when to say good-bye. I mean, if it's just someone you've met on the flight, you can usually say farewell once you get off the plane.

Sometimes it's awkward if you end up at the baggage claim or the taxi line together. But you can just kind of wave or nod and that's that.

That's all Flora was supposed to be: Someone I sat next to on a flight who I'd have to figure out how to say bye to. Maybe I'd see her at baggage claim and nod, or maybe I'd see her outside while we waited for our moms to pick us up and we'd roll our eyes at all the traffic.

But how do you say good-bye to someone you've spent thirty days in quarantine with? And *when*?

# 106. FLORA

I think I keep forgetting that the next thing after the airport is Oliver and me going our separate ways. His mom will pick him up, my mom will pick me up, and we'll be on our way to our respective parts of Brooklyn, our respective lives.

But I don't think I'll ever be able to think about my life being removed from Oliver's ever again.

I've listened to him breathe, sleep, brush his teeth, shower, eat, talk on the phone, text on the phone, talk to his girlfriend, fight with his girl-friend, break up with his girlfriend.

And now I have to figure out some way to tell him all of that before we get off the plane.

Before we get to baggage claim, where our moms are standing together, waiting for us, holding balloons.

Our moms hug us, and I look at Oliver over my mom's shoulder, and he's looking at me, and I still don't know what to say to him. How to say good-bye to him.

I want to kiss him. A real kiss. But I can't imagine he'd want to kiss me, formerly diseased Flora. The quaranteen.

"It's so good to hug you without wearing that stupid suit!" my mom says to me, pulling away, tears in her eyes. "Let's find your suitcase and get you home."

Oliver and I look at each other. He says, "So I guess—"

"Hey! It's the quaranteens!" someone yells. And even though we're in a loud, crowded airport, people hear him, look around, and then we're spotted.

I see my suitcase, grab it, watch Oliver do the same, and we're running with our moms to the parking lot.

People follow us, and Oliver and his mom go one way and my mom and I go the other. My mom quickly unlocks the car door, we throw the suitcase in, and we're off. I look around the parking lot, but I don't see Oliver or his mom or their car anywhere.

Even if we only live a few miles away from each other, he's not my roommate anymore. And he thinks I'm disgusting anyway.

"Bye," I say softly as our car turns a corner and leaves the parking lot.

# 107. OLIVER

I wonder if astronauts feel the way about their bedrooms that I feel about mine right now. They've been so far away, seen so much, changed so much, and their bedrooms look exactly the same as when they left.

I'm not the same Oliver who used to wear the Red Bulls shirt that's hanging up in my closet, or the same Oliver who has a shoe box full of baseball cards under my bed.

Something is missing. Someone is missing.

Flora.

I had so many chances to win her over. I had the author of the girl handbook in my very own hospital room and I wasted the opportunity.

I fiddle with my phone, spin it around on my bed, try to think about all the things Flora told me about how to win over the girl. I tried some in the hospital and they backfired. Maybe not backfired so much as just didn't work, because now I'm here and she's there.

A notification from Instagram pops up, and duh, social media. Girl handbook lesson number one.

Flora has posted a picture from today. It's of her room. Welcome home.

I wonder if she feels like an alien like I do. I could text her and ask her. But anyone can text her. I need to do something more romantic. Something more girl-handbook worthy.

I look through her pictures again, keep seeing pictures of the garden in her neighborhood.

I'm thinking about what I want to say to her, what I want to do for her, while I absentmindedly pull down the refresh button on her profile. I almost drop my phone. She's at the garden right now.

"Mom, I gotta go out! I need to pick up something at the drugstore!" I shout down the hallway as I pull my jacket on. I'm sweating already, so I quickly pull it off, then ball it up and stick it under my arm.

"Is everything okay, Oliver?" My mom comes out of her bedroom looking alarmed.

"Yes, it's fine, I promise. I just have to take care of something really important."

"And I shouldn't worry because . . . ?"

"Just, please, trust me."

She looks at me skeptically. "Okay. I'm going to try. But be home soon? It's getting close to dinnertime."

"Sure, okay."

"Love you, Oliver. So happy you're home."

"Love you too, Mom." I lean in so she can do her weird finger on my nose thing and then I'm out the door and on the subway on my way to Bay Ridge.

On the train ride, I keep refreshing the post, keep going over what I want to say to her. When I arrive in Bay Ridge, I make a quick stop at a pharmacy, and then I'm almost there.

Since Flora adds her location to all her photos, I know exactly where the garden is. I think I also know which statue is her favorite.

When I get there, her back is to the gate and she doesn't see me. She's looking around the garden, smiling, and she puts her arms out. She looks just like her favorite statue.

The light streams in through the trees and she looks radiant and beautiful. And I'm not going to be afraid to tell her that this time.

# 108. FLORA

Someone calls my name, and I jump. I thought I'd be alone in the garden. I turn around, and Oliver steps out of the shadows near the gate. It's so weird to see him outside a hospital or an airplane. Weird, and amazing. His blue eyes are sparkling, and I remember how they first reminded me of an open window on a spring day. The kind of spring day I'm standing in right now.

He takes a step toward me, and I see that he's carrying a small bag.

"But how did you"—Oliver waggles his phone at me—"oh, right. I post pictures of this place all the time, don't I? I never thought anyone was actually paying attention."

"I've been paying attention to a lot, Flora." Oliver's voice is gravelly, and I don't hear the wavering that I did when he talked to Kelsey.

"Someone really smart must have told you to pay attention to the details," I say.

"Very smart indeed," he says.

"And that same smart person must have told you how to give good compliments."

"She did."

"What a teacher you have."

"The best."

I feel a warmth spreading across my cheeks that has nothing to do with mono or a fever.

"So, what's in the bag?" I finally ask.

"Why don't you see for yourself?"

I open the bag. Oliver looks at me, grinning. Inside are packets of vitamin C, zinc lozenges, Airborne, and Emergen-C. But his smile tells me that he isn't making fun of me—that he doesn't think I'm gross or diseased or poisonous.

Something tells me he never really did.

I kiss him, and this time he doesn't pull away, doesn't look at me like I'm diseased. Because I'm not.

# Acknowledgments

While I was writing/attempting to write these acknowledgments, I convinced myself that I had pink eye, strep throat, and about five incurable diseases. Which is to say, I'm really good at procrastinating and really good at thinking I'm sick.

Scholastic Book Fair day was my favorite day of school as a kid, and it truly is a dream come true to have my first novel published with Scholastic. Thank you to everyone at Scholastic who made it happen, and especially to my editor, Orlando Dos Reis. He was amazingly patient with me in all my moments of doubt and insecurities as a first-time author. His incredible feedback guided my writing in directions I didn't know it could be guided in, and it was an honor to shape the story with his suggestions and edits. Thank you to Nick Eliopulos and David Levithan, for taking a chance on me, and for entrusting me with such a fun project. Thank you to Nina Goffi for designing a cover that I feverishly adore. Thank you to Melissa Schirmer, Jessica White, the production department, and everyone else at Scholastic who helped make this book a reality.

I couldn't have written this book without the support of my family and friends. Thank you, all of you.

Nicholas, thank you for the support, love, and encouragement. Not just while I was writing this book, but the entire time I've known you.

Which is a long time, and a lot of support, love, and encouragement. Thank you for being one of my first readers, and thank you for all the times you sat next to me on the couch while I was writing and talked out plot points, character aspects, and went over proper airplane and airport lingo with me.

Mila, your presence is in every page. I wrote so much of this book at night, with your video monitor propped up next to my laptop, watching you sleep while I typed. Thank you for inspiring me and encouraging me every single day. And thank you for the blueberry pancakes.

Mom, thank you for taking me to the library hundreds (thousands?) of times when I was little and for letting me read at the dinner table. Thank you for always believing in me, even when I didn't.

Greg, big brother, thank you for encouraging me to keep writing, for being so supportive, and for being such an inspiration.

Dad, wherever you are, I did it.

Cosmo Sagristano, Erin Cicatelli, Dawn Kuc, Bob Kuc, Natalie Kuc, Nico Medina, Billy Merrell, Oriane Wilkerson, Rudha Kerr, Rachel Losh, Lauren O'Neill-Butler, Kellie Porter, Molly Kolb, Tricia Callahan, Anna Teten, Jessie Shaffer, Autumn Stannard, Chrissy Denardo, Lindsey Keith, thank you for letting me freak out about the book at all stages, and for encouraging me when I needed it most.

And finally, thank you to everyone at Giocare, especially Bridget Clark, and to Cecilia Grace Figueroa, for spending time with Mila while I spent time writing. She's lucky to have gotten such wonderful care from you, and I'm lucky too.

Keep dreaming and believing, everyone.

# About the Author

**Katie Cicatelli-Kuc** spent over a decade as an in-house copyeditor and production editor for major publishing houses before becoming a full-time writer, freelancer, and mom. She has never been in quarantine nor has she had tropical mono, though she does spend entirely too much time looking up symptoms on WebMD. Katie lives in a yellow house next to a mountain in the lower Hudson Valley in New York with her husband, daughter, and two cats. *Quarantine* is her first novel. Follow her online at katiecicatelli.com.